CW00867504

A MESSAGE FROM CHICKEN HOUSE

The first thing you should know about *My Love Life and the Apocalypse* is that it's full of vintage culture from the 90s and 00s . . . and the characters go clothes shopping FOR FREE in post-apocalyptic but totally perfect shops! Who wouldn't love to live out their abandoned mall dreams? But there's so much more to this original and engaging novel: an emerging love story between a humanoid robot boy and a human girl with some awkward secrets and truly frightening truths. This is an end-of-the-world horror/thriller/romance mash-up with a difference – well, a whole *world* of funny, terrifying, thoughtful differences. Melissa Welliver is a startling new talent.

BARRY CUNNINGHAM
Publisher
Chicken House

MY LOVE LIFE AND THE APOCALYPSE

MELISSA WELLIVER

Chicken House

2 Palmer Street, Frome, Somerset BA11 1DS
www.chickenhousebooks.com

First published in Great Britain in 2023
Chicken House
2 Palmer Street
Frome, Somerset BA11 1DS
United Kingdom
www.chickenhousebooks.com

Chicken House/Scholastic Ireland, 89E Lagan Road, Dublin Industrial Estate,
Glasnevin, Dublin D11 HP5F, Republic of Ireland

Cover design by Micaela Alcaino
Typeset by Dorchester Typesetting Group Ltd
Printed and bound in Great Britain by CPI Group (UK) Ltd, Croydon CR0 4YY

1 3 5 7 9 10 8 6 4 2

British Library Cataloguing in Publication data available.

PB ISBN 978-1-913696-57-3
eISBN 978-1-915026-45-3

For my mum and dad
Kathy and Leon Welliver
For believing I could do it even when I didn't

1

Echo

AuroraBIO 3 Release 4.0

Copyright 2075-2080 Aurora Technologies Ltd

All Rights Reserved

BIO3 version 17.2

Gateway Solo 9550

System ID = TeenSynth0135

Build Time: 09/10/2179 09:09:52

CPU = Synth Mobile Quantum® III Processor - M 1066 GHz

1024 TB Positronic Brain RAM Passed

512 TB Human Biological System RAM Passed

2048 TB Memory RAM CATASTROPHIC FAILURE -

```
unable to run
4096 TB E-Mote RAM CATASTROPHIC FAILURE -
unable to run
512 TB HUMANKIND™ RAM Partially Enabled -
unable to update

System BIOS enabled
Video BIOS enabled
Sensory BIOS enabled
UMB Upper limit segment address: ERROR 404

[SELECT] to enter BIOS Setup
[SELECT] to boot up limited system with
CATASTROPHIC FAILURES
```

I opened my eyes slowly, the dying light of the day just enough to overload my optical sensors. The first thing I saw was the copy of *Coding for Dummies*, left open at the page I had stopped on. I was crashed-out on the floor of the library again.

God, what was I doing with my life?

I said God, but I didn't believe in him. I mean, of course I had a creator – the same as all synths did. We were property of Aurora Technologies.

Which, like the rest of the world, was . . . well . . . gone.

'Ouch.' I pulled my hand in defensively as a librarian

HUMANKIND™ synth stood on it.

'Apologies, Mr Echo Zero-One-Three-Five,' it said. It stepped over me as it spoke, focused on shifting its pile of books to the other side of the library. I watched as it moved, as straight-backed and graceful as a supermodel. Once, it would have identified as a male, like I did. From its faded hoodie to its pockmarked skin, it screamed Teen-Synth™. Once, it would have had a personality and feelings, like me, before it was reprogrammed like all the others.

'Doofus,' I muttered.

I jumped to my feet and picked up *Coding for Dummies* off the floor, hurling it as hard as I could at the HUMANKIND. I caught it right on the crown of its head and it fell to the ground like a sack of potatoes, taking the pile of books with it and scattering them all over the shiny parquet floor. The sound was deafening, alerting every bot in the area to the mess.

The cleaning bots came first. No human form to slow them down – because humans never did make small talk with the cleaners – they rolled into action on their tiny wheels from their hidden crevices in the walls, like mice. Their sleek, podlike structures unfurled into an array of metal arms and brooms and scoops as they arrived at the fallen HUMANKIND. They set about their business, which was to pick up the fallen books and check for any spills from the stricken synth's body. Not in case he was hurt, but in case anything damaged the pristine floor.

It was the job of the Paramedibots™ to see if I had damaged the HUMANKIND. The medibots rose up from the corners of the room, where they each had been sleeping in their dormant mode of a large brass box with a first aid kit glued to the top. They folded upwards into almost human form, faceless, bipedals dudes that stood thirty centimetres taller than me.

'Can I help you, sir?' The tinny speaker that made up the medibot's face spoke, a sentiment delivered in such a monotone that it was a wonder the programmer had bothered at all.

'I am undamaged. Apologies for any inconvenience caused,' the HUMANKIND bot replied as it finally stirred, after presumably running diagnostics for the last few seconds.

I didn't even feel bad. It was impossible to hurt something that wasn't conscious in any way, either emotionally or physically.

It stood up, retrieved the books the cleaning bots hadn't got to yet, and continued on its way to the book depository. It wouldn't even have a job if it weren't for me coming in every day. I liked to call it Gort, although it had obviously never seen the cult classic, *The Day the Earth Stood Still*. Shame.

Sometimes I wished I was as clueless as Gort. Life without an E-Mote chip was probably a lot simpler.

Three years had passed since my systems had first detected the E-Mote chip, lodged into my positronic brain so carelessly, like a tumour from the early twenty-first century. I wished I could remember who put it there, but the total noob that did the deed managed to break my memory bank, so I couldn't remember a thing from before I woke up. So now I was stuck, too human to access my robot functions, too robot to age out of puberty. Great.

Jeez, Echo, take a chill pill. I couldn't angst too much about the past or my short-term RAM might fill up and explode. Or something. I should be able to do basic coding on myself, but I couldn't remember that either. There were no humans left to fix it for me.

And that's a real bummer.

I left the bots to their devices – every pun intended – and headed down the steps outside the library.

For the end of the world, Earth was looking pretty damn good. I mean yeah, maybe most of the concrete was cracked open with weeds, and the football stadium was now unusable because there were so many trees growing there, but on the whole the city didn't look too shabby. The important stuff was still all right.

'Looking good, Robocop.' I clicked my fingers at a passing bot with the faded blue paint of the city police badge painted across its chest piece. Its voice box had broken long ago, but it still saluted at me as it passed.

I couldn't remember what it had all looked like before, but I had seen videos in the library archives. The same skyscrapers still stood in the middle distance, where the financial district used to be housed. The cars that littered the streets were kept clean and free of dust from the storms. There wasn't even any trash, what with no humans to make it. The plastic hadn't had a chance to biodegrade, not yet. Mostly, the bots were just shoving anything they found on top of the mountains of landfill outside the city limits.

The restoration bots may have run out of material for the roads, but they did a good job of cutting back the climbing ivy that sometimes threatened the foundations of the houses. There was just no substitute for the footfall of eight billion people, hence the concrete. I jumped across the cracked paving stones like I was a kid playing hopscotch. But, as usual, it did nothing to ease my mood. Someone once told me that if I stood on a crack, I would break my mother's back. I couldn't remember who it was. I couldn't even remember who my mother was, but I had to have some kind of parental. I was a TeenSynth, after all.

Most of the outdoor bots didn't use the walkways. They

were built to hover using magnets, an easier way to empty the bins and make it up a set of steep steps. They easily swung out of my way in mid-air as I hopped down the street. They didn't even talk, they were so basic. Their one function was to keep back nature so the cities would be ready for the humans again one day. Which was ironic because, and I'm just saying, that's how we ended up in this mess in the first place. But as long as the humans are safe, I guess.

If, you know, I could remember where we left them.

It's not like *nobody* knew where the humans were. The HUMANKIND bots were literally invented to keep them safe, and wake them when the world was deemed 'habitable' again. I had tried asking the bots, but they always answered me with that bogus robotic beeping sound: *access denied*. If I could get my E-Mote chip out, and could sort out the HUMANKIND programming mess that was wedged into my head, maybe I could remember too. But that was the problem when you did things in a hurry. The TeenSynths were developed over a really long time, to compensate, I guess, for the rise in infertility. There just wasn't time to finish the HUMANKIND programme before everything went to shit.

I stopped outside a shop with a flashing neon sign, *FreshFoods*, my stomach growling. I hadn't eaten since before I started my failed diagnostics attempt, and it had taken several hours to reboot my quantum core.

When I walked into the store I triggered the motion-sensor lights, which in turn flickered down each aisle until the place was fully lit. I also managed to trigger the annoying music system, which started to blast out royalty-free jazz interspersed with shop announcements.

'*Try FreshFood's home-grown cultured no-meat burgers. So good, you'll accuse us of murder! Available in aisle three.*'

I rolled my eyes as I moved on to aisle four. Aisles one to three used to house the fresh produce, but the cleaning bots had long since cleared out anything rotten. The only stuff left was in jars and tins; dried fruits in packets and sugary sweets too artificial to rot. I browsed the shelf until I came to the section I wanted and pulled off three tins of baked beans and a jar of red cabbage. And a bag of strawberry laces for, y'know, energy.

Almost as quickly as I removed the tins, the row moved forwards, pushed by some invisible force, like a giant vending machine. The shelf filled in the missing beans with more from behind, and it ended up looking as full as when I arrived. I went down to the basement once, to see how many tins I had before I starved to death, and a whole day passed before I even reached the end of the first conveyor belt of glass jars and cans. That was why I stuck to the city: 1,107 days later and I still hadn't eaten this metropolis out of baked beans.

'Hey, Deidre,' I said, stepping up to the vacant self-checkout. The till lit up and the familiar digital face of the young, blonde register girl filled the screen. She was hot for a bunch of pixels.

'Welcome to FreshFoods Superstores,' Deidre beamed.

'Oh, you know, so-so,' I replied. Deidre was only programmed to run through a set script, but in my head, we always had lots to say. 'How's it going with, what's his name, Drew?'

'Please place your items in the scanning area,' Deidre said. I did what I was told. She smiled again.

'Oh yeah, sorry, Dwayne,' I said. I leant on the top of her screen in a way I hoped looked sexy, in control. 'And he did what now? Deidre, you deserve better, girl.'

'That will be four hundred and fifty-five credits. Please pay by following the on-screen pin-pad instructions.'

'Well, you know you always have my number. You can call . . . anytime.' I whispered the last part and got out my wallet. Deidre froze, waiting for me to pay before issuing the next instruction. I pulled out a card labelled 'MRS B E SMITH' and tapped it to the pad.

'Insufficient funds,' Deidre said, still smiling. I sighed and tossed the card over my shoulder.

'Come on, bae. Don't be like that,' I said, tapping the next card in my wallet. This time, the transaction went through. Thank you, Mr G. Graham.

'Transaction complete. Thank you for shopping with us today.' Deidre smiled once more before the screen faded to black. I picked up my shopping and replaced my wallet. I knew I didn't have to pay any more, that there was no one left to pay, but that wasn't the point. Besides, I was the highlight of Deidre's day.

The street lights sputtered to life as I headed the familiar way home. The beans and cabbage banged against my leg as I walked and I sucked on the end of a strawberry lace. Another day, another failure. *Coding for Dummies* was my last hope, for obvious reasons. I had tried every other book in the library, every resource still operational on the server. Man, I couldn't even code like a dummy. Useless. I stopped, looked up at the street sign that I knew was looming above me. *Park Avenue.* The scene of my biggest failed attempt.

Not today. I moved past the street quickly, made sure not to look at what I knew was still there. I'd never been back there, even though I knew the bots had probably fixed it all up by now. Like nothing ever happened. But that could wait. There had to be something else I could try.

It started to rain so I broke into a run. Typical. At high school, maybe they called this 'pathetic fallacy'. I just called it pathetic.

Before I knew it I was back at my apartment building just as the rain was turning to hail. A bolt of lightning split the sky in two and I ran for the revolving door. I shook off the few hailstones that shifted down my neck after I took my hood off and caught my reflection in the dark glass, the windows turned to a mirror by the reception lights.

I looked wiped. There was a small breakout just under my bottom lip, and a five o'clock shadow crept in around my jawline, patchy though it was. Perpetual puberty was the enemy of a good beard.

I walked under the central chandelier and into the gold-plated lift.

'Welcome home, Echo Zero-One-Three-Five,' the speaker said as soon as the doors were closed.

I leant against the mirrored back wall and the lift propelled me upwards. I winced slightly when my ears popped.

'Floor one-zero-five. Penthouse.' The lift doors slid open on my living room.

I mean, obviously I live in the penthouse. And not just any penthouse, but the highest and most expensive penthouse in the city. I think it belonged to some sports guy before, but I don't even remember what team I supported, so whatever. Either way, it had a huge bedroom with a super-king; a TV that took up the whole living-room wall; and a hard drive full of . . . let's just say that if I did still have parents, I'd be grounded for a week if they found that hard drive. Maybe a month.

I flopped down onto the velour sofa and put my feet up on the marble-topped table, shoes on. Not exactly my taste, but furniture deliveries were a bitch post-apocalypse, so I had to make do. Bits of caked dirt from the street flaked off on to the table. The cleaning bots would take care of that in the night, while I slept.

I checked my vitals on my HUD – heads-up display. Low battery, but enough to do some reading before bed. *Or maybe . . .* My eyes slid along the wall to the cluster of wires at one end, towards where I knew the hard drive was plugged in. I pulled over the box of tissues I left out on the table and picked up the remote.

A flash of lightning blazed along the wall of glass that ran the length of the living room, followed by a crack of thunder so loud that I dropped the remote. All the lights flickered once and then went out, along with any chance of using the TV.

'Great,' I muttered. 'Hey, Rosie, what's the deal with the lights?' I said the second part louder, head dropped back, staring at the emergency lighting that lined the ceiling to the built-in speakers.

'Power surge. Possible electrical fault. Switching to emergency power,' a soft, almost sultry feminine voice replied. ROSIE – Remote Operational Site Integrated Engine. Another gift from our friends at Aurora Tech. Every building I had explored in the city seemed to have one, all still fully operational. Rosie controlled everything in the apartment, from the lights to the microwave. She would make sure I had enough power to charge, but that's it. No TV tonight.

I stood up and moved over to the window. Most of the city, laid out beneath my feet like a model town, seemed to be having the same problem. I had seen it like this before. Electrical surges were common during the storms.

What wasn't common was what I could see in the sky. What am I saying? It was downright crazy. I had never seen anything like it before. A streak of light, too long-lasting and slow-moving to be lightning, burnt across the black sky, high above the city.

A comet? No, it was way too big to be a comet. And even if it was, comets didn't move like that. The trail behind the object was zigzagged, like the thing was . . . steering itself?

'No way,' I whispered. I watched as it appeared to change direction again, heading south towards the city centre. It was definitely moving on its own, and from the trail, it had come from . . . above? From *space*?

But before I could think about it any more, another bolt of lightning streaked across the sky, followed by a boom of thunder. The bolt travelled towards the moving object in less than a second, and the flash of light as the two collided made me wince as it lit up the living room.

The next thing I knew, the object was a ball of orange fire, falling in a straight line from the sky.

Right into the centre of the city.

2

Pandora

I woke up in Hell.

Well, it felt like Hell. It was boiling, so hot that I was already soaked in a sheen of sweat. The first thing I did was try to sit up, and I instantly regretted it as I bashed my forehead on the glass panel above me.

'Ow,' I rasped. My mouth was dry, like I hadn't had a drink in a month. The window in front of me was covered in condensation. I tried to wipe it away but my arm was sealed tight next to my waist. My whole body was confined, and I couldn't even see my legs. Panic started to constrict my throat. Was this . . . a sleeping pod? No. This wasn't just a sleeping pod, it was a coffin.

'Hello?' I tried to scream but my voice wasn't there. A hairline crack appeared in front of my eyes, making its way across the glass, and I thought I could see an orange glow on the other side. *Fire.* Through the crack I could hear the low howl of an alarm.

Think. Where was I? I couldn't move my arms or legs, but I could just about lift my head enough to see the strange overalls I was wearing. All grey; an unflattering onesie with a neon-blue logo on the chest that I couldn't read upside down. Sweat patches made their way out from under my arms and down the centre of my chest. I had a pounding headache.

The window in front of my face was the only change in the smooth metal that made up the inside of the pod. What was this thing? I tried to unscramble my throbbing brain to remember the last thing that happened before I woke up.

There was an explosion, muffled, but close enough to feel. The pod vibrated and the spiderweb of cracks grew across the glass. I closed my eyes to protect myself but by some miracle it blew outwards. When I opened my eyes, I still couldn't see much as my head was strapped firmly to the backboard of my pod, but I could feel the full heat of the flames just outside of my view. The alarm was louder too, and I could make out the words repeating over the top.

'*Brace for imminent impact. Brace for imminent impact. Brace for—*' The voice was cut off as another explosion shunted the pod forward before it rocked back into position.

My pod. I knew what this was. After all of Father's efforts I was going to die anyway.

I tried to move but my arms were firmly pinned by my sides. I pushed my head forward as much as I could and looked down at the restraints across my chest and limbs. They were made from fabric and pulled tight in the middle like a seatbelt on Father's private jet, crossing over the grey jumpsuit. The one I'd had to change into before I could get into my pod. The one with the tiny blue spinning wheel over the breast pocket, and 'AURORA TECHNOLOGIES' printed in black underneath.

The pod lurched again and it felt as if I was free-falling. My stomach dropped like I was on a roller coaster, but the tracks didn't kick in to catch me. How long could I fall for? It felt like it would never end. The flames and the alarm and the recorded message all blurred into one until it felt like I was floating. I knew what that was from school. I had been falling for so long I had reached terminal velocity. So right before I die by hitting the ground at 300 kph, I'll feel like I'm floating.

I closed my eyes and drew in a deep breath. *Remember.* In through my nose. Out through my mouth. As I breathed in, I imagined a flower opening, each petal stretching out one by one to reveal the sunshine-yellow middle. I counted to four, and then held my breath until I got to seven. As I breathed out, on the eight count, the flower closed, and with it went the sound of the alarm.

I had to focus if I was going to get out of here alive. That was what Dr Kapoor would say. *Panic only creates more panic.* The breathing exercises were the only thing that could help me avoid a full-blown panic attack. And that was the last thing I needed right now.

I opened my eyes. The alarm filtered back through the brain fog, but it felt more manageable now.

Remember. Reaching behind my back, the fingers on my left hand felt for the emergency release that I had been shown when the scientists strapped me into the pod. If falling to the Earth at supersonic speed wasn't an emergency, I didn't know what was. I gasped as the straps came loose and more air filled my lungs, and then coughed as smoke tinged the back of my throat. The top half of the pod popped open, like a stable door.

Or an open coffin at a funeral.

The first thing I tried was climbing out of the pod, but my legs collapsed under my weight as soon as I released the last strap. '*You may feel a little weak when you wake up.*' That's what the scientist had said. '*It depends how much time has passed, and how much muscle wastage has occurred.*'

Panic seized my throat again. How long had I been asleep? My legs were like lead, useless things that wouldn't follow my instructions. No, that wasn't quite true. If I tried hard enough, I could wiggle my toes. The movement sent shooting pins and needles up and down my limbs.

'Parachute deployment failed.' The computerized voice cut through the alarm and brought me back to the present, dispersing the panic.

I needed to concentrate on what I *could* do, not what I couldn't. Parachute deployment failure did not sound good.

'Er, computer?' I shouted over the alarm, hoping the systems had some sort of AI programmed in.

'Yes, Pandora?' the computer responded, much to my relief. I almost laughed.

'Thank God. Computer, options for slowing down this pod . . . this pod thingy?' I stumbled over my words and kept my eyes on the number panel in the top right-hand corner, counting down to zero at sickening speed. *3,600 m . . . 3,500 m . . . 3,400 m . . .*

'I have found one option,' the computer responded. 'Manual deployment of parachute. Would you like to proceed?'

'Yes, proceed, proceed,' I screeched, my voice catching again. My legs weren't the only things that hadn't been used in a long time.

'I must warn you that manual deployment of parachute only has a four per cent chance of success. If this method succeeds, projected fatality scenario will change from definite to highly probable. This will also make your descent much more uncomfortable, which I can explain in more detail. Shall I explain, or do you wish to proceed?'

Definitely dead, or probably dead. There was no real contest. And nothing could be less comfortable than hurtling to your death.

'Proceed,' I shouted. 'What do I need to do? Quickly,' I said, my eyes never leaving the digital counter. *2,900 m.*

'Of course, Pandora.' The computer cut the alarm.

At first it was a relief to my eardrums, but then I realized how loud the flames outside the ship were, how high-pitched the sound of air particles whistling past the ship. I glanced back up to the monitor. *2,700 m . . . 2,500 m . . .*

'In order to enact manual protocol, you must pull the red lever to the left of the console. I will highlight it now.' A light to my left distracted me from the countdown to my death. In front of me, just outside my pod, was a console filled with buttons, switches and monitors, all of which were labelled with words that made no sense to me. All the lights that had been lit up were now extinguished, leaving just one: a huge red lever with a glowing handle.

'Don't have to ask me twice,' I breathed. I leant out of the pod, my fingertips just brushing the edge of the lever. *Shit.* I squirmed forward, my useless heavy legs holding the bottom half of my body firmly inside the pod. I gave myself an extra centimetre and managed to touch the full length of red plastic, but not enough so I could grab it.

The lever didn't budge.

My eyes flicked again to the monitor. *2,000 m . . . 1,800 m . . . 1,600 m . . .*

'Pandora, do you wish to proceed with manual parachute deployment? The time taken to deploy has limited your chance of survival to three per cent.'

'I'm doing it!' I screamed. That seemed to shut it up. With one last heave, I pulled myself over the lip of the pod and grabbed the lever, using my residual body weight to force it down.

The alarm started back up, but I only heard it for a second. Because after that, the roof blew off the top of the chamber and all the air was sucked out into the solid blue sky.

I tried to scream, but no noise came out. I couldn't breathe. The open roof worked like a vacuum, trying to suck me out, but the pod held my legs in position despite loosening the strap. Above, I could see the flapping material of the parachute. It was almost fully open, but I couldn't ignore the gaping hole in the middle of the fabric. I tried to look back at the console, to see if we had slowed down at all, but the sudden change in pressure had smashed the screen.

I moved and slammed into the back of the pod, winding myself as I reached for the strap. I had to strap myself back in if I was going to have any chance at all, and I didn't need a computer to tell me that. As I pulled the strap back closed behind my back, I struggled with the clasp. I felt even weaker than before, any trace of consciousness slipping out of the roof like the hatch, my mind scattering into the wind. At last, I heard the safety clasp click closed and let my arms go loose. At last, I could hear the alarm again.

'*Brace for imminent impact. Brace for imminent impact. Brace . . .*'

3

I had pressed the call button on the lift three times before remembering the electricity was out.

'Shit,' I cursed under my breath and I ran to the other end of the apartment, towards the emergency fire door. It clicked open and activated the emergency lights, which highlighted the 104 flights of stairs in a spiral below my feet.

'Awesome,' I muttered, taking the stairs three at a time. After the first two flights, my HUD reminded me that I needed to 'sleep', AKA charge up. The lettering had changed to red, meaning that I had less than ten per cent battery left.

'Plenty left in the tank,' I said out loud on the tenth floor down, more to convince myself than anything. I should be able to make it if I paced myself.

The sound of the object hitting the ground was loud enough for me to hear through the solid concrete walls of the stairwell. It was a low sonic boom that shook dust from the ceiling and into my eyes. How long had it been since I had seen it? A couple of minutes? It must have hit the ground fast. And hard.

I leapt down the remaining stairs and over the rail at the bottom before pushing open the fire exit.

It was chaos in the lobby. There was a chunk of warped metal big enough to take my head out in the middle of the marble floor. The thing had shattered the windows and glass littered the ground. Already cleaner bots were moving in to try and contain the mess, but some had toppled over and were writhing on their backs like overturned tortoises.

'Alert. Possible danger. Alert,' one of the concierge bots said, its wheels spinning uselessly in the air. I ignored it and ran to the door, realized it had been wedged shut by a mountain of broken glass, and instead stepped awkwardly through a smashed window to the side.

I had imagined there would be sirens like in a movie, but the streets were silent again. No need for sirens when there was no traffic to overtake. This was the first time I could remember there even being a need for the emergency drones. A whirring sound cut through the silence and I glanced up as a small bot glided over my head.

It was headed for the crash site, that much was obvious by the electric-yellow stripes that once alerted citizens to its presence, and made a statement of, *get the fuck out of my way*. I set off running, chasing the drone overhead as it traced the streets of the city and weaved in and out of the maze of skyscrapers. I was fast, but the drone was faster, and I struggled to ignore the flashing low-battery sensor on the edge of my vision.

My lungs strained under my tie-dye T-shirt and I used a precious breath to swear. Once again I found myself cursing the dude – or dudette – that left me unfinished. Not robot enough to be invincible, not human enough to pace myself properly. The thoughts raced by as fast as the buildings and I tried to ignore them. If anything, I didn't have the literal energy to worry about that right now. All I knew was that nothing had changed in years except for the number of dandelion heads that peeked out from the cracks in the pavement. Until now. I *had* to know what was in that falling star.

I slowed to a staggered jog as the drone raced over the iron fence of the park in the centre of the city, narrowly avoiding a collision with the top of the railings. The park was huge – there were corners even I hadn't found my way into yet – and overgrown, a mess of weeds and long grass and various poisonous ropes of ivy. I had seen the park in movies and on TV, and it didn't used to look like this. It used to be all manicured lawns and crappy pedal boats on a big-ass lake. Now it was just a forest.

I swallowed as I watched the trajectory of the drone. I didn't need to follow it now; the plume of black smoke was more than enough of an indicator of where I was headed. I was more worried about the other thing, the one that had forced me to lock up the park for good.

Slowly, using the break to catch my breath, I walked the edge of the park, trailing my fingers along the railings. The bushes on this side were as thick as a brick wall, but I knew there was a concrete path that cut a way through that I could follow if I wanted to. I reached the gate and fingered the thick padlock and chains. Through the bars, the path twisted innocently into the night.

In the distance, I heard a howl.

When you're the last thinking thing left on Earth, you have a lot of time on your hands. I had watched every movie in the library twice by the time I found the servers in a basement in the corner of the city. The building itself looked innocent enough, with a dusty sign I vaguely recognized. Most of the floors were just offices with busted PCs, but the basement was where the real treasure was. Hundreds of square metres filled to the ceiling with digital storage space. Thousands of hours of TV shows and films.

I had asked the storage bots to help me get it back online so I could stream whatever I wanted to any screen in the city, even my tablet. The servers for post-2015 were corrupted, but all the shizzle before that was still good. I watched whole seasons of early twenty-first-century shows and laughed out loud at hundreds of comedy films. Those characters had become my friends. But what I really loved, my absolute favourite thing to watch, were the nature shows.

Plants were abundant in my world. They grew out of every crack in the concrete, their will to survive stronger than the programming of the cleaning bots. But there weren't many animals left. I had seen the odd stray cat or dog, but usually once they were already dead, their cause of death made obvious by the sight of a second head or fifth and sixth legs. Basically, the world was polluted for a long time, and it wasn't good for the non-genetically enhanced creatures. My robotic side kept my biology from unravelling, but they weren't as lucky.

So I loved watching the elephants as they trudged across the Serengeti, or the dope panthers that prowled the branches of the rainforests. I had pored over old books and magazines and knew there was a zoo in the centre of the city, inside the park, so one day I set off to see if I could get in. I assumed it was locked like everything else, and of course it was.

I didn't mean to do it.

That didn't change things for now though. I reached down for the toolbox I had left next to the gate and got out the bolt cutters. I'd known I would need them again someday. I took a deep breath and cut the links. The chain fell to the ground with a loud jingle and I froze, waiting for the sound of padding footsteps.

'Here it comes,' I breathed, but by some miracle it didn't. Slowly I eased open the gate with an unnervingly loud creak, then I paused again. Listened.

Silence.

I had to be quick. If the threat of predators wasn't enough, I also had my low-battery warning still winking in the bottom corner of my HUD. Two per cent. Well, at least I wouldn't be awake when the mutated lions tore me limb from limb.

I entered the park, making sure that the gate didn't slam shut behind me. It was dark now, dark enough that the few overhead lights that still had bulbs flickered on and lit the path. Even some of those sputtered ominously. The park itself was a mess, worse than when I had shut it up. Weeds grew through the cracks in the gravel, and the grass either side was at least waist height. I couldn't see or hear any bots either. I suppressed a shudder as a million mental images of what had happened to them flashed through my mind.

Gotta leave it alone. It's not like they felt anything

anyway. And when I found out who was in the spaceship, I could maybe get them to help me fix the bots. And my chip.

I half jogged along the path, trying to get the balance right between hurrying to the crash site and preserving my battery life long enough to get there. I told myself it was a spaceship, because there was no other explanation. Whatever the thing was, it fell from the sky. In a bolt of lightning, for crying out loud. I once watched a movie about a really old dude and some kid who drove a car through a bolt of lightning to the past. Or was it the future? I shook my head. Thought processing was only going to wear down my battery faster.

I followed the path round to the great plume of fiery smoke that rose into the dark sky. The lightning seemed to have stopped, and with it, the freak weather. It was quiet now, the only sound that of my high-tops on the gravel. Which is what I was afraid of.

Another sound, this time a roar, cut through the darkness. And it was nearer than I'd have liked it to be.

I kept my breathing steady as my battery dropped to one per cent, turning my optical output a foreboding shade of red. What a cliché. I was like a walking video game. Although, if being stalked by a tiger while running towards a crashed spaceship *was* a video game, I'd sure as shit play it.

I blinked and the red dissipated. Couldn't worry about that now. Had to save my optical sensors for—

Something moved in the bushes to my right.

I stopped, the gravel crunching under my feet as I froze. For a split second, I prayed that I had imagined it, but the bush moved again. Slowly, like ink seeping out from the shadows, the lithe body of a panther crept out on to the path.

I tried not to barf as the street lights illuminated the creature. It had looked like a panther, but there was something else in there too. Something unnatural about the way the big cat moved its head; about the way golden hairs shone out from underneath slick, jet-black fur. It turned its head and my swallow caught in my throat, making me want to gag, but I held still.

In the lights, four pairs of eyes blinked back at me. Two sets of mouths. I wanted to scream, scream like I had all those months ago when I first opened up the zoo, but no sound came. The two-headed cat took a step closer.

Run! my brain screamed, but my feet ignored it. My mouth was so dry I couldn't open my lips and scream for help even if I thought it would matter. I'm just another bot to the drones. They were busy with the crash. Nothing could save me now.

The cat pulled its weight back on to its hind legs, ready to pounce.

'Greetings, Echo Zero-One-Three-Five.' The tinny voice of the safety bot was almost deafening in the silence, and both me and the panther turned to stare at the thing as it wheeled its way down the path and into the light of the street lamp.

The panther didn't waste any time. It leapt on to the bot and bit down so hard I heard the metal crack open under the pressure.

'Assistance. Danger. Assistance.' The bot managed to get out its last words before the panther chomped down on its voice box, sending screws and metal coils flying across the path.

That was my chance. I turned on one foot and ran as fast as I could off the path and into the darkness of the smoke-filled park.

Still panting, I ran for the middle of the field. Frankenstein's monster was down for now, but not out. I needed to get to the spaceship, check for survivors and then hightail it outta there.

It was even darker now, but the flames around the crash site lit up the craft that had carved a six-metre trench into the long grass. The fire would keep the animals away – at least, that was always true in the movies. I ran alongside the ditch, taking in the magnitude of what had actually just landed in my city. Although I'd kept telling myself it was a spaceship, I was still straight-up shocked that it actually was one.

Up ahead, casting dancing shadows in the firelight, was a huge hunk of torn metal. It was easily five times taller than me and just as wide. Great hulking holes let out billowing plumes of smoke and every now and then the flicker of blue-white electricity nearly blinded me. I ran past a parachute which was only attached by two lines, a red and white tent draped across the trench to my right. On the side of the ship, as I got closer, I could see there was the peeling paint of a logo. A blue spinning wheel against the letters *AT*.

Typical. Aurora Tech owned everything in the city, so why not space too? From the lines of programming in my head, to the rusted manhole covers on every street. That same spinning wheel. Those same initials. How can a country compete with money like that? No wonder nation-states didn't exist any more, even before the Big Sleep.

Finally, I reached the wreckage. Well, I say reached; the flames were so hot it was like an invisible heated forcefield surrounded the ship. I brought my hands to my face defensively and squinted through the smoke and bright lights of the broken electrics.

I hesitated. I had run down here so quickly, I hadn't thought to bring anything. How would I get them – him? her? – out? Could anyone even have survived a crash like that? I looked back at the trench, at the pieces of twisted metal and burning debris that littered the field. It was a rough landing. High in the dark sky, above the smoke, I could just about make out a flashing blue light.

The medibots. Of course. I totally forgot about the drones when I was, you know, wrestling with a big cat. Weren't they ahead of me, though? I remembered following them into the park. It soon became obvious they had gone to the nearest hydrant for water, which was way outside the perimeter of the park and down the street. Their bodies were artificially inflated to five times their normal size, an expandable belly protruding from the bottom of each drone, pregnant with water. The belly shrank a little as the drones approached each small fire, until eventually there was no water and no flames either.

At that point, the bots deemed it safe enough to approach the ship, and they switched to their fire extinguisher modes to put out the electrical fire. I lowered my hand as the flames got lower and the bots switched to floodlights to help them assess the damage.

'Well?' I asked, impatient for them to finish. If I had to wait for the medibots to call the all-clear, both me and any survivors in the ship would have died of old age. And I didn't age.

'Greetings, Echo Zero-One-Thr—'

'Yeah, yeah, get to the point,' I growled, standing on my tiptoes to see over the mass of metal at my feet. Gently, I touched the top of the nearest chunk, around waist height. Either it was cool enough to touch, or my heat sensors were down. Either was fine with me. 'Is there anyone alive in there?'

'Scanning,' a second medibot said, and the familiar tune of the scanning function started up. I knew the scan would only take a few seconds, but I couldn't wait any longer. I climbed on to the chunk of metal and picked my way towards the gaping entrance of the ship, lit by the flood-lights on the drone's apparatus.

'Affirmative,' the second medibot spoke. I blinked, my hands on the next hunk of metal, ready to climb. The bot's annoying beeping tone stopped, the scan complete.

'What did you just say?'

'In answer to your question, Echo Zero-One-Three-Five. Affirmative. One survivor of crash. One human female.'

My last breath caught in my throat. When I had seen the ship in the sky, the thought may have crossed my mind. Just for a second. But just as quickly, I had dismissed it.

Then why did you run all the way out here? Why did you risk your life by coming back here, if you didn't think it could be true? A voice in the back of my head mocked me and I silently told it to eff off.

I scrambled up the last piece of metal and, timidly, I peered into the open front of the ship. There, half propped up inside a metal box and wearing a singed Aurora Tech jumpsuit, was a teenage girl. All blonde hair and smooth, flushed skin. And then, suddenly, her blue eyes flickered open and she looked at me.

Somewhere deep inside my positronic brain, I felt something start to whir, something I hadn't felt before. Something that felt dangerously close to my E-Mote chip. In my chest, my heart felt like it swelled two sizes. A smile, a real, non-sarcastic smile, pulled at my lips. I couldn't even remember the last time I'd really smiled. I opened my mouth to say something.

'Emergency. Battery drained. Please plug in to energy source immediately to avoid memory damage.' The voice didn't come from my lips, but instead remained inside my head. I had just enough time to watch the girl's face crumple in confusion before I toppled backwards from the ship and hit the ground, hard.

4

I stared at the space where the boy had stood moments earlier, trying to ignore the pain shooting up my right leg.

I survived? I sucked in a breath and while my lungs ached, they complied with my instruction. The pod had been completely split in two, and reminded me of a sarcophagus, swung open and ready for me to step out.

The rest of the ship, or whatever it was I was in, was in worse shape. All the windows in the portholes had shattered, leaving a carpet of glass like fallen leaves for me to navigate over. My leg hurt, but not so much that I couldn't walk on it. I stepped out and marvelled at the twisted titanium that used to make up the front wall of the pod. I had been lucky – too lucky. My vision swam and I resisted the urge to vomit.

'Are you injured, human?' A medibot clung to the hole where the boy had been, peering in at me with its camera lens, so shiny I could see myself in it. I winced in the beam of its floodlight, and in response it dimmed slightly.

'I – no, I'm fine,' I stammered. My throat was red-raw, my voice harsh from screaming. I swallowed hard. 'You should worry about that boy, though.' I pointed towards the hole, over the shoulder of the bot.

The bot didn't move. 'You are the only human needing medical assistance within my jurisdiction,' it replied. Its voice was tinny. The best way I could describe it was rusty, but that couldn't be right. Medibots were serviced weekly.

'No, I-I'm fine,' I said, holding on to a smooth metal pole that was once part of the ship and pulling myself out of the compartment.

My leg complained and I winced, but once I was free of the pod my head was swimming more than my leg hurt. I tried to drag myself out of the open door, which was above my head, but it was hard. My arms felt like jelly and pins and needles ran the length of my body, but eventually I pushed up into the light.

I blinked. It was bright, really bright, and it took me a minute to understand why. There were two emergency drones, each with headlights, but it was the contrast with the darkness that struck me. It was night-time, sure, but the lights from the bots were almost the only lights I could see. I was in a field, surrounded by long grass and bits of broken spacecraft, but I wasn't in the countryside.

Once my eyes had time to adjust I could just about pick out an unfamiliar city skyline against the ever-darkening sky. Not long after sunset, then. I had seen blackouts before, back before the SpindleSleep programme, but not like this. Those blackouts were limited to certain areas of the city – usually poorer tower blocks – but there wasn't a single light on in a window of any skyscraper as far as the eye could see. The roads were lit intermittently with the odd street light, that much I could make out through the trees. But other than that, nothing.

I took a deep breath, remembering my breathing exercises. There, something else that was different. I almost choked as the fresh, rain-tainted air entered my lungs.

'Medibot,' I called. The robot had not left my side, hovering around my torso with a scanner.

'Yes, human?'

'Where's the smog?' I asked. My voice was still hoarse, but getting stronger now I could breathe fresh air. There was no faint smell of sewage, no tinge of smoke as the air hit the back of your throat. Everything just smelt . . . fresh.

'I'm afraid my programming does not allow me to understand your question,' the medibot replied, a spark emanating from its side that made me jump.

I didn't reply. Of course a medibot wouldn't know that. They were programmed with over a thousand different medical textbooks, but they couldn't hold a conversation like AI could. I needed a different bot, or even better, a person.

I held my hand to my eyes to shield them from the gleam of the glass skyscrapers that surrounded my landing site. My pod – or whatever it was – had crashed into the middle of a park. Maybe the city looked more familiar than I first thought, although all cities in this country looked the same since the second industrial revolution, so I couldn't be sure.

I looked up. There was no moon, and there were black clouds dispersing in front of a navy sky. But the thing that really got my attention were the stars. Stars, already tens of stars popping up in the early night. I had never seen stars in real life before. Even during rolling blackouts, the light pollution mixed with the smog was too strong. I had never seen the sky so clearly, and the feeling of wonder quickly turned to a knot of worry in my stomach. I had no idea where I was. This place was familiar but weird, different. It was Earth, but not as I knew it.

And where were the people? Apart from the crackling flames of the ship – and even that noise was quickly being replaced by the sound of the fire extinguishers from the emergency engineer bots – there was silence. No sirens screaming out to come and save me. No traffic noise, or children laughing, or people arguing. No planes or factories rumbling. There was nothing, not even birdsong, which I had been lucky enough to hear in the gardens at Father's office.

'What happened here?' I said, and this time my voice cracked with tears instead of a dry throat.

'I'm afraid my programming does not—'

'I know,' I screamed, and the medibot stopped. The tears spilt over and I swallowed hard, tried not to let panic consume me, all thoughts of deep breathing pushed from my head. Something was wrong, but I was alive. That meant someone else had to be alive too.

Right?

The boy. The memory of the boy, peering through the smoke and debris, flew to the front of my mind. Had he even been real? I looked around, trying to ignore the lumps of molten plastic and the deep brown of the freshly dug-up earth.

I spotted his shoe first. A bright green high-top with a white tick on the side. He was lying to the left of the pod, and looked like he'd fallen where he'd been standing, almost like he'd fainted.

My heart beat fast in my chest as I scrabbled out of the ship and climbed down to where he lay. The medibot fussed around me, protesting about finishing its scans, but I ignored it. The adrenaline that coursed through my veins was giving me more than enough strength.

Please don't be dead. Please don't be dead. Please don't be dead.

I finally made my way down from the wreckage and crouched next to the boy's body, forcing my ear to his chest and holding my breath.

Buh-boom. His heartbeat was dull but I could hear it, beating slowly inside his ribcage. I sat back up and studied his face, so relieved that I had stopped crying for a moment. He was handsome, with a strong jaw and only the faintest trace of acne under his patchy stubble. His dark features gave way to a pink backwards cap, which allowed a tuft of hair to poke through at the front. This was paired with a neon jacket and brightly coloured harem pants.

'What the hell are you wearing?' I muttered. His eyelids remained stubbornly closed.

'I'm afraid my programming—'

'Oh my God, are you still here?' I snapped, turning to the medibot. It hovered in the air, one of its propellers chipping slightly and making it list to the left. Its digital face did not blink.

'I wanted to let you know, human, that your vital scans came back within the acceptable ranges, if somewhat on the low side,' the medibot continued. 'There appears to be no long-term damage to your external or internal frameworks. Would you like me to debrief you?'

'For the love of— No, no I would not,' I said. The headache was creeping back in behind my eyes and with it, the panic. I wasn't alone, there was this boy, but he wasn't even awake. And where was everyone else?

'Sorry, medibot,' I muttered, pinching the bridge of my nose and feeling bad about my outburst. The bot was the only thing that had bothered to speak to me so far, even if it was annoying. 'Look, can you please just scan the other human?'

'I have already scanned all humans within my range,' the medibot replied.

OK. *Deep breaths, now.* It wasn't the bot's fault that it was an idiot. 'I mean, the boy. Right here? The one I am pointing to?' I jabbed a finger at the sleeping boy, half-heartedly hoping the motion would wake him up. It didn't.

'Human, are you referring to Echo Zero-One-Three-Five?' The second bot swooped in next to the first.

I frowned. Echo zero-what-what-what? I looked back down at the boy in his old-fashioned clothes. The realization washed over me, leaving me cold as I moved his chin to the left to get a better view of his neck. There, beneath his hairline, was a barcode.

'He's a synth,' I said, more to myself than the bots. The

dread grew in my stomach again. Where were the other humans?

'Correct, human,' the second bot said. 'To be exact, Echo Zero-One-Three-Five is an Aurora Technologies TeenSynth, version four-point-zero.'

'A TeenSynth?' I repeated. I looked back at the boy, at the flickering of his eyelids as REM sleep took over.

When I was still allowed to go to school, I had met plenty of TeenSynths. More controversial due to their price than what they were, the bots were invented to tackle the great infertility crisis in the West. We had even learnt about them in biology, about how their lab-grown organs were regulated by an electric, positronic brain. The goal had been to eventually graduate the bots into full, growing humans, so that their parents didn't have to trade in their bodies each year, but the project had been shut down due to lack of funding once the Emergency Powers Decree passed.

My friends always thought they were creepy, but I found them fascinating. I was never allowed to socialize with them, of course – being who I was, I was hardly allowed to socialize with anyone – but I certainly found it hard to tell them apart from the other students. The only giveaway was the barcode, which had to be on show at all times. But apart from that, we were the same. We both laughed, and cried, and had to do homework. For all intents and purposes, they were human. Mostly.

'OK.' I spoke to the medibot this time. I thought carefully about the wording of my next question. If I was right, I didn't want to waste any time, and clearly these bots weren't exactly bright. 'This TeenSynth is over sixty per cent human. Is there any way you can scan him and tell me why he is unconscious?'

The bots hovered for a moment, the only noise that of their propellers working to keep them airborne.

'Affirmative. I can scan and determine biological damage of TeenSynth Echo Zero-One-Three-Five,' the first bot finally spoke. 'I will need a human command to confirm—'

'Confirm, run the scan, quickly,' I babbled, shocked that I had somehow persuaded a robot to treat the synth like a human being. It was more than I had persuaded my classmates to do, anyway.

'Scanning . . .' Lights appeared on the bot's interface and a familiar beeping noise emitted from its speakers. After only a few seconds, the scan was complete. 'TeenSynth scan indicates several catastrophic failures. RAM memory, failed to initiate. E-Mote chip, failed to initiate. Cause of failures: unknown. Most likely cause of unconsciousness: lack of electrical power.'

'So . . . he's run out of battery?' I asked. The second bot moved its floodlight up and down, as if nodding its head. I looked back at the boy, and the rise and fall of his chest. So strange to think that he looked so real, so human, but all of his vital organs and processes relied on an electronic source. Who knew how long he had until his heart stopped beating?

And if there really wasn't anyone else, he was the only other conscious being left on Earth.

'What can we do?' I asked, my voice cracking again. I couldn't lose my only hope at finding out what had happened here, where all the others were. I had to save him. He was my only hope, and apparently, I was his.

'There are several possibilities for reviving Echo Zero-One-Three-Five,' the second bot said. 'Primarily, plugging TeenSynth into a power source will correct the issue.'

I looked down at the synth, from the top of his baseball cap to the tips of his size elevens. There was no way I could lift him on my own. And there were no lights on in the city – I had no idea where the nearest power source was.

Well, there was one person who would know. And he was out for the count.

I focused on the first bot, the one who had an open side panel and had scared me with the jumping electricity. Electricity that, really, was dangerous left unchecked.

'Would it be possible . . .' I spoke slowly, guilt burning in my cheeks. I knew it was ridiculous, but I felt bad asking the medibot to give its own . . . what? Not life, not really. I swallowed hard. 'Would it be possible to charge him – I mean, the TeenSynth – using, well, you as the power source?'

The first bot hovered despite the crackle of energy sparking from its open side. After a moment, the second bot intervened.

'Affirmative,' it said, and the first bot floated down to the boy laid out on the floor. Some semblance of meaning passed between the bots, something I could only assume was on some sort of electronic level. The broken medibot moved in front of me and I instinctively shifted back so it could access the boy's neck. Then, the broken medibot's light winked out, and the second bot took over.

Two metal arms protracted from the bot's main body, each equipped with a different tool, neither of which I could name. It made quick work of its comrade's corpse, popping the rest of the silver protective shell off to expose the wiring inside. It used one of the tools to snip a green wire, and then turned its attention to the TeenSynth.

A red laser point scanned the barcode and a soft click revealed the panel beneath his skin. The bot slowly peeled it back until the socket was on show, and then it jammed the green wire into the slot with less ceremony than I was prepared for. A blue spark appeared when the connection was made and for a moment, I thought the bot had short-circuited him. But after a few seconds, the boy took in a sharp gasp of air and his eyes opened.

'What . . . happened?' He spoke as if he had been running and was short of breath. I leapt to my feet, shocked at how quickly the boy had regained consciousness. The bot that had delivered the power remained motionless, but the bot with the tools quickly withdrew the wire and sealed back the patch of skin before the boy had chance to move.

'Oh, yes, erm, I think you passed out,' I said. The boy stopped panting and, slowly, rolled on to his back, his eyes meeting mine. 'I think you ran out of battery.'

For the longest few seconds of my life, nobody moved. Then, the boy's eyes grew wide, like he was seeing me for the first time.

'Holy shit,' he shouted, causing me to take a step back. He jumped up into a crouched position before getting to his feet. I had been right about not being able to carry him; he towered over me. 'Holy. Shit,' he repeated, his dark eyes moving from the top of my head to my scuffed regulation trainers.

'Um,' I stammered again, then bit my lip. Why was speaking up always so hard for me? I was fine with the service bots. They were the only things to talk to some days when Father had to work. But people? People were tricky. 'Are you OK? You looked . . . I wasn't sure if you were still alive for a moment there.' I gestured to the bot on the floor and the one that still hovered by his side, scanning him. The boy waved a hand at the bot and it backed up a few centimetres, but he didn't take his eyes off me.

'Am *I* OK? You thought *I* might be dead?' He stressed the pronoun and half laughed as he spoke. 'Are you shitting me? You just crash-landed to Earth, in a freaking spaceship! And you want to know if *I'm* OK?' He brought the heels of his hands to his eyes in disbelief.

A red flush of embarrassment burnt in my cheeks. 'Well, technically, half a spaceship,' I muttered, glancing at the debris that still littered the ground.

Had I really been in space? Is that where . . . where everyone else was? I pushed down the sheer terror causing my eyes to itch. Focus. One problem at a time.

He dropped his hands and stared at me for a minute before he burst out laughing, a warm sound that raised a smile out of me despite my embarrassment.

'Half a ship! Half a . . . You know, that's pretty funny. She's funny too, ladies and gents. What are the odds?' He held his hands aloft, like a spokesperson addressing an audience.

'Who . . . who are you talking to?' I asked. He stopped laughing and pushed his hands into his pockets, his face suddenly still. 'And what do you mean by "funny *too*"? Funny as well as . . . ?' I paused, waiting for an answer.

It was his turn for his cheeks to flush red. 'Oh. Right,

yeah.' I had caught him out, but I didn't understand how. He kicked at the dirt with his green high-top. 'Sorry, I've been alone for—'

He was cut off by a low, distinct howl in the distance that made the hair on the back of my neck stand on end.

'What was that?' I whispered.

'Something we need to move away from,' the boy said. He held out his hand, his eyes scanning the nearby tree-line. 'We need to move. Now.'

Despite everything, despite having more questions than ever before, I took his hand.

5

As I ran with her warm hand in mine, I couldn't believe what was happening. Sure, I had touched the HUMANKIND bots before – on a pretty dark day, I even tried hugging one – but this was different. This hand wasn't just warm, it was reactive. I squeezed the fingers tight and they squeezed mine back.

'What was that?' she asked again. For a moment I was so distracted by the sound of her voice – her new, unheard, human voice – that I didn't answer. Then we heard the howl again and I picked up the pace, half dragging her behind me.

'I'm not exactly sure,' I panted as we hit the treeline. 'I think it used to be a panther. Or maybe a wolf.'

'"Used to be"?' she replied, barely keeping up. I looked

back at her jumpsuit and realized that she must be struggling. One hundred years of bedsores will do that to a girl, if she's one of them, I mean. One of the humans that the HUMANKIND bots were always looking for.

'Don't worry about it,' I said. We ran out on to the gravel path and I stopped, again painfully aware of the loud crunching underfoot and the bright lights above. I checked my HUD and was relieved to see that the battery notification had gone. Thirty-eight per cent remaining. Not stellar, but more than enough to get home on.

Home. We had to get out of this park. I looked at the girl – she was doubled over, her hands on her knees as she panted. Hard. We could run like I had earlier, but there was no guarantee she would make it. It would be better to stick to the treeline, wait for the wolf-panther-thing to pass, and then slowly make our way out over the grassland.

The howl came again, and it was closer than I was comfortable with.

'Come on,' I whispered, dragging her into the bushes. She tripped on the gravel and I had to hold her up – her shoes were some sort of junky granny slip-ons, not built for running from mutants – and we ducked into the undergrowth, our backs against the long grass behind. In the silence of the park, our heavy breathing sounded louder than I would have hoped. At least a minute passed, and no more howls.

'So,' I whispered when I thought it was safe enough to talk; safety was relative right now, obviously, but I had to do something to drown out the pounding of blood in my ears. 'You an astronaut, or an alien?'

The girl smiled, her teeth perfectly straight. My heart stuttered and I instinctively checked my battery levels. Still well over thirty-five per cent. Weird.

'Neither,' she said. She gestured to her suit. 'I was part of the freezing programme. The one Aurora Systems ran? You know, at the . . .' She paused, her smile fading, her blue eyes distant. And her eyes were really blue, almost artificially so. She could easily pass as a TeenSynth. Maybe she *was* a synth. But no, the bots had gone straight for her. She had to be human.

My heart fluttered again, this time causing me to breathe in deep. Must get that checked.

'At the end of the world?' I finished for her. The smile returned, half as big, and she nodded. 'Yeah, I had guessed as much. We've been waiting for one of you to turn up.'

'We?' the girl asked hopefully.

A new feeling washed over me, something I didn't remember feeling before. I felt . . . I felt *sorry* for her. 'Oh, I mean me. Well, I think the HUMANKIND bots too, but they don't really . . . they can't care, exactly. It's . . . there's just me.' I looked away and scanned the path beyond the bush, avoiding her electric-blue eyes.

'Just . . . ? It can't just be you,' the girl replied. 'It can't even just be me. They said that we would all wake up together when it was safe. There has to be someone else.' Something in her voice caught and I bit my lip. Again with the feelings? I felt the lump at the back of my throat and swallowed it down. OK, this was getting really weird now. My chip must be more broken than usual.

'I dunno,' I said, witty and charming as usual. My cheeks flared. *I dunno* was the best I could come up with?

The girl was quiet for a moment and I used the time to check for signs of the big cat thing. I couldn't hear any gravel crunch, or twigs snapping. It had been a little while. Maybe it had gone?

'How long has it been?' she asked, and her question caught me off guard.

'What?' I said, turning to look at her. She had a small scar on her face, just above her eyebrow, which somehow made her features pop even more. My mouth went dry and I swallowed. Yeah, definitely a malfunction. I'd get a bot to check me over in the morning. Should never have let myself run out of battery like that.

'How long since . . . since we left?' she asked. *Oh, God.* There were tears in those perfect blue eyes. I had no idea how to deal with girls, never mind crying ones. I shifted uncomfortably in the bush.

'Hundred years, give or take,' I said. I looked at the

path, glad to have something else to turn my attention to.

The girl swallowed hard and I think – I know – a small sob slipped out from between pink lips.

'OK, I think we're good to move now,' I said. Anything to get me out of this situation. Maybe a change of topic would stop her from crying. You know, the topic of whether or not we were about to be mutant chum.

She didn't say anything else, thank God, and silently let me lead her along the edge of the path towards the exit. It wasn't far to the gate, but it wasn't close either. We just had to stay quiet and keep moving. The noisiest part would be reattaching the chain, but the gate had a master lock I could use while I did it. Just had to keep my fingers intact.

Up ahead, a set of iron bars blocked the way behind the bushes.

'OK. We need to go back on the path,' I said. When the girl didn't answer I turned to look at her. In the dim light, it was hard to see her face under all the soot. A tear track cut through the grime on her cheek. *Yikes.* She was no use in this state, so I was on my own. Well, that was fine. I'd survived a hundred years on my own so far.

Not with someone else to keep alive, though.

Gently, I pointed to the iron bars, and then to the path. She nodded. I let out a sigh of relief and led her out by her arm on to the gravel, after looking both ways first. Apart from the dark parts of the path where the street lights had failed, it looked safe enough.

We stepped out from the bushes and I let go of her arm, hovering my hands around her shoulders like I did after pulling a brick out from a Jenga tower. Not sure why I bothered playing; the bots always won anyway.

Once the girl seemed like she could stand up on her own, I gestured forwards and started to walk, and thankfully she followed. *All right.* We were doing all right. I looked ahead and could actually make out the outline of the gate in the gloom. We had travelled further than I thought. Me, and my new lady friend. In movies, chicks always dug a guy that saved them. That's kind of what I was doing, right? Damsel in distress and all that jazz.

I walked a little taller, straightening my back. The girl was going to be so impressed with me, especially when she saw my apartment. I remembered the hard drive and the tissues and cursed inwardly. Would have to move those before she noticed.

She. I almost facepalmed. *You moron*, I told myself. *You don't even know her name.*

'So, uh, what's your name?' I asked, trying to sound casual and instead asking in the same tone of voice that a waiter asks someone for their order. I had to rewatch some movies. I hadn't had time to practise my pick-up lines.

'Pandora,' the girl whispered. She was still crying but the sobbing had stopped. *Phew.*

'Pandora, that's a great name. Strong. Greek?' I asked, the heat rising in my cheeks again. *Greek?* Like anyone really knows stuff about their name. Like anyone actually cares.

To prove me right, the girl shrugged.

'I'm Echo,' I said, choosing to move past my own idiocy.

'Echo?' the girl asked. She wiped the tear from her cheek and looked at me. 'Isn't that your build, not your name?'

I blinked at her. I liked Echo, but yeah, I could see her point. My parents, the ones who adopted me and sent me to school and cared enough to spend a lot of money on me, would have had a real name picked out, but I couldn't remember it. Something else lost to the sands of time, blah blah blah. It had never bothered me, but suddenly Echo felt stupid and robotic and just plain wrong.

'Echo is a perfectly good name, you know,' I shot back. I felt it again, the familiar anger building up in my chest and balling up in my fists. It looked like my E-Mote chip was back in action – well, to the fullest extent it could be. 'I'm pretty sure it's also Greek. What makes your name any better than mine?'

I thought I was being clever, but the girl shrank back. 'I'm sorry. I didn't think. That was so rude of me, I'm – I'm sorry.' Tears filled her eyes again and her voice cracked.

Oh, no. More tears. I was surprised to find the anger melting away, to be replaced by that unfamiliar feeling of pity. I felt sorry for her, again. Was this what empathy felt like? I had never had anything to feel empathetic about before. Not even a goldfish.

'Oh, jeez. I'm sorry, Pandora,' I said. I reached out to – what? Pat her shoulder? I wasn't sure so I let my arm fall dead at my waist. 'It's totally rad. Both our names are totally rad.'

'You speak funny,' Pandora mumbled, knitting her fingers together and focusing on those instead as we walked along.

I speak funny? Yeah, says the girl who speaks so fancy that she sounds like a princess from an animated movie. I laughed. I was surprised even at that, which made me laugh more. Two real laughs in one night? Something weird was going on.

'What's so funny?' Pandora grumbled.

'Nothing,' I said. 'Just, you know. You tell me I have a funny name and then, in apology, tell me my speech is whack too.' I gave her a sideways glance and to my relief, she smiled. 'How do you know I'm talking funny? Maybe you're the one talking funny. It *has* been a hundred years since you were here, you know.'

'Fair point, well made,' she said. Her accent *was* unusual – she definitely sounded like she had money.

'Well, I am the smartest dude alive, you know.' I decided that funny was better than making her sad, and the laugh that followed made my heart do that weird flutter thing again. Maybe I wouldn't go straight to the bots in the morning. I was starting to kind of like it.

'Oh no.' Pandora's face fell and I followed her eyeline to the mangled robot that lay ahead, parts strewn across the path.

'Oh, don't mind him,' I said. It was the safety bot from earlier, the one that had unwittingly saved me from the panther-lion-thing. Poor dude. I knew it couldn't feel, but I still can't imagine a world where it would be fun to be pulled limb from limb. 'He kind of saved my life. It's a safety bot, see? It was built for that shit.' I pointed out the blue badge visible on the top half of the bot's main body.

Despite my best efforts, Pandora still looked sad. 'Do you think he suffered?'

I raised an eyebrow at her. 'Bots don't feel stuff. They don't have an E-Mote chip, or a brain or heart or whatever you have. They just . . . exist.'

Pandora nodded, but she seemed as gloomy as she had earlier. *Great. Bots are killing my vibe even when they're dead.*

'Gree-gree-greetings E-E-Echo-Zzzzz.' The noise made me and Pandora jump. The bot's voice box had come loose from its casing, which made it even louder in the quiet night.

'Shit,' I said, crouching on the balls of my feet. I scanned the ground, but there were too many parts to see which was the bot's voice box.

'Can I hel-hel-help you, m-m-miss?' The bot spoke again and seemed to be even louder as it malfunctioned its way through the sentence.

'It's alive,' Pandora said, and this time I did facepalm. She sank to her knees, sifting through the debris on the floor. 'We have to try and help him.'

'*Him?* Pandora, please, it's a bot,' I pleaded, my eyes flicking from the gate to the darkness of the trees. 'It's not alive, and this isn't helping. If anything, the damn thing is ringing the dinner bell.'

I hissed the last part and Pandora looked up at me, eyes wide in recognition of what I had just said. Almost on cue, the sound of growling made us both turn slowly around.

Under a flickering street light stood my worst nightmare. It had the body of a wolf but the golden eyes of a lion. It was huge, almost as big as the panther-thing from earlier. Drool pooled from its mouth, which had two sets of teeth. The weirdest part, though, was the legs. There were six, four on one side and two on the other, making the thing look like a photograph that had overexposed.

'Pandora. Get. Up,' I whispered.

She didn't move.

'Pandora, get your butt off the floor before I pick it up.'

I spoke louder, the need to whisper long gone.

The creature snapped its teeth together and Pandora sprang to her feet.

'What now?' she asked, pure terror in her eyes.

'Run!'

She turned on her heel and took off into the darkness, but I knew from earlier she would be too slow. Before the wolf could lean back on its many legs to give chase, I picked up the nearest piece of bent metal from the ground.

'Hey, *Coyote Fugly*,' I called, and the wolf took its eyes off Pandora's fleeing form. 'Come at me!' I held my position as the wolf started running, a mixture of fear and adrenaline holding my muscles taut. *Just a little longer. Hold your nerve.* The wolf closed in, and just before it pounced I ducked, letting the thing jump right over my head. Metal in hand, I slashed at the wolf's exposed underbelly, catching one of the extra legs and spilling hot liquid across my shirt that I knew would make me throw up if I looked at it.

The creature howled, a primal scream that made Pandora turn and look back to see what had happened.

'Keep running!' I shouted, because my feet were already moving, my high-tops pounding the gravel as I left the creature behind me. I had wounded it, but it wasn't dead. No doubt I had just made it mad, and who needed six legs to run when it had five perfectly good ones left?

Pandora didn't need telling a third time. She turned and carried on towards the gate, now so close I almost felt relieved. We had done it. We were nearly at the gate. We just had to run through and pull the lock down. I could chain it in the morning, to hell with that tonight. I could see that it was closed, the way I had left it, and despite the obvious dangers I wished I had left it open.

I risked a look over my shoulder – the wolf was so close I could see its amber eyes glowing in the dark area between two street lights. I was right. It was mad as all hell.

'We're not going to make it!' Pandora screamed as I caught up with her.

'Just don't look back,' I yelled. We reached the gate and I threw myself at it, my momentum almost pushing the thing open. As quick as my trembling fingers could, I threw back the rusted bolt and pushed open the gate with a loud squeak. The noise seemed to piss off the wolf even more, and it howled so loudly I thought it was going to burst my eardrums.

'Go!' I yelled. Pandora shot under my arm as I held open the gate, then I followed, turning in the same movement to slam it shut.

I pulled the outer bolt across just as the wolf slammed into the bars, the force knocking both me and Pandora to the floor. I banged my elbow hard against the pavement and sat, stunned, as the gnashing teeth rained slobber down on to my high-tops. The wolf was strong, forcing the gate back on to its hinges, but I knew from experience that the bars were stronger. After a few useless chomps, the wolf pulled its mouth out of the grille, howled, and stomped away into the darkness of the park.

'We're alive.' Pandora spoke first. I stood up and helped her to her feet, and she actually fist-pumped the air. 'We're alive!' she said again, and she threw her arms around my neck, squealing into my hair.

I stood stock still for a second, and then hugged her back, feeling her warmth through the thin fabric of her suit. My heart skipped again, and I smiled as I breathed in the smoky smell of her hair.

Yeah, maybe Pandora wasn't so bad after all.

6

I woke up in the king-size bed I had passed out in, with the beginnings of dawn creeping across the plush carpet from under the heavy curtains.

It took me a moment to remember where I was. The decor of the room I was staying in was almost the complete opposite of my childhood bedroom. Instead of framed posters of French plays, the walls were covered in gold reflective wallpaper and posters of half-naked women. There was a huge TV covering the whole opposite wall, and the bedsheets were red satin, not the cream cotton of my own. Echo had told me that this was some famous football player's apartment, and insisted that he hadn't chosen the pictures on the walls. It had been cute the way the conversation turned his ears pink, though.

Echo. I wasn't sure if it was because he was half bot, but he just seemed easier to talk to than the other boys at school. Oh God, was that racist? Can you be racist against bots? I sighed, the embarrassment coming over me again like it did last night when I hugged him. I never did stuff like that, but I was just so happy to be alive. Hopefully he'll have forgotten by now.

Breathe. Dr Kapoor's voice floated through to me as the anxiety threatened to take over. *In, one-two-three-four.* I held my breath and started to count before a thought hit me. Dr Kapoor – she was probably dead, too, unless she got on the programme like I did. Would she have got on the programme?

Out, seven-and-eight. I couldn't think like that. I was catastrophizing again, that's what she would say. There was every chance she was in her own pod, safe and sound, with all the others.

Wherever they were.

I slid my legs over the edge of the bed and made my way to the gold-plated en suite, attempting to inspect myself in the mirror. I had showered last night once we got in, the smell of smoke and sweat clinging to my clothes, but I still looked tired this morning. Was it possible to still be tired after a hundred years of sleep? I pulled at my pale skin, dark beneath the eyes with bags.

I was thin, even thinner than I realized in the shower

last night. To be expected, I supposed, after so long in stasis. I had been too tired last night to eat, but this morning I was starving. My mouth watered at the prospect of orange juice and fresh eggs, thick toast and lashings of butter.

After I washed my face and brushed my teeth, I headed for the walk-in wardrobe. Unfortunately for me, the only clothes available were for a man at least twice as tall and twice as wide as me. I had ended up sleeping in a shirt so oversized it could pass for a night dress. I rooted through the drawers and finally found another large shirt and a belt to cinch it in with. We would have to go shopping this morning.

Shopping. With a pang, the events of the night before came crashing down on me again. Were there even shops any more? Yes, there must be. On the short walk to the apartment, Echo had explained that the majority of the bots had kept working all these years, that the electricity was still on and the stores still full of stock. There would be somewhere to get clothes, and food, but then what? What was the point? Echo said he didn't know of anyone else that was still out there. He said he hadn't spoken to another human being in over a hundred years.

I swallowed the panic that was rising in my throat and leant on the edge of the dresser. I needed to do my breathing exercises again. *In, one-two-three-four.* We couldn't be the only ones. If I was here, someone else had to be. *Out, seven-and-eight*.

My father would be safe, somewhere. He had to be. As the president of Aurora Tech, my father was the most important person in, well, arguably the world. *In, one-two-three-four.* Yes, what I needed was a plan. I just had to work out where the other pods had landed, and find my father, and we could work out what to do next together.

Out, seven-and-eight. And then everything would be all right.

Once my heart rate had returned to normal, I made my way out into the living area. It was all one space, a huge cavern of boys' toys and electronic entertainment. When we had come in last night, Echo had dashed about, picking up bits of rubbish and packing away a games console or something. Not that I really cared about the mess. Who did he have to keep it clean for? It had been very sweet of him though.

The blinds were drawn so I flicked the light switch. Echo wasn't around.

'Rosie, can you open the blinds?' I called. Echo had explained to me that Rosie was still operational, and had used her to close the blinds the night before. Apparently, there had been a power surge, but everything seemed to be working now. Echo explained that they were common. No change there, then.

'Certainly, Pandora,' Rosie replied. I had programmed her with my details the night before after being left alone in my room, glad of some semblance of normalcy to help me drift off to sleep. Rosie had run my whole life before all this. Even now, she immediately set about raising the blinds and I covered my eyes as the sunrise temporarily blinded me.

The view was sensational. Last night, there weren't enough lights on across the city to truly appreciate it, but now the sunlight moved between the buildings like a cat stalking through long grass. The sunrise oranges and golds lit up the towering skyscrapers and rebounded across the dense living-room carpet. I had never seen the sky so clearly: pinks and blues and reds streaked across the clouds in the morning light. Last time I had looked out of my window, my last day on Earth, the usual haze of pollution had blocked the sun out until it was a dull coin of light in a grey sky.

'Oh, you're up.' I started, as I hadn't noticed Echo enter the room. He was already dressed in another strange get-up, this time a geometric bomber jacket and tight acid-wash jeans. He raised an eyebrow and lowered his eyes, taking in my own makeshift dress, and for a moment I blushed.

'I don't quite have the selection of clothes you do,' I said, pulling at the edge of the giant shirt that skimmed just above my knees. Did I imagine it, or did Echo blush too? 'I hope not all the clothes in the stores are in your . . . unique style.'

'Oh no,' said Echo, bouncing across the room and flopping down on the oversized couch. 'Sorry, chica, but this style is taken. Took me months to put together this look.' He picked up the remote and the television that covered one whole wall clicked on.

The home screen said *Welcome back, Echo*, and suggested a long list of what he might want to watch next. To my surprise, most of the titles were in the *Watch again?* list on the left-hand side, a series of tiny stills from the shows and the telltale red line of progress maxed out along the bottom. One of the stills maxed out across the screen during the moment of inactivity, and a clip played silently in the background.

'Hey, that guy dresses like you,' I said, perching at the other end of the sofa. The boy in the clip was dressed almost identically to Echo, except his outfit featured a gold chain around his neck.

'Yeah, that's my idol. The Fresh Prince. I'll take that as a compliment,' Echo said, popping his oversized collar.

'Where is he the prince of?' I asked.

Echo raised another eyebrow at me. 'Of Bel Air.'

'Where is Bell Hair?'

This time Echo laughed. 'You don't know the Fresh Prince?'

I shook my head. At the bottom left corner of the screen the episode title and season of the show were listed. Under that, there was a date. *1992.*

'Why would I have seen this? This show is ancient, look at the date,' I said, pointing to the bottom of the screen. 'It's like, nearly a hundred years old.'

'More like nearly two hundred, actually,' said Echo quietly, and my retort caught at the back of my throat. He was right, everything was ancient now. And Echo had been alone for so long, no wonder he had seen everything. Even the classics.

'You OK?' Echo broke through my thoughts and I managed a small smile.

'Yeah, I'm fine. I think I just need to find out where everyone is, that's all.' A shadow darkened Echo's expression and I tried to laugh it off. 'I know what you said last night, that you haven't seen anyone else. But have you really looked everywhere? Even outside the city?'

Echo thought for a moment. He opened a drawer in the mirrored coffee table and got out a bag of strawberry laces, pulled one out, and chewed on it thoughtfully. 'I've never had a reason to leave the city,' he said finally, and something about his tone told me he was reluctant to admit it. 'Oh, shoot. Sorry. Want one?'

'No, thank you. I think those jelly-type sweets usually have gelatin in. I'm a vegetarian.'

Echo scanned the back of the pack before slowly nodding and withdrawing the offer. We'd have to go shopping for more than clothes, then.

'And anyway, now we have a reason. To leave, I mean.'

'We?' Echo repeated. He grinned and I couldn't help but feel a little better. His smile had that effect on me – was that a robot thing, or a human thing? Or should I not even think about that? 'I like the sound of that. The Adventures of Pandora and Echo. We'll need a theme song, but I can think of that on the way.'

'Sure,' I said slowly. If Echo wanted a theme song, then he could have a theme song. 'Well, I've been thinking. First, we need to get me some clothes that actually fit, and some food. And then we can ask a HUMANKIND bot where to go.' I had done a report on the emerging HUMANKIND project at school, just before everything went to pot. The bots were being created with a similar model to the TeenSynths, meaning they would be both biological and robotic. That meant their artificial systems could measure the environmental impact of the world on biological structures, and they could decide when it was safe for humans to return. They also had to know where the other cryogenically frozen people were. That was their job.

Echo frowned. 'I can help with food and clothes, but those HUMANKIND idiots? They've never told me shit.'

He took another bite of his lace. 'Maybe they don't even know.'

It was my turn to frown. 'I'm pretty sure they do. That was their whole purpose, in case we had to initiate SpindleSleep. I remember my father talking about it.'

'Your dad? Was he a programmer?' Echo looked intrigued, but I knew I had said too much. When people found out about my father, they treated me differently. I couldn't ask for a cleaner slate than the one sat in front of me, munching his way through a pack of reconstituted sugar, and I didn't want to ruin it just yet.

'Something like that. Say, Echo, I'm rather peckish. What's for breakfast?' I asked.

Echo laughed, bits of lace spewing across the table. 'You're looking at it,' he said, gesturing to the drawer stuffed full of candy.

'Is there nothing . . . like eggs?' I asked, my mouth filling with saliva at the thought.

Echo stopped laughing, his eyes wide. 'Eggs? Dude, I can't even remember the last time I saw an egg. And even that was in powdered form. I haven't got a little farm in the games room, ya know. There isn't anything as fresh as eggs in the whole city.'

I blinked. How could I have been so stupid? Obviously there were no animals. There were barely even crops when everything ended. That was the point of SpindleSleep, so the world could recover. So things could live again.

I grabbed a pack of Red Hots and tore them open. As I ate, I explained to Echo about my plan to find my father.

An hour later, we were in the platinum lift racing down to ground level. I tried to ignore the pop of my ears as we descended, although it didn't seem to bother Echo. Once on the ground floor, we stepped out into the lobby that I had only seen briefly the night before.

I remembered the smashed glass but in the daylight it looked even worse. The chunk of metal from . . . goodness knew where on my pod was still lying on the floor, too heavy for the simple cleaning bots to move. They were already sweeping up the mess and another bot was scanning the window frame, presumably in order to replace the glass. The sight of familiar things put my stomach at ease after the churning trip of the lift.

The bots, with their sleek silver bodies and mechanical appendages, were one thing – but that wasn't what startled me as we walked through the ruined lobby. A boy who looked the same age as Echo and me stood in what had once been the revolving doorway of the building. But no, it couldn't be a boy. From its upright stature and blank expression, everything about it screamed robot.

'Greetings, Echo Zero-One-Three-Five,' said the bot. I turned to look at Echo, who narrowed his eyes at the bot.

If I didn't know any better, I'd say he and that bot had a past, and not a very good one.

'Hey, Gort,' Echo said through gritted teeth and a false smile. 'Well, I can guess why you're here. News travels fast over Wi-Fi.'

'Indeed,' the bot responded. Its voice was distinctly human and yet the tone was devoid of personality. It looked like a TeenSynth – but clearly it had been stripped of its personality and converted into a HUMANKIND. I shifted uncomfortably. Near the end there had been talk of converting the bots we already had to save resources, but I never knew if they went through with it. Clearly they did. I wasn't sure how I felt about that.

'I am here to speak to the human, Pandora,' the bot – Gort, had Echo called him? – replied. Rosie must have uploaded my information to a main server, and now the HUMANKIND had sought me out. Made sense, and saved me some time.

'Hello. Nice to meet you. I'm Pandora,' I said. Gort stayed perfectly still, and I wasn't sure he had heard me, so I carried on. 'Erm, I'd quite like to locate other humans? Perhaps the ones from . . . well, from wherever I came from?'

Echo widened his eyes a little.

Gort moved suddenly, a mechanical movement that betrayed his biological limbs. He strode across the room until he stood uncomfortably close to me, and I heard the whirring of a processor deep inside him.

'Scan complete. Identity confirmed. You are one hundred per cent human. Welcome back to Earth, Pandora,' Gort smiled, a mechanical smile that didn't reach his eyes. I swallowed, unsure what to say.

'He's never that nice to me,' Echo said, flicking the side of Gort's skull. He didn't flinch. 'Then again, I'm only sixty per cent human. Bit bigoted, but I'm not one to hold a grudge.' I smiled. Echo's humour was like nothing I had come across before, human or bot.

'Bigoted? I think the correct term before I was frozen was technophobic,' I said.

'Technophobic. Yeah, that works. Stop being technophobic, Gort.' Echo held a sarcastic edge to his tone. 'And hey, listen up. Pandora needs to know where her fam are at.' Echo took over and I was glad, even though I only had half an idea of what he was talking about. 'I know you never told me, but she's your human overlord so, like, spill.'

Gort blinked, the mechanical smile wiped from his lips in an instant. 'The location of the cryogenic laboratory where Pandora was stored is LOCATION NOT FOUND.' Gort shrieked the last part so loudly I backed up until I was against the closed lift.

I turned to Echo and he looked as confused as I did.

'That's weird,' Echo said. 'He's never told me, because I

am but merely a lowly synth, but to not tell you?' I knew he was joking, but I still felt guilty at the way he mentioned his robotic parts. 'Maybe *you* need to ask him.'

Panic constricted my throat and I coughed to clear it. Talking, again. Not my strongest suit. But then again, Echo had assured me that 'Gort' was just another bot. I had to give it a good go. 'Robo— I mean, HUMANKIND,' I said in a voice I hoped imitated the superiority of my father. Echo snorted at my mistake but I shrugged him off. 'I am a human. You were designed to serve me. I require information. Where is the laboratory that I came from?'

'Oh ex-squeeze-me, your highness,' Echo said. I glared at him.

'The location of the cryogenic laboratory where Pandora was stored is LOCATION NOT FOUND,' Gort repeated, deafening us again.

I felt it, the panic creeping up like a physical thing, threatening my airway. 'That's not good enough. Tell me where they are.' My voice was high-pitched, frenzied, and I saw Echo take a step back out of the corner of my eye. I jabbed a finger at Gort's chest. 'Listen, you. I did not survive a fall from space just to be told it's the end of the road.'

'Correction, Pandora,' Gort replied. 'You have not come from space.'

This time, I was angry. 'Well, I, I mean . . . yes, yes I did.

I fell from the sky less than twenty-four hours ago. Echo saw me, he can corroborate that.' I turned to Echo and clearly something about my expression caused him to just nod in response, hands up in surrender.

'Negative,' Gort contradicted me again. I heard another low whirring sound before he continued. 'Human Pandora is not emitting enough radiation to have resided in space for any significant amount of time. Human Pandora may have fallen from the sky, but not from space. The HUMANKIND project was initially engineered to support a space exodus, but rolling solar storms in the late twenty-first century made space travel too dangerous. The HUMANKIND project therefore pivoted to underground bunkers, a fail-safe. Bunkers were built inside launch silos in case space launch was possible, but it was deemed safer to stay on Earth and weather the climate change. It is more likely – ninety-four per cent likely, to be exact – that your pod launched unexpectedly, recently, and then malfunctioned.'

'Malfunctioned?' I repeated dumbly. I looked at Echo, but he just shrugged. 'What does that even mean? Gort, can you at least tell me where I did originate from? If not space, then where?'

'Calculating,' Gort replied. He stood stock still with his eyes closed, his lids moving rapidly like he was in REM sleep. After a few seconds, he opened them again. 'Information downloaded from server. Calculations complete. Judging from the trail left behind by your pod, and the angle of trajectory after you landed, it is probable your point of origin is between seven hundred and seventy and eight hundred kilometres south of this point.'

'South of the . . . so, maybe I was the only one who launched, as opposed to the only survivor?' I asked, tears brimming in my eyes. The relief was palpable. It had occurred to me as I tried to sleep that perhaps my pod had been part of a larger ship that broke apart on re-entry, and that the other people I had been frozen with – my friends, my father – had been killed or scattered to the winds. The thought that they might still be alive, still asleep and safe somewhere, made my heart swell.

'Uh, are you OK?' Echo said. I had almost forgotten he was there, and he looked worried. I laughed through my tears.

'I'm very well, thank you, Echo,' I said, the tears spilling over. He took a step back and I wiped my cheeks. 'Happy tears. I mean, I had hoped that the HUMANKIND could help more, I'm not sure if they have become corrupted or what, but this is still good news. Maybe I can find my father.'

'You think so?' Echo asked, looking strangely hopeful. Why was he so excited to meet my father? Had he worked out who I was? No, impossible. I was always kept out of the press. I had to be mistaken – maybe Echo was just happy for me.

'Right,' I breathed. I stepped past Gort and my foot crunched broken glass. 'Come on, we're going to need supplies.'

'Supplies?' Echo asked. He ran to catch up with me as I strode across the lobby.

'Hey, Echo. Have you ever driven a car before?'

7

As I pushed the cart around the store I couldn't help but think of the commercials I had found on the servers a few months back. Apparently, before, TV shows had been punctuated by commercials, telling peeps to buy stuff and do stuff with money they didn't have. At the very least, it made sense of the timing of some of my shows, which were weird lengths like twenty-two minutes or forty-one minutes. The reason for that was because there would be like, fifteen minutes of ads. Which seemed crazy to me. Who wants that?

So I had set out to find some of these ads on the old video sites. They were mostly boring and informative, some dude in need of new shoes or something. Sometimes they were kind of funny, using superheroes to do the laundry or whatever. But there had been this one with a husband and wife arguing while they went around the grocery store. And that's what this reminded me of.

'What do you think of this one?' Pandora asked me for, like, the millionth time. She was holding up a red top that looked identical to the other red top she showed me five minutes ago.

'Yeah, that's rad,' I said, hoping I sounded sincere. I had never been so bored in my life. This mall was identical to all the others I went to. Everything under one big, friendly, Aurora Tech-owned roof.

Pandora had insisted on coming straight to the store after Gort told us about the sleep-lab bunker she had come from. In all honesty, I thought it was pretty vague. Eight hundred kilometres south? There was wasteland for days out there. I had seen it on maps. How would we know if we were going in the right direction, or avoid missing it? How did we even know what this bunker looked like? But Pandora seemed excited, and that was better than her crying.

Maybe she would even hug me again.

I hadn't been able to stop thinking about that hug since last night. And ever since, I just didn't feel so bad any more. Maybe it was the new sense of purpose or maybe it was just that it was nice to talk to someone, but it was sorta . . . nice, y'know? Plus, when my systems booted up this morning, the log showed a change to my E-Mote chip:

```
4096 TB E-Mote RAM Partially Enabled -
unable to update
```

Maybe it was coincidence. Maybe it was my tinkering the other day, or even the hard reboot from running outta juice. Whatever it was, my chip was better. Not fixed, but better.

'OK, and this is just an idea, feel free to decline, but,' Pandora appeared from behind a clothes rack holding up two grey backpacks, 'matching bags. Yes? No?'

'Groovy,' I said, with a thumbs up to back up my statement.

'I have no idea what that means but I'm going to assume it's a yes,' Pandora almost squealed as she loaded up her cart. 'Shopping might be the one thing I'm rather good at. I'm going to the changing rooms. Meet you in the grocery section?'

There was a reason I had suggested the strip mall a few blocks from my house. One, it had everything we could ever possibly need – as the jingle liked to remind me every half hour – and two, it gave us a good chance of finding a working car without running into . . . well, you know.

Pandora had asked me if I had driven a car before and what I told her was only really half a lie. Had I driven a car before? Yeah, exactly once. Why did I never drive again? I told her it was because I could walk everywhere I needed, that I needed to keep up my hot-bod physique, but that wasn't strictly true either. It was because during my one and only time in a car, I had crashed into a brick wall and nearly killed myself. And that car was still there, at the corner of Dennison Road and Fifth.

Had I meant to crash? Was I relieved when my systems rebooted, and I saw the programming bots checking my vitals? Maybe. It wasn't something I liked to think about.

Instead, I was relieved to head off to the store aisles. It occurred to me that Deidre was probably working today – she was the clerk at all the Aurora Tech-owned stores – but I would have to avoid her or I might scare Pandora off. Besides, when Dee saw my new girl, she might get jealous.

I cruised down the empty fresh produce aisle until I was going fast enough to lift my feet off the floor and ride the cart. At the end of the aisle I made a hairpin turn and rushed into the next aisle – confectionary. I loaded up the cart with the bare essentials – strawberry laces, a couple of jars of red cabbage, plus some sachets of dried stuff. Pasta, meals for one, lentils, anything that said *just add water.* Then I grabbed a couple of bottles of water too. I had seen enough zombie movies and played enough video games to know how to loot a store. I had no idea what was out there, and that scared the hell out of me. Best to be prepared. Finally, I wandered down the liquor aisle and was just eyeing up a bottle of single malt when Pandora appeared.

'You drink single malt?' Pandora said. I looked up and *damn*, she looked fly. She was wearing combat pants and the red shirt, complete with leather jacket and aviator shades. She had already shouldered her pack and she handed me mine to start packing with the contents of the cart.

'Of course I do,' I replied, not even convincing myself. 'All the greats do. James Bond. Scotty. Uh, that guy from *Columbo*?'

'Are they friends of yours, from before?' Pandora asked, packing some of the trolley contents into her bag.

I was about to laugh until I realized she was being serious. 'Friends of . . . yeah. Sure. Some of my best guys,' I said, sighing. The Educate-Pandora-on-the-Classics marathon would have to wait. I turned my attention back to the whisky. 'Probably shouldn't drink and drive, though.' I replaced the bottle on the shelf.

'Hey, wait,' Pandora said. She caught my hand while it was still on the bottle and electricity tingled under my skin, right where her fingers were. Another malfunction? Whatever it was, it felt good. 'We should take it. You know, in case of an emergency. Alcohol is a must for first aid and cleaning a wound.' She took the neck of the bottle and gently pulled it from my hand before putting it in the waiting backpack.

'Right. Emergencies. Smart,' I said, grinning back at her. She pulled a piece of blonde hair that had fallen from her ponytail and tucked it behind her ear, and all I could think was how much I wanted to reach out and touch it. Not in a creepy way, more in a 'how the heck can you be real?' kinda way.

Yikes. OK, now I sounded like a psycho. Definitely a small malfunction.

'Are you nearly ready?' she asked. I blinked away my thoughts and nodded.

'Yeah. You add any more to this cart though and we're gonna need a bigger boat.'

'A boat? I thought we were driving,' Pandora said. She grabbed a tin from the cart and put it in her bag, the picture of confusion.

I sighed and added *Jaws* to the list. 'Don't worry about it. I'll help you pack these. Then the fun starts,' I said, taking the bag from her and packing the pasta.

'The fun?' Pandora asked. I flashed her what I hoped was a wicked grin.

'We're going car shopping.'

Once we were packed up, I bypassed Deidre – sorry baby, you know we would never have worked – and headed out to the parking lot.

Considering the end had been nigh, there were a lot of cars still in the lot. Clearly some people heard about the climate collapse and thought, screw it, Oreos are my only hope and I will die trying to get some.

'What was it like?' Pandora asked. She had been quiet for a while by that point, ever since we left the store. I just assumed it was sort of the calm before the storm, the anticipation of hitting the road, but she looked nervous.

'What was what like?' I asked. I had spotted a freaking *Ferrari* in the corner of the lot and wanted to check it out as a first point of refusal. It was so rare to find any old classics, especially after Aurora Tech took over the last of the car manufacturers in the late twenty-first century. This was a treat.

'Well, to start, straight after. The . . . the bodies.' Pandora whispered the last part and I stopped, confused. I raised an eyebrow. 'You know, after the sudden freeze, and the heatwave? We knew it was coming, but to live through that . . . I assume you had a bunker? And then coming out to . . . what was left . . . it must have been awful . . .' Pandora trailed off and put a hand on my arm, which felt nice and tempted me to go along with her story. Just for a second.

But obviously I didn't. I'm not a total sleazeball. 'I don't remember any of that,' I said, shrugging my shoulders. Pandora dropped her hand. *Damn.* 'I don't remember anything before the bots found me at the edge of the city

– took a while for them to repair the weather damage to the centre of town and venture out that far, I guess. I was in the basement of some burnt-out house, nothing left but me and some burnt timber. The medibots scanned me and from, I dunno, levels of wear and tear and stuff, think I was out for, like, ninety-seven years. That was . . . three years ago now? No clue how I got there after everything went to shit. My memory – like, my robotic memory – is corrupted. I can't remember anything past three years ago.'

Pandora blinked. 'Three years alone is still a long time, though.'

I shrugged, but something tugged at the edge of my mind. An old dude, beardy, but I couldn't quite make out his face. He's saying something to me but there's no sound, so I gotta lip-read. I think he says, *I don't want you to be on your own.*

And then, just as fast as it was there, the face is gone. I shake my head. That was weird. Luckily, Pandora didn't seem to have noticed. She looked lost in her own thoughts.

'So you haven't . . . you haven't *lived* for a hundred years?' She used quotes around the word 'lived', which made me laugh.

'Well, I mean yeah. Something obviously kept my positronic nervous system going, because my cells kept renewing. I'm kinda like a 3D printer, everything just renews so I don't age. A human brain would have been sweet if they'd worked out how to clone one, but I wouldn't still be buff if I had me one of those. But, like, I was basically asleep the whole time, or I just don't remember. I'm not, like, a creepy old dude in this young hot bod, like in those vampire movies. I'm not much older than you, up here.' I tapped the side of my head.

'I'm sorry, *you* watched those vampire movies?' Pandora smirked. She seemed relieved, which made me relieved. I turned to keep walking towards the Ferrari.

'Yeah, yeah. You actually know those ones? I saw on the servers they were still pretty popular, even in the late twenty-first. I just wanted to know what the fuss was all about.'

'Oh yeah?'

'It gets lonely being the last dude on Planet Earth.' We reached the Ferrari and I dug in my pockets for the small tool kit I had picked up in the store. I looked at Pandora and she looked sad again. What had I said? Was it the last dude thing? I didn't like it when she was sad.

'Anyway, don't worry about it. And as for the bodies? Yeah, I thought it was weird that there weren't any around. But I asked Gort once and he said they were all cleaned up by the bots. They weren't, like, raptured or nothin'.'

Pandora's face lit up again. 'And now you believe in the Rapture?'

'Is it any worse than watching nine-plus hours of vampires? Now make yourself useful and hold this a second.' I passed her the lock pick, which I had fashioned out of two screwdrivers and a paperclip.

The cars left behind at the end of the twenty-first were all electric, like me – well, like forty per cent of me. Despite sometimes hating being part bot – and sometimes hating being part human – it did come in useful. I lifted my hand to the locked door and rested my palm against the handle. Closing my eyes, I tried to get in the zone, the one where I could hear the gentle hum of the car's electricity banks. Sometimes the batteries were too dead from lack of use, but some manufacturers were smarter than others. My old Italian friends at Ferrari were some of those smart dudes.

'What are you doing?' asked Pandora. I opened one eye and took the makeshift tool.

'Let's just say I've done my share of grand theft auto during this apocalypse,' I lied. I pushed the tool into the lock of the car and focused all my energy into my palm. 'A lot of these old-school car-battery manufacturers were actually owned by Aurora Tech. They used the same batteries and systems that they used in me, even if the outside was all someone else. Further, better, faster and all that. If I really concentrate, I can hear when the lock falls into place and I can also tell how full the battery is from the sonic frequency output. This one, for instance, is dope.'

'And dope means . . . ?'

'Dope means we are good to go,' I said. I clicked the last lock out of position and the door popped open, revealing the red leather seats beyond.

'So, you were able to do all that with your . . . I want to say robotic side, is that offensive?' Pandora chewed her lip.

I laughed. 'I'm not easily offended. And I know I'm one of a kind. I mean, I guess Gort and the other bots can technically commit GTA, but they wouldn't, because their coding doesn't let them break the law.'

Pandora raised an eyebrow.

'OK. It's like this,' I said, leaning back next to the unlocked door. 'Gort is a TeenSynth like me, right? So we look the same on the outside, all patchy facial hair and bad skin. But,' I paused as Pandora laughed, and then composed herself, 'on the inside, we're different. Aurora Tech didn't have time to create a whole new robot army, so they repurposed the TeenSynths. I read about it on some old news sites that the library archived. A lot of mad adoptive parents, for obvious reasons.'

'That's awful. I had no idea they resorted to . . . to that. They told us that they would build new models for the HUMANKIND project,' Pandora said, her brow furrowed. She looked upset. Better push along.

'Must have run out of EasyGrow organs. Look,

Pandora, don't worry. Gort doesn't remember anything or feel sad. See, that's the difference. I have my E-Mote chip and memory drive, Gort doesn't. Aurora Tech took those out so the HUMANKIND bots wouldn't feel lonely, I guess. I can see the HUMANKIND chip in my head, but . . . it doesn't seem to work. Kinda messed up my E-Mote chip and memory while it's in there too. But that's OK. I've made new memories, and I clearly kept my awesome sense of humour. That's more than old Gort can do.'

'So . . . they messed up the installation of your HUMANKIND upgrade?' Pandora asked. She sniffed, still on the wrong side of crying, but her curiosity had got the better of her.

'Correct-a-mundo. At least, it seems that way. Until I find a programmer – and let me tell you, there really aren't many at the end of the world – I'm stuck this way. Lucky for you.'

Pandora smiled. Man, she had a wicked smile. 'It is rather nice to not be the last human being alive,' she said.

I grinned back at her and tried not to get too excited about that comment. She saw me as human? Dope. 'So, let's get to it, m'lady.' I bowed and gestured to the passenger seat. Pandora rolled her eyes and ignored me, instead moving to pop the boot and put her bag inside. Sassy. I liked this new side of her. Maybe she was starting to open up.

Once I had squeezed my stuff in next to hers, I had to admit the space was a little tight, but a Ferrari? I wasn't missing my chance to drive a Ferrari.

'OK, so what now?' Pandora asked once we were sitting comfortably.

I adjusted the mirrors and checked the wings – the Ferrari was a good look for me, I looked fly – and pushed the button to turn over the engine. It took a couple of clicks, but I was right; there was still power in the bank. We would have to juice her up before we got into no man's land, but these babies could cover 500 kilometres, no sweat. More than enough to get us to another station.

'Let's see what we're working with here,' I said. I fiddled with the touch screen on the dash and spotted a GPS. I don't know why I got my hopes up. When it flashed on, it just said: *No satellite signal in this area. GPS not available.*

'The satellites probably broke up a long time ago,' Pandora said, and I nodded. She pointed to the corner of the screen. 'But look, a compass. We can at least use that to head south. It's not like we have an address anyway.'

'Boss,' I said, impressed. She was right. At least the compass would make it easier to sweep the area south of the city. I put the car into gear, revved the engine, and placed my hands on the steering wheel.

'So . . . shall we go?' Pandora asked. She lowered her

aviators to look at me over the frames.

I swallowed. I had jacked cars before, to look for supplies and old music players and other cool stuff, and that one other time . . . but never to leave the city. This place was my home, or at least as close to a home as I had ever gotten. There was so much to explore here, I had never even considered leaving before. More TV shows than I could ever watch, more books than I could ever read. Strawberry laces on tap. I flexed my fingers on the wheel.

I could lie. Say that the car doesn't work, buy myself some time. Pandora had told me herself that she didn't know the first thing about driving, which made sense. She must have been rich to afford one of those eee-zee-freeze tickets from Aurora Tech. I had seen the newspaper articles, back when I had tried to learn more about the world I just woke up in. Only hella dollar bought a space in the bunker. She was probably used to being driven around by a servant, or some shit.

We could hang out in the city for a while. Yeah. Watch some movies. Maybe I could even try and get the old cineplex working. Gort might be some use for once. And then maybe, eventually, Pandora would forget about this crazy road trip and we could make a life together. I wasn't so bad to look at. We could totally make it work.

'Echo?' She placed a hand on my arm and I realized I

hadn't said anything in a long time. I looked at her, into those pretty blues, and I knew. I couldn't do it. Pandora needed to find out what happened to her dad, for better or worse. I'd spent almost three years looking for mine. I would kill to know where I came from, why I wasn't updated and erased like the other synths.

In my chest, something warm and tingly spread from where my heart was. Another feeling I hadn't felt before meeting her.

'Sorry, P. I was just thinking, you know what this road trip needs?' I pulled a small cell from my pocket and flicked to the music app. There was no phone signal, but the rest of it still worked. 'A soundtrack.' The phone found the car's wireless speakers in seconds and the playlist I had spent years compiling blasted out. *Rad*.

Pandora grinned. 'Nice. Didn't take you for a classical music fan.'

I feigned shock and clutched non-existent pearls. 'Classical? Please. Someone needs to educate you on a little thing called grime.' I turned the volume up to max and clicked the handbrake off, pulling a one-eighty as I zoomed past the crusty old cars and out of the car park towards the freeway.

And nearly ran Gort clean over.

I slammed on the brakes as soon as I saw the dude standing in the entrance, which threw me and Pandora forwards so hard I nearly hit the windscreen. Man, seatbelts save lives, dude.

'What the—? P, you OK?' I asked, rubbing the back of my neck. If I had whiplash, Gort was paying my non-existent medical bills.

I checked over Pandora and while she was a little shaken up, she seemed fine.

'I'm all right,' she confirmed, a little breathless. She stared at Gort, who was still standing in the road like a traffic warden on steroids. He even had his palm up like a freaking stop sign.

I unbuckled myself and jumped out the car. 'Dude, what are you doing? I nearly killed you, yo.'

Gort lowered his hand and walked over to the passenger side. I did not like where this was going.

'Apologies if I startled you, human Pandora. Apologies, Echo Zero-One-Three-Five,' Gort said, although he didn't look at me. He spoke directly to Pandora's window. 'Human Pandora, I believe that, after running some more calculations, I have narrowed the search area of your escape pod launch location to thirteen square kilometres. As a HUMANKIND bot, it is my duty to assist you safely to said location, as it may hold further information about my primary objective. I heard you asking Echo Zero-One-Three-Five about possible vehicular transportation, and using a basic probability algorithm, I traced—'

'OK, I think we got it, Gort,' I said through gritted teeth.

Gort straightened up to look at me over the roof of the car.

'I'm sorry, what is he saying? It's hard to hear him through the window,' Pandora asked through my still-open door.

I gave Gort my best death stare before leaning back into the car. 'He's saying he thinks he knows roughly where your pod launched from, so he wants to tag along. Seems to also think it might tell him where the cryolabs are, or at least give him a clue. Remember I told you they can't remember? Well, Gort's entire existence hinges on fixing that.'

'Well, then, he should absolutely come. If Gort thinks he can find the labs, and my father, he needs to be with us.'

Pandora looked downright excited, all wide-eyed and smiley, which was a bit of a gut punch to be honest. So much for our romantic road trip.

Then again, the quicker we found the frozen dudes, the quicker I could remember some stuff too.

'All right. Gort, come round here and get in the back. Pandora already called shotgun.' I pulled forward the driver's seat to allow access to the tiny back seat beyond. Gort folded himself into the back neatly enough, but the way his knees touched his chin reminded me of one of those clown cars.

'Are you OK back there, Gort?' Pandora asked once I was back in the car.

I adjusted the mirror and tried not to laugh when I saw him concertinaed across the seat. 'He's fine. Let's go. And Gort, no talking over my choons. The driver makes the rules.'

'Affirmative, Echo Zero-One-Three-Five,' Gort said, and he switched to standby mode.

It was *almost* as if we were alone.

As we sped through the city, I looked up at the hollow shells of the buildings, the familiar streets and hydrants and bots. We nearly hit a security bot as we rushed by but he was too slow to even notice us. Pandora opened the passenger window just as we passed my apartment block, surrounded by bots trying to fit new windows. She surfed her hand through the air and I swallowed the lump in my throat.

Stupid. It would be here when we came back. That's what the bots did – maintained the cities for the return of the human race. Maybe I would even get to keep my apartment.

'You OK?' Pandora yelled over the music. She looked genuinely concerned. *Damn.* Must be written all over my face. Can't have that.

'Never better,' I said, and flashed her my pearly whites.

Then she reached across the gearstick and squeezed my knee.

My heart pounded against my chest and it reminded me of the wolf creature, throwing itself against the bars of the park. I felt something shift in the pit of my stomach and I immediately pictured the scene in *Alien*, when the little guy busts outta the dude's chest. Surefire way to stop any sexy vibes, a gross worm-thing totally owning a guy. The feeling passed and I breathed a sigh of relief. *Be cool, man*, I told myself, but I could see my stupid grin in the rear-view mirror anyway. Driving a fast car down an empty road, pretty girl on my arm – well, sorta – it was better than watching my movies. It was like I was in one. I kicked into high gear and Pandora laughed as we raced past the last skyscraper and towards the edge of the city.

8

We drove all day, until the sun crossed over the road in front of us and started to touch down on the other side. We couldn't drive for ever. For one, we needed to recharge the car, and for another, we needed to sleep. The city was vast, but now we were in the suburbs, and layer after layer of identical, empty houses spread out on all sides.

I saw the sign first. If Echo saw it at all, he didn't say anything, and Gort was still . . . asleep? I wasn't sure exactly, but his eyes were closed and he hadn't said anything since he got in the car.

'Maybe we should stop for the night,' I said. 'Take the next left. I think I know a good place to rest our heads.'

'You know a place? Around here?' Echo raised an

eyebrow but kept his eyes on the road. 'OK, Miss Daisy. I'm listening.'

'Miss who?' I frowned at him. 'You say some very strange things, Echo.'

Echo rolled his eyes. 'Never mind. Just tell me where to turn and I'll follow your lead. I'm interested to see where a rich girl at the end of the world thinks is a good place to chill.'

I pointed out the turns when I saw them, all helped out by the rusted signs. Echo was driving too fast to really read them, so even he was surprised when we finally turned into the empty parking lot and under the partly faded signage of the campus.

'*Aurora Tech University.* Seriously? You been here before?' Echo parked across two spaces right in front of the main building, which was made of red brick and covered in climbing ivy.

Well, almost covered. In the setting sun I could see the reflective surface of two maintenance bots that hovered around the walls and cut at the greenery with their scissor hands.

'I came to visit once. Last year, when I was choosing where to apply to. It's a good school,' I said.

We hopped out of the car and Echo reached for the nearby car-charge port. Another reason I thought this was a good place to stop. Gort seemed to reanimate the moment the car parked, and he squeezed out of the back of the car after Echo with no questions.

'We are not yet within the search zone, human Pandora,' Gort finally said, presumably after scanning the area.

'No shit, Sherlock,' Echo muttered. 'Did I mention how glad I was that you tagged along?'

'Echo, stop being rude,' I hissed through gritted teeth. I turned to Gort apologetically.

'P, it's cool. Gort couldn't give a monkey's about what I say. Ain't that right, Gortmeister?' Echo snorted and tapped the side of Gort's head, like he was another car at the lot, waiting to be stolen.

I shook my head at him.

'If Echo Zero-One-Three-Five is referring to my lack of an E-Mote chip, then he would be quite correct, human Pandora. I feel nothing, and nothing can hurt my mental well-being.' Gort blinked at me and despite his words, something in my heart felt heavy.

'Well, just because you don't feel bad, doesn't mean you should have to endure bad things being said to you,' I said, resting my hand on his arm.

Gort didn't even blink.

'All right, now you're making *me* feel bad,' Echo said. I turned to look at him and his cheeks were a little red. 'Yo, uh, sorry Gort. I'll try to remember to be nicer.'

'Do not change your mannerisms on my account, Echo Zero-One-Three-Five. Unless of course you want to impress human female Pandora, which given your rising heart rate, seems to be the case. If I am correct, I would recommend doing as she asks, should you intend to attempt traditional mating—'

'OK, yes, all right, thank you, Mr Encyclopaedia.' Echo cut Gort off and I tried not to laugh. He turned to me. 'He's got that all wrong, by the way. Spends too much time in the library, that's his problem. I just . . . I'm not . . . so tell me more about this university of yours? Surely all the schools were basically the same once Aurora Tech took them over.'

Echo pinched the bridge of his nose and avoided eye contact, which only made it more difficult not to smile. Did he like me? I supposed that up until now he had been on his own, so maybe he would like anyone at this point. But I did feel sorry for him, and he did seem to have learnt his lesson about being nice to Gort the hard way, so I allowed the change of subject.

'Yes, I suppose that's true. But this campus is very old. Older than even Aurora Tech.' I popped open the trunk and shouldered my pack. 'Trust me. This will be a great place to spend the night.'

'Whatever you say, m'lady,' Echo said, half laughing at me. I sighed. I'd show him. He grabbed his own stuff and

Gort just brought himself. We were halfway across the cobblestone quad outside the main building when we were stopped by a bot.

'Hello there, prospective students.' The bot had a soft feminine voice and was humanoid in structure, but stood at least thirty centimetres taller than any of the three of us. Its head was one smooth surface like a mannequin, but the front was a flat screen where a digital female face beamed at us with flashy white teeth.

'Well, that's not terrifying,' Echo said.

'It's probably just activated because we're moving across the quad. This is where you would start a campus tour, if you were visiting the university. That's how you can tell if it's the right campus for you,' I said.

Echo rolled his eyes. 'I've watched enough TV to know what a campus tour is. I've seen universities, too. So come on then, robo-girl, show us the ropes.'

'I do wish you wouldn't be so disparaging about your own kind,' I said. I turned to the bot with an apologetic smile, but her digital face didn't even register that we had spoken. I then looked back at Gort, who also didn't seem to register, his eyes glassy.

Echo held up his hands in mock surrender. 'Sorry, P. You might be right about Gort, but . . . that thing? It's another level,' he said, and the way the bot's visual interface flickered was a little more than unnerving.

'It's . . . She still deserves common courtesy. Just because someone isn't listening doesn't mean you can be cruel about them,' I said, hoping I sounded more confident than I felt. To my surprise, Echo's shoulders dropped. Victory.

When I was younger, my mother used to take me out to the rallies in the capital, back before Aurora Tech was a full governing body. She had been a scientist, working on the ethics committee at Aurora Tech, when she met my father. He was just a salesperson then, but he was fast moving up the ranks. His bonuses opened up a world of possibility to my mother, who had been born into poverty, and he carved out a life for us where we were happy. Everything changed when Aurora Tech cut the ethics team from the company.

At first, my father supported Mother in her quest to get her job back. But, as the severance package grew, and more and more people were let go, he tried to persuade her to stay home. He said it was too dangerous out there, and that I needed her. That he was making enough money to support us, which was certainly true even then. And at first, she complied.

Then came the announcement of the PLEASURE-BOT division, a movement that had been knocked back time and time again by the ethics committee. And that's when, while Father was at work, we would go to the rallies. I don't remember much except the brightly coloured banners and the sound of thousands of voices, singing as one. There must have been bad times, police breaking up the protests as we had seen on the news in history class, but I didn't remember those bits. I just remembered Mother's happy, shining face looking down on me, and the feel of her slender fingers threaded through my own.

That all stopped once Father was promoted to the board, of course. The new bodyguards never let us out of their sight. He kept us safe, and it's not like one woman and her child could have stopped the wheels of progress. Father was supportive; the decision was just taken out of his hands.

'My name is Stephanie, and I am so honoured to be your host today. We're just going to have so much fun together as we explore our amazing campus.' Stephanie startled me out of my reverie and flashed us another smile just as Echo made a vomiting gesture by putting his fingers in his mouth.

'May I ask what your names are, and what you are interested in specializing in while you study with us?' Stephanie asked. Her face froze then, waiting for an input reply. Even I had to admit it was a little uncanny.

'Oh, me first.' Echo cleared his throat and I was just pleased he was finally taking an interest. 'My name is Steven Spielberg, and I'd like to major in Film Studies, please. Show me the home theatre in this bad boy.'

'Your name isn't Steven,' I hissed, but it was too late to change it now.

Stephanie's face finally moved. 'I'm sorry, Steven. I could not find the subject "Film Studies" on the curriculum at any of our campuses. Can I offer you another selection?'

'No movie degrees? Really?' Echo sighed.

'Most of the degrees Aurora Tech offered in my lifetime were all career focused. I'm afraid they didn't really consider movies as a career,' I shrugged.

Echo chewed on his lip, thinking for a moment. 'All right, Steph. How about Robotic Engineering?'

'Oh Steven, it is just so exciting that you have selected that.' Stephanie seemed to smile even more than before. 'I simply live for Robotic Engineering. Ha, ha, a little robot humour for you there. Right this way.' Stephanie turned on her huge legs and started to walk quickly away from the quad and around the side of the building, causing me, Echo and Gort to run to keep up.

'Robotic Engineering, huh?' I asked him as we jogged through the neat treeline that lined the walkways.

'Humans are allowed to study medicine and biology. Don't see why I can't take an interest in robotics.'

'Will this bot take us closer to our search radius for the launching station, human Pandora?' Gort asked, the only one of the three of us that didn't sound out of breath.

'Oh, erm, not quite. But we need to rest, and it'll be good to stretch our legs. Plus, it might be fun for you to learn about something new?'

'Fun,' Gort spoke slowly, like the notion was new to him. 'I am not sure about this concept of "fun", but I will accompany you, human Pandora, to wherever you need me to go.'

'Great,' Echo said, deadpan.

As we passed more beautiful buildings, covered in ivy and gargoyle statues and stained glass, Stephanie would pause occasionally to tell us about them.

'This is the cafeteria. Here for all your dietary needs, requirements, and all that good stuff.'

'This building is the gym. It caters for your physical health, any injuries, all that good stuff.'

'Up next is the library. We have teams to support study, and help with things like dyslexia, short-sightedness, all that good stuff.'

'I think someone has to break it to Stephanie that not all stuff is good stuff,' Echo said. I elbowed him in the ribs. 'Ow. What?'

'Be nice.'

'Hey, I would have said that if she was human too. Equal-opportunities banter, over here.'

Finally, we entered one of the buildings on the far side

of campus. This one was much more modern than the others, with a grey facade and solar panels on the roof. We entered through the revolving glass door and stepped over a cleaning bot in the hallway, who had been released from the walls as twilight set in, before Stephanie led us upstairs to a glass door. It was locked.

'Welcome to our robotics lab. Here at Aurora Tech U, we pride ourselves on having the best and brightest tutors. They are committed to training up the next generation of robotics engineers. Like yourself, Steven.' Stephanie smiled and her programming froze again.

'Any of these tutors still around? Or even their bots?' Echo cupped his hands and stared through the glass into the laboratory beyond. It looked pretty empty. There weren't even posters on the walls.

'I'm afraid I cannot detect any staff members on campus right now, Steven. But I can show you some of our prototypes if you like. Which area of robotics are you interested in?'

Echo frowned. 'What do you have for me, Steph?'

'Well, today we have a live demonstration of our PLEASUREBOTs. We are the leading institution of graduating programmers for those who want to move into the sex and pleasure robotics industry. Would you like me to—'

'No, no, God, no. Stop the tour. I'm out.' Echo covered

his ears with his hands and walked quickly down the hall away from us.

'Of course, Steven,' Stephanie said, and her face froze again.

I looked at Gort, who was silent as usual, then chased after Echo, Gort's footfalls just behind mine as he tried to keep up with me. 'Echo, please wait.' I circled the banister and ran back down the stairs, my heart in my mouth. To joke about his robotic side was one thing, but to hear about how it was used in other ways . . . I couldn't imagine how awful that was for him.

'Echo, stop. Please. I understand why you're so upset. Coming here was a mistake, I don't know what I was thinking.' He pushed open the glass door at the entrance and ran out into the warm night. The sun was just setting and all the lights had flickered into life, casting long shadows as we ran along the walkways.

'I know what you were thinking.' Echo finally stopped in front of the library, so Gort and I did too. 'You were thinking that I'm like you, but I'm not. I'm different, and I always will be. You human, me robot. You engineer, me . . . me prototype.' He sighed and sank down on to the steps of the library.

'Can you give us a minute please, Gort?' I asked.

'I can time one minute for you, human Pandora. Sixty, Fifty-nine—'

'No, sorry. I meant, would you mind sitting on that bench in the quad until I come get you? I need to speak with Echo alone.' I pointed out the bench and tried to keep my tone even. It wasn't his fault that humans had stripped him of any contextual intelligence.

Once Gort walked away I closed the space between me and Echo and sunk down next to him, but he wouldn't look at me. 'I'm sorry, Echo. Truly. Some people back in the twenty-first were absolutely abhorrent.' I shivered at the thought of such a programme at a university even existing. 'But you're wrong about one thing. Biological parts were never used in the . . . in the PLEASUREBOTs. It was banned after the introduction of the TeenSynth and ChildSynth programme. They were never given a positronic brain, either. You are not, nor were you ever, one of those things. You were created for a family, to be a person. Not a slave.'

He looked at me then. 'You really believe that?' His eyes were wide with hope.

I smiled. 'I don't just believe it. It's true. My mother used to work on the ethics committee for Aurora Tech, and my father pushed for the biological parts ban on her behalf.'

'Makes sense your ma and pop worked for them. From what I've read, seemed like Aurora Tech were the only ones handing out jobs near the end of the twenty-first,' Echo said.

I shifted uncomfortably on the stone stair. I wasn't ready to talk about exactly how involved my parents were with Aurora Tech, so I didn't go into more detail.

'Here, let me show you the real reason why we're here. Something that I loved about this place when I visited before,' I said, changing the subject.

I took his hand and pulled him up the remaining steps of the library. It was still early, so the doors were open and the lights flickered on when we tripped the sensors. A faceless bot tried to welcome us to the library but I ignored it, instead making my way across to the glass case at the far-left side.

'What's this?' Echo said. He still sounded a little down.

'It's our history,' I said.

Inside the case was a large slab of broken pottery. In the middle of the slab was a crude drawing of a mammoth, with tiny stick people and single-line spears decorating the jagged edges. The plaque next to the piece read:

THE NIGERIAN POT.
ON LOAN FROM THE AURORA TECH SCIENTIFIC SOCIETY.
THOUGHT TO BE FROM THE NEOLITHIC PERIOD,
AROUND 6,000 YEARS OLD.

'It's . . . it's a broken pot, Pandora,' Echo said.

'It's more than just a broken pot. It's our shared history. This pot was created thousands of years ago, by our ancestors. The same ancestors that survived and procreated all the way until the engineer that created you, and Gort. All the way until my parents were born, and created me.' The words caught in my throat at that last part. I couldn't think of my mother now though, and especially not my father. This was about Echo.

'So what you're saying is, we're . . . related?' Echo raised an eyebrow at me and I laughed.

'No, not related exactly. Just that we are the same. We're both human, even if you have some robotic parts. We both wouldn't be here if it wasn't for our ancestors . . . Oh, look, I don't know. I just thought it was inspirational. Well, I did before I showed you.' I nudged him and managed to coax a smile out of him.

'Nah, you're right. It's pretty cool to think that some dude painted that so long ago, and now look. Here we are. It may be the end of the world but at least we're still alive.' Echo shrugged and met my eyes. 'Thanks.'

Gort was still waiting for us on the bench when we left the library, despite it being dark.

We went looking for the dorms then. We needed to rest. We couldn't have been more than 300 kilometres out from the city, and Gort had suggested my pod had come from 800 kilometres or more. After getting to the dormitories – which had been kept fresh with new bedding, thanks to the cleaning bots – we unpacked and immediately found the bottle of whisky Echo had been eyeing up in the store.

'I mean, it's unlikely we'll actually need to clean any wounds at any point, right?' Echo said, popping the cork. 'Gort, you want some, buddy?'

Gort blinked at the bottle. 'Alcohol is detrimental to human health. Human Pandora, I would advise against alcohol intake at this time.'

'Sometimes alcohol is used to aid human health,' I said, exchanging a look with Echo. 'It can be used medicinally to cure shock, or to relieve anxiety, in moderation of course.'

'Totes,' Echo said, which I assumed from the glint in his eye meant he was backing me up. 'Come on, Gorty. Have a sip. Call it an experiment. If your human side really has gone from up here' – Echo tapped the side of his head – 'then maybe it won't affect the other human bits that are left.'

'I believe this is what humans refer to as "peer pressure", Echo Zero-One-Three-Five,' Gort said. But to my surprise, he held out his hand for the bottle. 'However, if human Pandora is partaking, I must at least test the strength of the liquor in question.'

'Well all righty then.' Echo leapt off the single bed and thrust the bottle into Gort's outstretched fingers.

Gort took three large gulps of the amber liquid. My eyes watered at the thought of the fiery drink being imbibed so quickly.

'Ah. That was . . . Is it normal to feel quite nauseous after drinking, human Pandora?' Gort handed the bottle back as the colour drained from his cheeks.

'Wait until it hits your bloodstream,' Echo said.

I was no stranger to alcohol. It wasn't scarce in the twenty-first, because it was a good way to forget the crumbling world we lived in. Aurora Tech even abolished alcohol taxation once they came into power, one of my father's first initiatives. Often my best friend – my only friend – Lexi would get hold of some and invite me to some party or other so that she could get a lift in the company car.

That didn't mean I wouldn't get drunk quickly.

But not as quickly as poor Gort. He sat in silence for twenty minutes, slowly swaying from his perch on the opposite bunk, before quietly excusing himself to the en suite bathroom. Echo found him asleep on the toilet lid an hour later. We decided it was best to leave him to sleep it off.

After my head was officially swimming, and my inhibitions weren't quite as high as they usually were, I let Echo persuade me to take two of the single beds out into the quad.

We carried the beds as far from the outdoor lights as possible, lay back, and stared at the sky. The Milky Way was an inky painting across the black abyss. I'd never seen it before, except in satellite photos.

'I'm totally shook that my old boy Gort drank so much he passed out,' Echo said once we were settled, hands behind his head as he stared at the sky. 'I never knew he could actually have fun.'

'Really? You've known one another for, what, three years?' I asked. My vision was blurry, but lying down was helping and the stars were giving me a point of reference so I didn't just fall straight out of the bed.

'Me and Gort? Not really,' Echo said with a small hiccough. 'I dunno, man. It feels bad now I say it, but I just assumed that he had nothing interesting to say to me. He always seemed so, like, bland and stuck-up. But it ain't his fault he has no memory. I mean, hey, me neither.' This seemed to make Echo laugh until he could barely hold the bottle any more, he was so doubled up on his bed.

'See? You learn new things every day. *In vino veritas.* It means "in wine is the truth". You just learnt something about Gort, and in turn, something about yourself.' I couldn't tell any more if it was the alcohol trying to sound wise, or me.

'But we ain't drinking wine. If wine makes you smarter, whisky must be making me a freaking genius,'

Echo said, and then we both laughed until our sides hurt.

We were quiet for a while, and I was convinced Echo had fallen asleep until he spoke again.

'Say, Pandora.' Echo slurred a little as he passed me the bottle. 'Do you think there's life up there?'

'What? Aliens?' I asked. I laughed and choked on the whisky as it went down, then took a minute to regain my composure. 'No. I think it's just us. I think that's why no one came to save us from ourselves.'

'So you think we're alone?' Echo hiccoughed again. I could see from here that his eyes were closing. 'That's depressing, bro.'

'Yeah, I think we're alone,' I whispered.

Echo drifted off to sleep in less time than it took for me to replace the cork and put the bottle down. I rolled over, listening to the cicadas chirp in the night, and tried to believe that it wasn't just us left, that there was a point to our journey.

I had to believe we weren't alone on Planet Earth, too.

9

'Hey, you never answered Stephanie's question,' I said. I adjusted the rear-view mirror and winced as the sunlight reflected back in my eyes. Damn, this hangover was legit.

'What question?' P asked.

She hadn't said much since last night. Maybe she was mad I had fallen asleep on her, but woah boy, that whisky was strong stuff. I had been happy when she suggested we left the rest of it behind. Pandora was worried about leaving the beds out, but that was a bot job. Besides, it wasn't like anyone else would need them soon.

Although, since her pep talk, I could kind of see what Pandora meant about the bots. I could maybe, just sometimes, be a little lazy. And I did sort of treat them the same as slaves. And at that point, was I any different to the psychos who made those sex bots? I wasn't sure any more.

Plus, was it just me, or had Gort seemed a little face-palm-esque this morning? He'd certainly been quiet when we went to get him from the bathroom. And right now, he was pretending to be on standby, but I could see his eyelids moving a little too much. Can't kid a kidder, brother.

Anyway, it sure was nice of Pandora to cheer me up after Stephanie put me in a bad mood. And that pottery fragment was lit. Maybe we *were* the same. Plus, when she held my hand, my skin tingled again. Malfunction or not, it felt nice.

After scrounging up some grub from the cafeteria, we wanted to hit the road in good time to cover the remaining kilometres. Which hadn't really allowed for my head to stop throbbing. And I had the weirdest dreams last night after me and P had our existential alien crisis. The old bearded guy was back, the one I saw when we stole the car. Only this time, I was talking to him. *Well, I guess the world can't wait. I am a hero after all.* That's what I said. But mad, I think I was crying too? I mean, talk about drunk dreams. And a hero? Me? Not my style. But if this creepy dude could stop haunting my brain, that would help. Maybe my chip really is super damaged.

'You know, what you would study if you were going to

go to Creepy Tech University?' I asked again. I reversed from the charge station and pulled out of the parking lot and back on to the road.

'Oh. That's easy. I had already applied for Psychology,' she said. She didn't elaborate, but I was just glad she was talking again. Maybe she was as hungover as me.

'What, really?' I said. I shifted gear and got some speed on, opened my window a crack. The fresh air made me feel more human. Well, as human as I could manage, anyway. 'Why?'

'So I can help people. I want to— I wanted to be a therapist.' Pandora looked sad again, I could see in my mirror as her face fell. Couldn't have that.

'So, um, did you learn much about it? Psychology, I mean?' I shut my mouth to stop any more stupid falling out.

Pandora turned away from the window. *Phew.* 'A little. I use one technique a lot. A breathing exercise. If I ever get anxious, I just breathe in, *one-two-three,* then hold it for four seconds, then breathe out, *seven-and-eight.*' She closed her eyes as she demonstrated and I watched as her shoulders physically relaxed.

You know the drill. Count backwards from ten.

Woah. That was weird. Not seeing things any more, but I definitely heard something. A familiar voice too, but I couldn't place it. Man. I need to recode my chip when we next stop.

Pandora opened her eyes so I focused on her, not on the voice. 'There. Seems to work for hangovers too. Well, a little anyway. Would you mind if I rested my eyes for a while? I didn't sleep well last night.'

'Oh. Sure thing,' I said, turning the music down. I glanced sideways at her as she made a pillow out of her jacket on the window and closed her eyes. I couldn't tell her I was hearing things. *I'm all she's got*. Maybe I shouldn't have said to sleep al fresco last night. She didn't not sleep because I made her take her Zs outside, right? Not that I could ask, because she was asleep in seconds, judging by the slow rise and fall of her breathing. I turned my attention to the rear-view mirror and my other road trip buddy.

'Hey Gort. Gorty? I know you ain't sleeping back there. Listen, I gotta ask you 'bout something,' I said, careful to keep my voice down. That said, P was even starting to drool now, so that wasn't gonna be a problem. Damn, even when drooling she looked pretty.

Gort opened his eyes, and hold up – was that a sigh I just saw? I swore he damn near rolled his eyes at me. 'Yes, Echo Zero-One-Three-Five?'

'I uh, so like . . . listen. I just wanted to say, bot to bot here, that, like, I guess I'm sorry.' I rushed the words out at the end, but I got there. Like, dude, 'sorry' is my least favourite s-word, but I knew when I was beat. 'I'm sorry I haven't given you a chance in, well, three years. You're actually kind of OK, you know, sometimes.'

'Well Echo Zero-One-Three-Five, while I don't fully understand your reasoning, I understand it is human etiquette to accept a heartfelt apology. So I do accept.'

I caught his eye in the rear-view again. 'Yeah? Well, that's big of you, man. I wouldn't have been so lonely all this time if I'd just made the effort. I just thought we were too different, y'know? You were the bot and I was the . . . well, I don't even know. And you're not just a bot either. So, yeah, sorry about that.'

'You were lonely, Echo Zero-One-Three-Five?' Gort asked. He tilted his head like a puppy listening to a command from its owner.

'Well, um, yeah. No intelligent conversation in over a thousand days? Weren't you lonely?'

Gort seemed to think on that for a minute. 'I do not think HUMANKINDs are programmed with the understanding of loneliness. But from my research into humanity and possible locations of the cryogenic labs, I have come across the term. And it is possible that at times, especially before these last two days, that yes, I did feel some semblance of what you refer to as loneliness.'

I laughed. 'Well, no shit. Would you look at that, Gorty? I think you're starting to become a real boy.'

But Gort didn't reply. Instead, his eyes went wide as

dinner plates and he pointed ahead to the road in front of us.

I just had time to tear my eyes away from the mirror and see the half-eaten carcass of a mutant strewn across the freeway before I swerved. Pandora screamed. Hell, even I screamed. The car went into a death spiral, spinning and spinning until I heard a sickening crunch of metal and we were thrown to a stop at the edge of the tarmac.

'Holy shit. Are you OK?' I asked Pandora. We both had our seatbelts on and, miraculously, we all seemed fine, Gort included.

'I'm fine. I'm OK. Thank you,' she said, although I thought she was hyperventilating a little. 'I'm not . . . not sure the same . . . can be said . . . about the car.'

'OK, here's what we're going to do. You stay here and do your breathing thingy, I'm going to check the car. You OK with that? Gort, you stay here with Pandora.'

'Of course, Echo Zero-One-Three-Five,' Gort said.

Pandora nodded, so I unclipped my belt and tried not to puke as I got out of the car. My head was spinning bad enough before the accident. That was just karma being cruel.

I walked around to the back of the car and spotted the problem pretty quickly. The back wheel had hit something when we spun out, probably the nearby pothole, and it had completely burst open.

I sighed. I knew from when I opened the trunk before leaving the city that the Ferrari didn't have room for a spare tyre, just a puncture repair kit. And this was gonna need more than that.

'Stupid mutant,' I muttered. I stared back at its hulking body, just chilling as if nothing had happened.

And it really couldn't have happened in a worse place. We had been driving long enough to leave the burbs, and there really weren't many buildings around at all any more. I had been speeding too, so it would take way too long in the heat to walk back to the university. There were no cars there, anyway.

'Shit,' I shouted and kicked the car, which only made my feet hurt.

'Is everything OK?' Pandora leant out of the passenger door and I tried not to wig out.

'Well, the car is busted. And we're in the middle of nowhere. And – and I think I may have just found a solution . . .' I trailed off, my eyes hitting a sign just to the left of where we crashed:

Aurora Airways Airport
Next Exit

Pandora followed my line of sight and spotted the sign. 'Good idea. There will be cars there, or at least a spare tyre.'

She hopped out of the car, now totally cool as a cucumber, and came round to get her pack. *Man.* Maybe I had to give this breathing thing a try.

We decided to leave Gort with the car, because even in the apocalypse it felt too weird to leave a Ferrari unlocked and alone in the middle of the freeway. Plus, he could hit the horn and scare away any mutants that came back for the carcass, but still stay safe inside the car. I could be smart sometimes, you know. And this way, Pandora and I could have a little alone time.

It only took us fifteen minutes to reach the exit for the airport, but it took another twenty for us to find our way in. Airports were huge, much bigger than they looked in the movies. Pandora seemed to know her way round well enough, and worked out that we would need to go through check-in to reach the tarmac where the planes and cars were kept. The entrance was blocked off with these huge concrete slabs, and I tripped over one trying to get around it. *Smooth, Echo.* What a ladies' man. 'They fence off the part with the planes, because it's – or rather, it was – too dangerous. The easiest way will be if we pretend to check in. Then we can use one of the gates to get on to the runway and look for a part that will work,' Pandora said. She hadn't noticed my fall. Small mercies.

'Good plan, Batman,' I said, ignoring her puzzled look.

We approached the first check-in desk and an ancient

hologram flickered into life. Well, what would you know? She had a different uniform, and she was wearing more make-up, but I would recognize that face anywhere.

'Hey, Deidre. Long time no see,' I said, then paused. P looked at me like I was crazy this time. I tried to laugh it off. 'Ha, just playing along. If we have to check in, we gotta get past these guys, right?' I pointed to the sealed security gates to our left, the ones with a sign above them that said: NO ENTRY PAST THIS POINT WITHOUT BOARDING CARDS.

'Right,' Pandora said slowly. 'OK. Then where are we going?'

'Oh. Yeah. Pick a destination, gotcha. Uh . . . Paris?' I said, instantly regretting it. Paris? Chick would think I'm way too keen. City of Love, and all that.

'I've always wanted to go to Paris,' P smiled and my heart flipped over. Damn E-Mote chip. 'Two tickets please, Deidre.'

Wasn't it always just so awkward bumping into an ex when you're with your new girl? I waited for her to respond – sometimes, poor Deidre's wireless connection could be a little on the slow side – and tried to ignore the warm feeling in my chest.

That's when it happened again. It was that stupid dream dude again, the one that was haunting me. This time, I could see him a little better, but he wasn't sad. It only lasted for a second, but I think we were . . . watching TV together? My favourite pastime, spent with a stranger? Nah, no way.

I squeezed my eyes shut, tried to make ghost-beard go away. Because, sure, it had crossed my mind that maybe I knew him in the before times, but that meant he was dead, right? And I don't wanna get messed-up over some dead dude I don't even remember. Gotta focus on the very real and alive girl in front of me.

Sorry, Deidre.

'Paris. We have a flight leaving in ERROR LOADING DEPARTURE TIMES.' Deidre bugged out the same way Gort did when he tried to tell us about the labs. No more information to download at the end of the world. 'If you would like to proceed, please tap your payment card to the scanner.'

'Oh no. Payment? Echo, we don't have any money.' Pandora bit her lip and stared at the closed gate longingly.

Cue her knight in shining armour. AKA, *moi*.

'Chillax, Pandora. I got this.' I smiled and rooted in my jacket pocket for the wallet I always carried with me, the one loaded up with cards I had found around the city. This one's on you, Mr G. Graham.

'To confirm two flights to Paris, please press your payment card to the scanner,' Deidre said.

I held up the wallet like Braveheart holding up his

sword, and quickly dug out a card to press to the scanner.

Two tickets printed out of the desk, the same tickets we needed for the security barriers. It was a breeze after that, mostly because there were no queues or security bots at passport control, which I thought was a little weird. At least it meant we didn't need passports, too. Pandora explained they only asked for those as you entered a country, not on the way out. Weird.

Yep, P certainly knew her way around an airport. I tried to imagine all the fancy trips she must have taken, back in the twenty-first. Maybe she had seen the pyramids. Maybe she had even had a private jet. Anyway, I was glad she was a rich chick, because without her I wouldn't have had a clue how to navigate this place, never mind where or what the 'gates' were. We found our way past the closed-down bars and bookshops to the first one, pressed our tickets to it, and bingo, we were out on the tarmac.

It only took us about thirty minutes to find a buggy with enough juice to get us back to the Ferrari, along with a wheel that could work as a replacement. I thought it would be fun, just Pandora and me, but I was surprised at how bad I felt for leaving Gort on his own, especially after our deep and meaningful about loneliness. In my chest, my heart felt heavy. Another feeling I didn't remember, but I knew instinctively what it was. Guilt.

We boarded the buggy and followed the airport

signage back out to the main road, the security badge that had been left inside enough for the bots to raise the gate and let us out. Good old Gort would be just fine. He was a bot. He knew how to look after himself. And this was maybe the only chance I would get to be alone with P, so why couldn't I enjoy it?

Girls, man. They mess with your head. And your heart, even if that heart is controlled by a broken E-Mote chip. I caught a glance of the wind ripping through P's hair as we cruised down the road at a stable top speed of 65 kph, and man, this was sort of fun. Even in a jumped-up golf buggy stolen from an airport.

The good vibes didn't last long. I could tell something was wrong as soon as the Ferrari was in sight. The driver's door hung open, and the road was as silent as a horror movie when we cut the engine on the buggy.

The back seat was empty.

'Do you think something happened to him?' Pandora asked after checking every crevice of the car, including underneath. She was totally freaking out, even pulling up the floor mats to check as if Gort could shrink himself down and hide under there, and her voice was all high and squeaky.

I scanned the road. No blood, which was a good thing. And no obvious signs of a struggle. Pandora finished ransacking the car and looked at me, her eyes shining. I couldn't let her panic, no matter how hard my heart hammered against my ribcage. Panicking wouldn't find Gort.

'Maybe he thought he saw something, or he could get to the launch site faster without us? He's a HUMANKIND. He wouldn't do anything to jeopardize his, like, primary objective or whatever. And I think if a mutant got to him, it wouldn't clean up after itself. The evidence points to Gort just . . . leaving.' I sighed and looked in both directions across the barren, empty wasteland. We hadn't seen him on the way up in the buggy, and we had been gone over an hour. He could be anywhere by now.

'Listen, Gort knew where he was going. And we still know from his directions to keep heading south until we reach the search area. It's not as specific a spot as he would have shown us, but it's something. Hopefully we can pick him up on the way,' I said. I tried to sound cool, but inside I was sweating. Why would he think walking was faster than the car? Did he really not think we could find a wheel?

Now wasn't the time for panic. P needed me to not panic.

Relief wasn't the word when her frown finally smoothed out. 'All right,' she said, 'let's get this wheel fixed so we can get moving.'

10

As we left the outskirts of civilization, the buildings became more spaced out and smaller in stature. For an hour or so after the airport, we drove in relative silence, and I let the wind rush through my hair and the music pound in my eardrums. Echo was right, we would just have to hope we would meet back up with Gort when we got closer to our destination. He had survived a hundred years in this wasteland, he could survive another few days.

I hoped.

We pulled into a charging station about six hundred kilometres out, according to the ancient and broken GPS anyway. Echo switched off the engine, plugged in the car, and headed inside.

'Where are you going?' I asked.

Echo shrugged. 'It'll take about ten minutes for the battery to fully charge. Who knows when we'll next pass a station? Thought I would go and rustle up some candy for the trip.' He turned and jogged into the store before I could say anything else.

It was terrifying being alone. With my father in a job like his, I had hardly ever been on my own. There was always a security detail or an assistant or a driver to take me where I needed to be. Even at night, it was comforting to hear the shuffle of feet as my bodyguard, Scott, tried to stay awake on the other side of my bedroom door. Echo had been with me the whole time at the airport and the university, even though they were eerily empty otherwise. I didn't even remember the last time I had been alone. Probably when my mother died and we went to see the open casket.

Pollution-related cancer got nearly everyone in the end, but my mother wasn't even forty. Father did everything he could, paid for every possible experimental treatment, but it was too aggressive. In the end, she went quickly, which was in itself a blessing. I was ten.

After that, it was just me and Dad, the two of us. I didn't see him much once he made CEO, but his promises to get straight back to work after her death were what helped pay Mother's medical bills. I was sent off to boarding school until I was fifteen, when he became president of

Aurora Tech and it became too difficult to guarantee my safety away from his security forces. My protection was his highest priority, and it came at a price.

I shivered and pushed down the memory, trying not to think about how parallel the pods felt to the sight of that coffin. I also tried not to think of Father and everyone else in their similar coffins, frozen down to their brainstems, waiting to wake up.

Something moved outside my window and I turned quickly, hoping it was Echo, but it was just a cat. I watched as it chased a dead leaf across the tarmac.

'Here, puss puss puss.' I leant out of my open window and rubbed my thumb and forefinger together. We had a cat at home, but it was really more the servants' cat. It had been there longer than we had.

The cat turned to look at me and I gasped, my hand instinctively going to my mouth to hold in the scream that might also slip out.

It was hideous. From the back, it had the regular sleek, black form of a cat, but from the front it looked like it had burnt its face on a hot frying pan. The nose wasn't fully formed and its eyes – or rather, eye – was one molten mass in the middle of its face. It meowed, a sad cry that didn't sound natural, and I could see that its mouth was twisted up into its jaw, exposing crooked teeth.

'Hey.' Echo opened the driver's side door and I would

have hit my head from jumping if I hadn't been belted in. He slid into his seat slowly, his hands up in surrender. 'Woah, sorry. Didn't mean to scare you. They had Red Hots is all.' He sat down and passed me the familiar box, which I grasped with trembling hands. He waited for me to tell him what was wrong.

'The . . . cat,' I managed, pointing out the window. Echo leant out of his seat to see.

'Oh yeah. Cute. More of a dog person myself though,' he said, turning over the engine.

'Cute?' I scoffed. The cat, meanwhile, had taken one look at the roaring engine and run off. 'It only had one eye! It barely had a mouth. That was anything but cute.'

Echo pulled out of the charging bay and on to the freeway again, keeping his eyes on the road. 'Don't you remember the wolf-thing in the park? Why do you think I don't eat any meat, or that the streets aren't full of stray dogs and like, runaway chickens? Most of them don't survive birth. Too much pollution and now the gene pool is whack, that's what Gort told me anyway.'

I did remember the wolf-thing. How could I forget? It'd had extra limbs and run with a gait that didn't match its body. Come to think of it, he was right. I hadn't seen many animals at all, or heard birdsong in the sky; even insects seemed scarce. When we were briefed on the SpindleSleep project, they said they would freeze more than just people.

Crops, seeds, even animal embryos would all be carefully selected, in case a species had died out during the Big Freeze, or the continuing drought, or the endless floods.

'Hey, look.' Echo slowed the car down at the next intersection and when I looked up from my lap I could see why.

Ahead, two army-green trucks blocked the road, flanked either side by huge camo-coloured tanks. I had seen tanks before – there was always one stationed out on our front lawn – but Echo seemed transfixed.

'They are fucking A,' he said, coming to a stop. 'That cruiser tank is the exact model I used to spawn on to on . . .' He saw me looking at him and trailed off, his cheeks red. 'Uh, just a video game I played. Not a lot. Just to see what it was like, you know.'

'Well, do you remember the controls?'

Echo raised an eyebrow at me.

'This road leads south,' I explained, 'and those things are blocking the way. We need to move them.'

Echo grinned and punched the air. 'Righteous,' he said, which I assumed meant he was happy about the development. I tutted as he jumped out of the car, but I followed suit. It might be quite cool to sit in a tank. Father had never let me get near.

'Look at this thing,' Echo said, jogging over to the nearest one. Either side of the road were huge concrete breezeblocks, stopping anyone from driving around the blockade. We would need to move the tank first, and then one of the trucks into its place, if we wanted to keep going south.

'You take the tank, I'll take the truck,' I called out to Echo, who didn't need asking twice. He had already climbed up to the open hatch of the vehicle. 'But be careful. I'll be really mad if you accidentally blow my head off.'

'Roger that, ma'am.' Echo saluted – a little too realistically – and dropped down into the body of the tank.

I could hear his echoing footsteps and muffled cries of 'awesome!' as I made my way to the truck. I heaved myself up the huge step and pulled open the door, just managing to squeeze on to the leather seat beyond. I wasn't confident enough to drive on the freeway, but I knew enough from watching Echo and my drivers to be able to roll a truck back a few metres.

Why was there a blockade here anyway? We hadn't seen anything at the university or the airport. I pressed the start button and was relieved when the engine roared into life. I didn't know what I would have done if the thing was out of battery. I moved the stick into reverse and wiped down the dusty windscreen. From high up in the truck, I could see the long, low outline of a school, just down the east road, which wasn't cordoned off. Outside were neat rows of yellow school buses, as well as a couple of white marquees with red crosses on the side. There were also more tanks and army vehicles.

A thought crossed my mind and I blinked hard to block it out. When we were told about the SpindleSleep project, they said that the extreme weather conditions would kill the remainder of humanity quickly and painlessly. No one could survive more than a few seconds in the extreme temperatures predicted, the head scientist had told us. He had even shown us a graph. The scientists couldn't have got it wrong, could they?

I had to take my mind off it. Instead, I focused on adjusting the rear-view mirror so I could avoid Echo when I had to reverse. It was stiff, but it eventually moved with a sharp tug, revealing the back seat of the truck.

There, still dressed in camo gear and sat bolt upright on the seat, was a bright white skeleton.

I screamed. I screamed but I still couldn't move, the sight of the skeleton too much to bear. My throat went hoarse and I remembered where I was, that I could get out of the truck, and I scrambled for the handle.

'Pandora?' Echo had poked his head out of the tank hatch and swivelled round to look for me. Once he caught my eye, he pushed himself out of the top and clambered down the side of the tank even faster than he had climbed up it.

I finally found the handle and threw the door open,

forgetting about the huge distance from the door of the truck to the asphalt below. The force of my weight, of my sheer panic to escape the corpse, meant I stepped out on to air and tumbled head first towards the ground. I braced my arms over my head.

'Pandora!' It was Echo's turn to scream as I heard the sickening thud of my skull crack against the road.

The shockwave reverberated through my bones, from the top of my head to the tips of my toes. Within a second, my arms burnt and I saw blood as I brought them away from my head. I was splayed out across the road, my head pounding and all the skin taken off my forearms, but surprisingly my head didn't hurt as much as my arms did. I must have braced in time, but God, the rest of me was in agony.

'Fuck, Pandora, are you OK?' Echo was there, hovering his hands over my arms and head like a witch casting a spell.

'Is it bad?' From the expression on his face, I had my answer. As if saving Echo the effort of answering, something liquid trickled down my forehead and turned my vision red, stinging my eyes.

'How many fingers am I holding up?' Echo asked. He felt for my hand and placed a bottle of water there, and I used it to wash the blood out of my eyes. When I could see again, he was holding up three fingers.

'Why do people always hold up three?' I mumbled. Now I could see again, while the pain wasn't ideal, it felt less terrifying. 'It's so easy to guess three. Law of probabilities.'

'If you're talking about math, you must be all right,' Echo said. 'You OK to stand?'

I nodded and felt his strong arm slink around my waist. Despite the pain, I felt a small flutter in the pit of my stomach as he easily lifted me to my feet with no effort on my part. Standing made the blood rush from my head and I stumbled slightly, meaning I was face to face with Echo, so close our noses were touching. I held my breath. He really was handsome.

'Sorry.' Echo spoke first, breaking the spell. He stepped back, but not until he was sure I could stand without assistance. 'Thought I had you there. Can you walk?'

'I think so,' I said, slightly sad when the warmth of his arms left my skin. 'But where are we going? We can't go back to the car. No way to get round.' Blood dribbled down my arm to my elbow before dripping on to my combat pants. 'Plus I think I have to do something about this.' I sucked a breath between my teeth as I lifted my arms. It really stung.

'Did you see the medical tents by the school?' Echo asked, and I nodded. It was obvious. There would be everything we needed to patch me up there.

'Let's go. Quick, before I completely ruin these pants,' I

said. I walked gingerly, my arms out like a robotic chicken, my feet shuffling along the road so as to not wobble my head too much.

'You're lucky you didn't crack your egg wide open,' Echo said, slowing his pace to walk with me. He didn't even smile at my faltering gait, which I was grateful for. 'What made you so jumpy? Not another cat, was it?'

I bit my lip, images of the soldier rushing back to the forefront of my mind. 'I saw . . . a person. A dead person,' I clarified and Echo's eyebrows went from surprised to concerned.

'Woah. Like a real dead dude?' Echo thought about it for a minute. 'So weird when we didn't see any at our other stops. Like I said, the bots cleared all the ones from the city, but I guess even bots make mistakes. Maybe they missed one?'

'Maybe,' I replied, focusing on my breathing to bypass the pain. *In, one-two-three-four. Hold six-seven. Out seven-and-eight.* 'Or maybe there weren't really any bots out here.'

'No bots?' Echo snorted. 'I wish. If I knew there was a paradise where I wouldn't run into any more of Gort's buddies, I would have moved out years ago. What makes you say that?'

'Well, I know that even with the blackouts in the city, it was nowhere near as bad as in the countryside. I saw it from my window at night. Outside the city walls it was just . . . black.' I slid him a sideways stare and saw his jaw was set, completely focused on getting to the school. 'I don't think they had enough electricity out here to keep everything going as long as we did. I think it was really bad out in the sticks. You know, at the end.'

I blinked back the tears that stung my eyes. Useless to cry for them now. That soldier died a hundred years ago, more maybe. Tears weren't going to bring him back.

'I think it was bad everywhere, from what I've read,' Echo replied.

We were at the entrance to the school now and passed the sign set into the edge of the road: *Aurora Tech High School.* I rolled my eyes. It must be the most common school name in the whole world.

We walked soundlessly as we approached the tents and the tanks set up in the faculty car park. It was completely silent in the midday sun, without even a breath of wind to ruffle the material of the tents. Not everything had survived. Some of the trucks were rusted to the point that a wheel or two had fallen off, leaving them lopsided, and a few of the tents had blown over at some point. Mould crept up the bricks of the building beyond and I was glad it was dry enough and hot enough to cover the smell.

The worst part, though, was the bodies. The truck had just been the beginning. Some were hanging out of car doors, like they had toppled where they sat; others were strewn across the car park, crawling towards the building. Some wore uniforms like the soldier in the back of the truck, and some wore the blue and green scrubs of doctors and nurses. All of them had been reduced to bone. It was like a sick joke set up by a high school kid, one who had stolen the skeletons from the biology lab and set them up to look like people. But these *were* people. Once.

I turned away from Echo and vomited up a rainbow of candy and Red Hots.

'Oh, jeez,' Echo said, half-heartedly rubbing my back while holding his face as far from the smell as he could. I didn't even have the energy to be mortified. I wiped off my mouth and took a swig of the water.

'I need to sit down,' I said, suddenly so tired that I felt I could sleep for ever.

Echo nodded, his lips pulled into a tight line. 'Yeah, no shit. Come on, let's find you a bed.'

He half carried, half dragged me across the car park, his arm tucked firmly under my armpit. It didn't feel the same as it did before. Now, all I wanted was his promise of a nice comfy bed and sleep. We stopped outside the nearest medical tent and he paused, unsure.

'Wait here,' he said. Still holding me up, he pulled over a cracked plastic chair with the toe of his high-top and sat me in it. It sagged slightly under my weight but held its own. Unsurprising, really. Plastic would be all that was left once even the trucks and bricks and skeletons had gone.

Echo disappeared into the tent for a few minutes. Or maybe it was hours. If it weren't for the beating sun, it would be hard to tell. I focused on staying awake as I heard him huffing and puffing beyond the curtain of fabric. At one point, something fell and smashed, but a few more shuffling sounds told me he was OK. Finally, he came back out.

'OK, come on,' he said. He was sweating, like he had been working out. I almost giggled at the thought, and the mental image of Echo with his shirt off. Why was everything so funny suddenly? As Echo lifted me from the chair and into his arms I laughed out loud. My arms were ticklish. Big, red, ticklish patches.

We entered the tent and inside were three makeshift hospital rooms, just camp beds with curtains pulled round them. At the end was a bed without a curtain, perfectly made up and ready to fall into.

Echo lifted me up like a groom lifted a bride to step over the threshold. I marvelled at the thought of a white dress. White as bone. As he lay me down, I saw through the crack in the curtain to the bed beyond. There were two skeletons, one on top of the other, still dressed in their scrubs, one lower jawbone falling into the other's mouth.

'They look like they're having fun!' I squealed, laughing again. Echo looked at where I was pointing and pulled the curtain shut.

'Yikes. Sorry, dude, thought I got them all.' He turned back to me. So strong. So handsome.

'Maybe we could have some fun.' I was slurring now and felt drunk, like I was back at the college campus. I reached out to grab Echo's belt, but misjudged the distance and missed, banging my red-raw elbow on the bed frame. 'Ouchies.' The pain was so shocking tears sprang to my eyes.

'OK, bedtime for you,' Echo said, and even as he spoke, my eyelids felt heavy. I let sleep take me.

11

I'd never seen a dead body before.

I braced myself for the second day running, pacing back and forth in front of the doors of the school. I hadn't worked up the courage to go inside yet. It was bad enough out here, dude, without seeing like . . . what? Dead kids? That was not what I signed up for. But I needed to go inside. For Pandora.

She was messed-up. She had been in and out of fever dreams for like, a day and a half now. Sometimes, she seemed wide awake, and even chatty, but then she would say something dumb like 'I like chihuahuas' and fall back asleep.

Maybe she had a concussion. What was the rule? Let them sleep or keep them awake? I couldn't keep her awake if I tried.

I knew where I would find answers: the school would have a library. When the world ended, a lot of the servers for like, Wikipedia and shit weren't labelled as essential, so they weren't kept online. I was lucky to get my movie and TV server working at all. So for everything I needed to know, I went to the library.

And yo, libraries are dope. They have all the books for all the things. You wanna learn Japanese? Library. You wanna try and fix your internal code so you remember the catastrophic event that nearly killed you? Library, my dude. And it's not just books – they have tons of other stuff. Like they had all these newspapers on teeny-tiny microfilm, and you gotta use this huge, like, TV-microscope thing to read them. That's how I learnt about how the world ended.

I remember, back in the city library, I found this really old archive full of all these articles warning people about a 'cataclysmic climate event'. I asked Gort about it once. He said it was a theory about super-severe weather changes due to global warming. A big event like what took out the dinosaurs. Gort said there was something like a ninety per cent chance that at some point, from what the bots had recorded from debris and air pollution changes and stuff, there was a heatwave so intense it killed any living thing left outside in a matter of minutes. And it probably happened more than once, with no warning.

Yep, deffo don't wanna see what's in that school building. Nope.

I glanced back over at the tent where Pandora was sleeping. I had cleared the skeletons from the bed next to hers – although that was pretty funny in, like, a sick joke kinda way – and tried to get some shut-eye, charging myself from the dregs of batteries in the army vehicles. But I was starting to run outta juice.

'Echo?' Pandora called and I ran back to her, glad for another excuse not to go into the school. Maybe she was having one of her lucid half hours.

When I entered the tent, Pandora was trying to sit up in bed.

'Woah there,' I said, running over to stop her fussing with the pillow. 'I think it's a little soon to try sitting up. You've been out for a while.'

'Well, now I'm not out, I'm . . . in?' She muttered the last part and winced as her brain tried to power through the sentence. 'I want to get up.'

'That's what you said last time. And then you told me that Care Bears are all evil and fell asleep again.'

'What?' she said. Her cheeks flushed pink. 'I haven't said anything really embarrassing, have I?'

I thought about a couple days earlier, when she laughed at the skeletons on the next bed and asked to get freaky. I tried not to grin. What can I say? The chicks dig me.

'Not really,' I said. I already knew that she liked me. I didn't need to humiliate the poor girl.

'Good,' Pandora said. She settled back down on her pillows, relieved. 'So, did you do these?' She pointed to the bandages on her arms.

'Just call me Dr Kildare,' I grinned.

'I don't know if I'll ever get used to your turn of phrase,' Pandora replied, and I let it slide. It was just nice to hear her talk again. I felt a tingle of electricity pass from my chest to my head and quickly checked my HUD. *E-Mote updating.*

'No fucking way,' I blurted out loud, and Pandora raised an eyebrow.

'What? What is it?'

'It's OK. It's just – let me break it down for you,' I said. A few days ago, I was way too embarrassed to even let the HUMANKIND bots know what I was going through, but I couldn't help it. I felt . . . like that bit in *The Shawshank Redemption*, where Andy crawls through all that shit and stands there in the rain. If I didn't know better, I'd say I was excited.

'So us TeenSynths, we're mostly biological, right? But we also have the robotic parts, to make our brains function and stuff like that,' I continued.

Pandora nodded. 'We learnt about TeenSynths at school. I know the rough outline of how they – how you, how you work.' She corrected herself and I grinned harder.

'Right. Because without the positronic brain, and the memory, and the E-Mote chip, I'd just be a vegetable. But three years ago, when I woke up, I was in bad shape. Some bots had found me at the edge of the city, sitting in a basement, no idea how I got there. They charged me up and tried to wake me, thinking I was a HUMANKIND.

'When they realized I wasn't, they sorta just . . . left me to groove to my own beat, you know? And I just sorta had to work out what happened on my own.'

'That must have been terrifying,' Pandora whispered. She reached out for my hand and rested her fingers over mine. The feeling was literally electric.

'I dunno. Yeah, I guess. I never really thought about it before,' I said, and something weird happened. My eyes began to itch. And like, there was something in my throat, but I didn't need to cough.

I needed to cry.

E-Mote update 57% complete. The message flashed up again at the edge of my heads-up display and temporarily shocked the crying feeling from my system. How was that possible? Where was it even updating from?

'You've really been through a lot,' Pandora said. 'You know how, before all this, I wanted to be a psychologist?' Her question brought me back into the room. She was still holding my hand.

I decided not to tell her what was going on with my updates. I wasn't sure I even knew that myself. Keeping one eye on the percentage ticking up in the corner of my HUD, I said, 'Yeah, why?'

'Well . . . I didn't tell you the whole truth, before, about how I got into it. When my mother died, I didn't handle it very well. And my father, he was always busy with work, so he didn't really get it. I ended up seeing a therapist. I wasn't really into it at first, but she really helped me through a difficult time. She's the one who gave me the breathing exercise. I still see her now – I mean, I saw her then. A hundred years ago. I guess she's dead now.' Pandora swallowed, but thank God, she didn't cry. 'It's what made me want to become a therapist. I want to help people like she helped me. Not that it would do much good now.'

'Your mom died? Man, I'm sorry, P. That really sucks,' I said. I mean, I never had a mom, but I can imagine that they were pretty dope and suddenly not having one might even be worse than never having one at all.

'Thank you. It was a long time ago. A lot of people weren't well back then, especially in the cities. But still. Thank you.' She gave my fingers a squeeze and she might as well have squeezed my heart, the way it flipped.

'Do you miss them? Your mom and pops?' I asked.

'Yes, very much so. But in different ways,' Pandora said, and she went still, her body language telling me not to ask any more about it.

'And hey, what do you mean, *it won't do much good now*?' I asked, switching up the subject. She was still holding my hand. 'I think wanting to be a therapist is kinda dope. Helping people and all that. I've never really thought about other people before.' I knew I sounded savage, but it was true. I had only been thinking of me, and where I fitted in, and who I wanted to talk to. Man, I even felt bad for Gort now. I threw a book at him, took him clean out. Never tried to strike up a conversation. He was like me once. Dude, I really hoped he was OK out there, on his own.

E-Mote update 97% complete. The message flashed up on the edge of my vision and I let it sink in. Was that why I was feeling bad for Gort? Maybe the update was busted or something.

'I mean, because there's no one left to help,' Pandora said. Her voice was deadpan, emotionless. She sounded like me on a bad day. I squeezed her hand harder.

'You're helping me,' I said. She looked at me, and damn, those pretty blues got me every time.

Another message to my left: *E-Mote update downloaded. Installing.* Weird. I thought maybe it would hurt more, my first real update, but I felt fine.

Oh shit. Pandora was still looking at me. Gotta say something smart. She probably thinks what I said was dumb, and I know why. 'Look,' I continued, 'I know I'm not really a human, that all my feelings and stupid words are run by lines of code, but I think you're helping me all the same. I feel better since you got here.' Woah. Did I really just say that? *Just put it all out there, why don't you, Echo?* So much for playing hard to get.

Pandora smiled and something moved in my heart. It felt, I dunno, bigger somehow. Her smile made me smile.

'Oh, Echo. You're one of the most human people I've ever met.'

Well, that did it. I grinned so hard I thought my teeth were gonna fall out of my head. All this time, I'd been so obsessed with the mechanics of my robotic side. No one had been here to remind me I had a human side too. All I had been focused on was the pain and confusion and memory loss. I was obsessed with moving on. Maybe I could, with Pandora.

E-Mote update installation complete. The message flashed up in the corner of my vision but I didn't need it to know it was true. My heart danced in my chest like it was at a disco. Pandora looked better than before, and there was colour in her cheeks – or was she blushing?

I leant forward, careful not to move her too much. My fingers were still laced in hers. How did they do this in the movies again?

'Is this OK?' I asked, my voice barely a whisper.

Pandora licked her lips – whoo boy, that drove me wild – and nodded. I inched forward again, this time until my nose was a centimetre from her face. Even after days of lying in bed, she smelt good. She smelt like fresh sheets and antiseptic. She smelt alive.

'You can touch me,' she whispered, her breath tickly on my face. And I leant in, my mouth on hers, and I expected it to be gross but it was amazing, totally dope and strange and free. My heart did another happy dance and I sucked in a deep breath of air through my nose, because I couldn't breathe in anything that wasn't her, and it only sent me deeper. Her hands were in my hair, round my neck, and all I could think was, this is way better than being like Gort.

Then I pulled away. I had to, because the party in my mouth and chest wanted to move into my pants, and even a dude who has been alone for a century knows that isn't cool on a first date.

'That was . . . very human,' Pandora said, smoothing down her hair.

'I'll take that as a compliment,' I said. I was teasing, and she could tell. She smiled.

'OK. Well, the treatment was unconventional, but I think I'm ready to get up now.' She pushed herself back into a sitting position and I moved round the bed to help her. I held her elbow, careful not to catch her nasty-looking grazes, and she swung her legs out from the covers until her bare feet hovered above the floor.

'Still hanging in there?' I asked.

She closed her eyes and took a deep breath, then nodded. 'I'm good. Can you help me put my shoes on?'

I bent down to slip on her boots and tie her laces while she checked my bandaging job. The scabs on her arms had pretty much dried out, and luckily weren't too deep. Her head was a bit gnarlier, but it wasn't bleeding any more, and didn't need stitches – according to the leaflet I read, anyway. Maybe she had just needed some time.

Soon she was dressed and on her feet without my help, which was a relief to say the least.

'Any longer here and I would have had to carry you the rest of the way,' I said as we shouldered our packs. 'I'm nearly out of juice.'

'Out of . . . ? Oh, right.' Pandora shook her head. 'Your batteries. I completely forgot. But you're OK?'

'For now. Most of the cars and stuff had some power left in there. But uh, I do have some bad news.'

I walked slightly ahead and out of the tent, not wanting to see her face when I told her. I didn't just spend the whole time thinking up ways to avoid the zombie school library. I had also tried to move the trucks and tank, but there just wasn't enough power. The little that they had I had siphoned off once I had drunk out the parking lot.

'Let me guess. The road block.' Pandora joined me and

winced against the bright sunlight, but she didn't look surprised. 'Yeah, I guessed as much when I saw the body. If it still had power, why did he stay there during . . . whatever happened?' She shuddered at the thought despite it being hot as hell. Sweat dripped into my eyebrow and I thought about something else I wasn't looking forward to.

'We'll have to walk until we can find a new car,' I said. I thought of the pile of empty water bottles next to Pandora's bed. We didn't have much left. 'And if we're doing that, we gotta find another strip mall or something. There has to be one around here. It's a school, right?'

Pandora nodded, her mouth drawn into a line. 'I thought that might be the case. What we need is a map. Bound to be one here somewhere.'

'Good plan, Batman.'

'Who?' Pandora asked, heading for the first tent, labelled 'CHECK-IN'.

I wrinkled my nose. 'P, when we find your fam, we gotta get you versed on classic cinema.' I thought she was ignoring me, but she let her fingers catch in mine when I caught up, and I tried not to grin too much.

Inside the tent was the jackpot. The tables were all messed up, but there were no dead people – an honest to God miracle at that point – and there was a map of the local area still pinned by rusted pegs to the corkboard walls. We took a few minutes to find the road we had taken and work out how far we had travelled. Eight hundred kilometres, give or take. Gort had estimated around that as the beginning of our search area, so we didn't have far to go.

Even better, there was a mall nearby.

'Score,' I said, pointing to the square on the map. 'We can totally load up here. It's huge, see the scale? One of those outlet malls you get outta town. There'll be tons of stuff there.'

'Then that's where we go next. It's even on the way. And if we go now, we'll make it before night-time,' she said, and I swallowed. I had heard some creepy-ass howling in the night here. Out in the sticks it was practically a desert, so my guess was some sort of mutant coyote, but I wasn't willing to hang around to find out. It hadn't found us so far, but a mall sure beat hiding out in tents.

And maybe there was a mattress store. With double beds.

We had a last look around for anything I had missed – Pandora found another water bottle and a portable battery for me, but that was it – and we set off down the highway. When we squeezed between the truck and the tank, I saw Pandora pause, but she wouldn't let me help her. She had been hurt so bad when she was last here, and she just kept going, like a total badass. I knew there was a reason I stuck with her.

It was hot, so we didn't talk much as we walked.

Instead, I tried not to think about the water sloshing around in my pack. Man, my mouth was dry. We'd only been walking for about an hour, but my lips were so cracked by the time we found the mall that I thought they were going to fall clean off.

Once we saw the sign for the turn, Pandora broke into a sort of half run and I followed her. It would be cooler inside the mall for sure. There were no cars in the parking lot, so we headed for the huge double doors under a marble arch. Fancy mall for fancy people. Maybe we could find fancy food and drink here, like champagne.

But as we approached the doors, I could see something was wrong. The usually unbroken reflection of the sun was scattered across the entrance. Broken glass. Both me and Pandora slowed up as we got nearer, glass crunching beneath our feet.

Inside, the mall was as dark as a cave. A really fucking ominous cave, like from a horror movie.

'We don't have a choice.' Pandora read my mind and pointed at the sky. Despite the heat, she was right. The sun was about to dip below the horizon.

'I heard them too,' she added in a whisper. I swallowed hard. The coyotes.

'Sure,' I said. I tried to style out the shake in my voice. 'Into the murder mall we go. After you.'

12

'Pandora, babe. I can't believe Dad took the car to work today,' Lexi groaned. She was speaking from my tablet screen, which was propped up while I did my make-up. 'Today of all days.'

I tried a clear lip gloss and instantly regretted it. 'Oh, right. Did you need me to send a car around again?' I said. I pressed my lips against a tissue to get the make-up off and glanced at the screen, where Lexi's pout had turned into a dazzling smile. She only ever called me when she wanted the car sent round, which was more and more often recently.

'Oh, babe, would you? I'll be your best friend for ever.'

'Weren't you my best friend for ever yesterday, when I lent you that top?' I sighed as Lexi stood back to admire herself in her mirror, her look complete with the very expensive designer top

that I hadn't even had chance to wear yet.

'Oh, you slay me, bitch. You love it,' Lexi said, and I went back to cleaning my face. She wasn't wrong. I did love it that she needed me so much. It was hard to make friends when your father was who mine was. Although 'friend' was a loose way of describing our relationship, which was more or less a one-way street.

'Hey Lexi, I actually wanted to talk to you about something,' I said, the familiar swell of anxiety flipping my stomach over as I edged my university prospectus out from my pile of girls' magazines.

'Sorry, babe. Gotta go. Gotta fit in my HIIT workout before school. You'll send that car, yeah?' She turned to camera one last time, finally tearing her eyes away from her reflection.

I swallowed, nodded. I was dreading telling her I didn't want to go to the same college as her, never mind that I wanted to study something other than fashion. Besides, she would probably just say I was 'bringing the mood down'.

Lexi made all the decisions: what we talked about; what we wore; where we went; and what college we were going to. Same campus, same subject. And that was usually just the way I liked it. Fewer decisions meant less responsibility on me. But I couldn't ignore this. I loved psychology, and biology. Luckily we were in different classes for those in school so I could lie to her about how good my grades were. Now that I thought about it, that was probably the reason my grades had improved.

'Great. See you at school, bitch, love ya, byeeee.' She blew me

a kiss and cut the video call.

And I was alone again.

I sighed and wondered what Dad's schedule was like today. Whether he was even still in the house. Aurora Tech needed its fearless leader, after all. Especially at times like this. The company waited for no one, not even the CEO. We couldn't even produce food or run transport without Aurora Tech – one of the many downsides of a mega-corporation taking over every aspect of life on the planet, as the news liked to remind us.

'Your father would like to see you in his office, Pandora.' Rosie's voice came through my tablet the instant Lexi hung up. So, not completely alone then. It was hard to be alone when surrounded by so many bots.

The request was highlighted by an on-screen exclamation mark emoji that danced around. He had probably been calling for the last half an hour.

'Rosie, respond.' Rosie's interface lit up my tablet in green, awaiting my next command. 'Tell him I'll be right there.'

I flicked Rosie's notifications off the display and switched to the news channels on my socials. The same hashtag was still trending worldwide: #GaiaGivesUp. I scrolled through the images that had swamped my timeline over the last few weeks. Pictures of the rainforest, which had burnt until there were only four hectares left last year; pictures of the UK and mainland Europe, where major flooding had created 150,000 refugees.

In India, monsoon season had been so bad that the economy

fell apart. A nuclear power plant had exploded after trying to run on a skeleton staff, and radiation had poured into the already rising water levels.

The drought and resulting wildfires in Australia had wiped out nearly ninety per cent of their ecosystem. KOALAS NOW CONSIDERED EXTINCT IN THE WILD, *a headline screamed from my sidebar. There were people in Australia now starving, and they had introduced a rationing system and martial law.*

And all of it was happening because of my father. The people had tried to reason with him when the board decided to decommission the individual governments, but the company had stood firm. There was no need for patriotic identity when all the land was owned by Aurora Tech.

And here at home, people were adding a new hashtag: #LightsOut. I saw it every day when I looked out from my bedroom window, which had a view over the whole capital. Entire sections of the city in darkness, sometimes for weeks at a time. The oil had run out decades ago, and we hadn't switched over to renewable energy as quickly as other countries. Not that it had helped much. You can't build a windfarm on a clifftop that's about to fall into the sea.

I put my tablet face down on the table and hesitated before plugging it in. Our house was unaffected by the rolling blackouts. The perks of being in charge.

I went to the window now. It was daytime, so obviously I

couldn't tell whether or not the city and the towering skyscrapers that had been built so rapidly in recent years had managed to generate enough electricity that day, but I doubted it. It was hot, a heatwave in February, and people were getting restless. Every day, my driver took a new route to school, the gates guarded by more guards with heavier guns. I hovered my hand over the grate in the window ledge, the one where the AC came out. Cool air, keeping the temperature of the room comfortable.

I was fairly certain that no one downtown was enjoying AC right now. At the gates to the house, a crowd was gathered, but that wasn't anything new. People had always protested here, even when it was called the White House and the president of a country had lived here, not just a company. The protestors were a constant presence that banged on the dark glass of our cars as we came and went. Sometimes they threw things, but I wasn't worried. The glass was bulletproof.

I narrowed my eyes as the crowd suddenly surged towards the gate like a wave headed for the shore. Something wasn't right. I could see from here that the people had stopped chanting in unison and instead were shouting, their faces little red circles behind the bars. I reached for the window before I remembered it didn't open.

A flash. A dull bang. One of the guards had opened fire on the crowd, and even from this distance I saw the small figure fall to the ground. I stopped breathing, my breath caught in my throat.

The crowd got angrier. Several at once ran at the guard, who started shooting again. Flash. Bang. Flash. Bang. More bodies on the ground. Other guards were running across the lawn, rushing up to the top of the watchtowers either side of the gates. There were maybe forty or fifty servicemen in black suits with guns, but they were heavily outnumbered by the crowd outside the gate. There must have been hundreds, maybe thousands of them, a sea of angry red faces and placards:

TURN THE LIGHTS BACK ON!
THE 1% GET 99% OF THE FOOD!
JUSTICE FOR THE REST OF US!

I stood, rooted to the spot, unable to tear my eyes away as protestor after protestor went down. Guards lined the railings and shot through the bars, stopping to reload when necessary, but it was like trying to pop a room full of balloons with a single toothpick. They just kept coming. There was a wall of them, climbing over the bodies of the dead, some reaching the top of the gate before they were picked off.

And that's when the gate caved in.

'Ms Pandora?' The door of my room opened so violently it hit the wall and made me jump. It was Scott, my bodyguard. As burly as his job title would suggest, he filled the doorway with his dark shoulder pads.

I stood stock still, looking between him and the scene outside. The crowd was pouring in now, getting picked off one by one by the guards, but slowly more were getting through. I watched as one went down only a stone's throw away from the official entrance of the house.

'Please.' I blinked, hearing a pleading in Scott's voice that I hadn't heard before. He had been saying something to me but I hadn't been listening. He crossed the space between us in two huge strides, his size elevens making imprints in the plush carpet.

'OK, time to go. Sorry about this, Ms Pandora, but we're out of time.' Scott grabbed the top of my arm and steered me out of the room. I didn't resist, and it wasn't the first time he had led me like this. Usually, it was just to get through a pack of press photographers, not to walk around my own house.

'Where's my father?' I croaked, finally finding my voice as we turned into the formal dining room.

'He—' Scott's grip on my shoulder got firmer as we heard the sound of breaking glass. 'Shit. They're inside. This way.'

He yanked so hard it felt like he'd pulled my arm out of its socket as we turned out of the dining room and into the back hallway. There was broken glass on the floor and a body, not security, lay bloody and broken and still on the carpet, a neat bullet hole in the back of their head. The sour taste of bile filled my mouth and I was glad I was being held upright.

'Zero-niner, this is Papa Bear. I have Goldilocks secure, what's your whisky, over?' Scott held a finger of his free hand to his ear as he walked, whispering into his mic.

'Copy, Papa Bear. We are secure in the Little Straw House with King Grizzly. Bring Goldilocks to extraction point, over.'

Standing this close to Scott, I could hear everything the agent on the other end of the line said.

'Wait,' I hissed. I dug my heels into the carpet and Scott turned to look at me. It was like my brain had been on pause, and finally started working again. 'What about Lexi? I said I would send her a car. She still thinks we're going to school, and—'

'The Waters family all have tickets,' Scott said, pulling on my arm to get me moving. 'They're probably already in situ.'

'Tickets?' I stammered, and my confusion was just enough to let Scott keep pulling me forwards. I heard more glass breaking, this time closer and accompanied by shouting. Scott looked back, bringing out his handgun and pointing it behind us just as someone appeared at the end of the corridor ahead.

'Look out,' I screamed, pointing at the man with a large gun and blood down his front.

The man aimed and shot, but Scott was quicker. He fired off two controlled rounds and the man went down immediately. Scott stopped, his grip on my arm loosening.

'Good shot,' was all I could think to say. I tried not to think about another body soaking into our carpets as I turned to look at him.

Something was wrong. Scott's skin was pale, his eyes cloudy. My own eyes traced down his body until I saw it. A red bloom of blood, spreading out from under his suit jacket. He opened his mouth, groaned and sank to the floor.

'Scott!' I sank down next to him, the tears already running

hot down my face. Behind me there was shouting, but I didn't pull my eyes away from him.

'It's OK,' he said, struggling to keep his eyes open. 'It's OK, it's OK, it's OK.'

It didn't look OK. There was so much blood that it was pooling behind his shoulder, staining the carpet and the edge of my skirt.

'I don't know what to do.' I burst into tears, panic making my vision swim more than the crying. Scott had been shot. There were crazy people running around the house. Ten minutes ago, I was putting on lip gloss. Now I was squeezing blood out of my clothes.

'Take . . . this.' Scott tried to move and I protested but somehow he managed to shrug me off. He reached into his pocket and pulled out what looked like a credit card.

'What is it?' I sniffed, turning the card over in my hands. It was smeared with his blood. On one side was a magnetic strip and on the other was a picture of a white spinning wheel. Underneath were the words 'AURORA CRYOGENICS'.

'Take it to . . . the panic room . . .' Scott wheezed. He was so pale his lips were blue, but he used the last of his strength to grip my wrist. 'Do you remember . . . ?'

'What? Yes, yes. I know where the panic room is, I remember,' I said, new tears flooding down my face. When Father was appointed, the first day we moved in, they showed us the panic room. In his office, to the left of the desk. The door that was flush

to the wall and that you would only see if you were looking for it. The biometric system that was preloaded with our retinas and thumbprints.

'Go. It's OK. Go,' Scott said, and then he was gone.

'I'm sorry,' I sobbed. I gave Scott's hand one last squeeze and let it drop to the floor with a dull thud.

Those words seemed to be the only thing that kept me going.

'I'm sorry,' I whispered as I stood up, tucked the card away, and stumbled out of the corridor.

'I'm sorry,' I said as I tripped over the limp body of a civilian on the stairs to Father's office.

'I'm sorry,' I screamed as gunfire cracked over my head at the top of the stairs, and then silence. I ducked, grabbing my ears, but kept moving once I was sure whoever it was had stopped. Or had been stopped.

'I'm sorry,' I mumbled once I got to the office. I slammed the door shut behind me and barricaded it with Father's chair for good measure.

I was still apologizing as I scanned my eye and stepped into the room that revealed itself in the cavity of the wall.

'I'm sorry,' I said to the guard that met me there, who held up his gun until I showed him the bloody card that Scott had given me.

'Miss? We have to get you to the escape tunnels now. It's the only way out of the building, come along. Miss?' the guard babbled, but I could barely focus on him.

I gave in to the exhaustion and passed out just in time for him to catch me.

'Pandora, wake up.' A familiar voice forced my eyes open.

I sat bolt upright, the feeling of falling still haunting my limbs and stomach. I turned and found Echo staring at me, his hands a tight grip around my shoulders, his face full of confusion.

Scott. That day. Worrying about the same stupid stuff, like Lexi and clothes and a lift to school. It all seemed so trivial now, so pointless. I had to do better. I had been given a second chance.

'What did I say?' I asked, but I knew. Dr Kapoor had helped me through my old nightmares, through the terrors that had me screaming at night and made me shout out Mother's name. But I said other stuff too, and clearly it had started again from the look on Echo's face.

'You were yelling something about your Dad? That you were sorry?' Echo said. He still had hold of my shoulders, and from the tight pinch of his fingers I must have been really making a racket.

'Oh, right,' I said dumbly. Images from the dream – the memory – flashed through my mind.

'You were trying to run, I think. Well, you were all tangled up in the sheets, anyway.' Echo let go of me and sat back. He was dressed only in his shorts, like he had run in in a hurry. We had found a bedding store that hadn't been too seriously looted, and managed to barricade the doors with a mattress and a bedsheet before finding separate beds for the night. I liked him, but I wasn't ready for that. Even if he was the last boy on Earth. Besides, the beds were in the same showroom. And Echo had said he would take first watch for . . . whatever was out there.

'That makes sense,' I said. Echo stayed quiet, waiting for me to carry on. For someone who hadn't been around people much, he was an excellent listener. 'I was dreaming – well, more remembering – about the last day on Earth.'

'Trippy,' Echo replied, and I had to smile. He had a way of making things less serious, less scary. It's what I liked most about him. I studied the curve of his jaw in the half-light, the way it faded into thick, two-day-old stubble. I think I liked that almost as much as his sense of humour.

'Trippy indeed,' I said. I opened my mouth, then closed it again. Echo didn't need to hear this.

'Wanna talk about it?' he said, reading my mind. He crossed his legs at the end of my king-size bed, waiting. Patient. Not that much different from my therapist, really.

I hesitated. Sure, it was easy to speak to Dr Kapoor, because she was being paid to listen to me. Whenever I tried to talk to my father, or Lexi, or even Scott, they had always been too busy. From what I knew about her, my mother would have made the time, but when she died I was too young to have the same sort of questions. And yet here he was, Echo, a boy sentenced to an eternity alone at the end of the world. And he wanted to hear about me.

'Actually, yes. I do,' I said, and I explained every detail to him. I told him about Scott, and Lexi, and the final moments in that house before everything fell apart. Echo nodded at all the right parts, and listened. Poker-faced.

'That sounds . . . intense,' he said. He reached out and hovered a hand over my knee, asking with his eyes if it was OK to rest it there. I nodded and he did. I loved that he always checked.

'Any more intense than waking up at the end of the world with your memory erased?' I asked. I raised an eyebrow.

'You know what, it's a close second,' Echo said, a smile playing around his mouth. 'But that's life. My mama always said life was like a box of chocolates. You never know what you're gonna get.'

'I thought you didn't remember your mother?' I asked. He had also put on a weird accent for that last part. I realized too late it was another reference I just wasn't going to get.

Echo sighed. 'I don't – it doesn't matter. I mean, we all got crazy lives. Sounds like yours was maybe a little crazier than most. What exactly did your dad do to earn that kind of dollar?'

I hoped he couldn't see my expression in the dimness. My father. I knew the question had to come up at some point. But if I told him, how could he ever look at me the same way? Would he be angry?

Even worse: would he be impressed?

'My f— I mean, Dad,' I repeated, the intimate nickname foreign on my tongue. I scrambled for a coherent lie. But none came. This was it. The truth I hoped would never come out. 'Well, I—'

'Quiet.' Echo leapt across the bed in the darkness and clamped a hand across my mouth, knocking the breath from my lungs. I was so shocked I didn't stop him, just stared into his eyes as he pushed me down into the pillows and came to lie beside me.

'Don't you hear that?' he whispered.

In the distance, something delicate smashed against a hard surface. Someone – or something – was in the mall.

13

'Shit, sorry,' I whispered, removing my hand from Pandora's mouth. She sucked in a huge breath and said nothing.

I strained every muscle and fibre-optic nerve ending to listen to what was going on in the lobby of the mall. I was sure that was where the noise was coming from. Something smashed and Pandora jumped against me, her body pressed close to mine.

Well, this wasn't exactly the way I was hoping we would eventually fall into bed together.

Focus, dude. There were animals out here, that much was certain from the nests in some of the stores. And the way the food hall had been ransacked, reeking of pee.

The weird thing was the lights. I could feel the hum of

electricity straight through the walls once we were inside, but all of the light bulbs had been smashed at some point. The chandeliers at the entrance; the overheads in the stores; the emergency exits – all gone. Like someone had knocked them all out when they looted the place. At least I was still able to plug in. In the city, the bigger buildings like the supermarket had their own solar panels so they didn't have to rely on the grid, and I had to assume the mall had the same thing.

That's a point. If Pandora's screams were enough to wake me when on charge, they sure as shit were loud enough to attract our unwanted company. Hiding might not be an option. I needed more info.

'Stay here,' I whispered. Pandora opened her mouth but I interrupted her. 'I mean it. No point two of us getting caught. Need you to stay safe so you can rescue me if things get bad.' She knew I didn't mean that, but she nodded anyway.

I tried to ignore the terror running up and down my legs like pins and needles as I crossed the floor of the showroom. The update to my E-Mote chip had done some great stuff, but with the good stuff came the bad. Before, I didn't really feel much of anything except occasionally a bit murdery towards Gort. But ever since the update, I had felt happy, then *really* happy during the kiss, and now I was afraid. I had never been afraid before, because I hadn't really cared if I made it through the day or not. Now, someone else was relying on me. I had to do this, even if I shit my pants while doing it.

I reached the door we'd barricaded with a mattress earlier. Either side of the barricade was a safety-glass display window, decorated with bedspreads printed with a cartoon I didn't recognize. I crawled into the display space and lay low to the floor, edging my way to the front of the display.

The bed store was on the second floor, which was accessible via a set of unmoving escalators that led to a mezzanine level of the mall. I could just about look over and through the glass railing that semi-remained in its runners along the edge of the balcony and into the lobby below, but it was unlikely whatever was down there would be able to see me if they looked up.

I narrowed my eyes and tried to adjust them to the gloom. The mall had a partially intact skylight, and the sun was just starting to paint the sky pink, so it wasn't completely dark . . . but it was pretty damn close. And there was deffo something down there. The crunch of something on the broken glass was loud even from my hiding place. The thing was large, and dark. A mutant coyote? Like something from the city park? I shuddered at the thought. It moved into the open part of the mall, where a chandelier had long since fallen into the dry fountain.

Then it split into three separate parts.

'Holy shit,' I breathed, my breath fogging up the window.

'Holy shit, what?' A voice came from behind and I almost knocked over a mannequin as I struggled to keep my heart in my chest. Pandora was crouched behind me, her eyes like two jewels in the darkness.

'Maybe as in "holy shit, what are you trying to do, give me a fatal shutdown?"' I stilled my breathing and checked back over my shoulder. The sound of our conversation would be muffled by the mattress, surely? But when I checked the lobby, there was nothing there.

Double shit.

'What did you see?' Pandora pressed me again and I shuffled out of the window display.

'I dunno, but whatever it is, there's three of them,' I hissed. Pandora's eyes widened even more and I tried to temper myself. It wasn't her fault. She had lived in a mansion with a bodyguard her whole life, until a few days ago. I hadn't left the city, sure, but I knew about the mutants.

'Maybe they didn't hear us,' I said. I hoped I sounded more convincing than I felt. 'A lot of the mutations aren't for the better, you know. A lot of these poor little dudes are missing eyes and ears and all sorts of bad stuff. I think if we stay here, they might go away.'

'They *might* go away?' If I could see her, I'd say Pandora's face just went white. 'How big are they?'

'Not big,' I answered a little too quickly, but when I thought about it, they weren't huge. 'No bigger than me or you. We can take 'em.'

'I don't want to "take" them anywhere,' Pandora hissed. She seemed mad, but she was probably more scared. I know I sure as hell was. I reached out and found her hand in the darkness. She squeezed my fingers so hard I thought she had popped a knuckle.

'We're safe in here,' I whispered, definitely not sure that we were safe in here.

As if they were literally just trying to kill my vibe, right on cue, a clicking sound came from outside the store. The sounds were close together. Footsteps? Claws on marble floors? I backed away from the window and dragged Pandora's limp body with me.

I couldn't have her freeze on me now. 'P, you gotta listen to me. Stay very quiet, and very still.' I was whispering so close to her ear that my lips brushed her earlobe. Maybe her freezing wasn't the worst. Maybe the creatures really would go away.

'Clear,' a voice rang out and I reeled back, checking Pandora for any sign she had spoken.

But it didn't sound like her voice. It didn't sound like any voice I had heard before. It was low, and gruff, and totally belonged to an old dude. Pandora's eyes widened. Something dropped in the pit of my stomach.

'It could be a TV,' I whispered, a frantic feeling leading my words. 'Or a stereo or something.'

'All the televisions were looted when we got here. Anything expensive or electronic was gone,' Pandora said. Her voice was rising, the excitement palpable between us. The tension hit me like a car hitting a brick wall at 100 kph.

And she was right. We had spent over an hour checking out every store for supplies. The electricity worked, but nothing remained. The lights were on and no one was home.

Until now.

'Anything on the south side?' The voice again. It echoed in the empty lobby.

This time, we heard the crackled response of a walkie-talkie.

'Clear, boss. Approaching the north stairs now.'

'Roger that,' the first voice said.

He was close, just on the other side of the mattress. There was no way he would leave that alone. It was too out of place, too obviously moved. When we had made the barricade, it was for mutant desert creatures, not . . .

What? Am I really about to say it, to meet my second one of these in five days, after years of nothing?

'He's human.' Pandora spoke the words I was too

chickenshit to even think.

I swallowed a dry lump that rose to my throat. 'It could still be a trick.' What was I so afraid of? Hadn't we set out to find the humans? Granted, I assumed they would all be in popsicle form, but hadn't we found the very thing we were looking for? Wasn't that good?

Then why was I begging Pandora with my eyes not to call out?

'It's not a trick,' Pandora said. She stood up and spoke loud enough that it made my shoulders tense up. 'It's my people.' She turned and walked towards the door.

My people. Yeah, should have seen that coming. But it still sat like a dagger in my heart. *My people.* As in, not me. Not someone who isn't all human. Real, proper humans. Humans that aged and didn't wear lime-green high-tops and didn't need to charge their batteries at night. Those sorts of humans.

'In here,' she called out, pushing her weight against one side of the mattress to try and force it aside. When she couldn't, she turned to me. 'Aren't you going to help me?'

That was a good question. Should I help her? My head said *hell no*. Why should I? But my heart drove my feet across the floor and positioned me next to her at the mattress.

I moved the barricade with ease and realized it probably would have been no match for a mutant coyote anyway. Beyond the entrance to the store, I heard the quick tap of feet moving towards us. More than one set. Pandora and I stepped out of the store and into the path of the three dudes I had seen, dressed all in black like commando characters from a video game.

They had guns like them too.

'Woah.' I put my hands up and Pandora did the same. I could see out of the corner of my eye that she was afraid, and maybe even . . . regretful? Hell, who wouldn't be? We were safe, and now we were being held at gunpoint. Was it bad that I felt a little bit vindicated?

I decided it was. Get out alive now; tell P *I told you so* later.

'We don't want any trouble, bro,' I said.

I addressed the man in the middle, mostly because he had the biggest gun. Their leader? He looked super different to how Pandora had looked. I mean, he was a dude, obviously, but he looked wrecked. Skin hanging off bone, his eyes sunk into hollow sockets, he looked like he hadn't eaten in a while. His comrades looked no different. Pandora didn't look this rough after crashing at hyperspeed into the ground.

'Bro?' The leader dude almost laughed, which made my chest tighten. It wasn't a funny laugh for sure.

'I've never heard one talk like that before,' the second goon said. He gripped his rifle and readjusted his aim at us. 'Shall we shoot 'em? Can usually get a couple rounds in 'em before they malfunction.'

Malfunction? 'Wait. She's human. Not HUMANKIND. Don't shoot.' I realized how pathetic I sounded, but the way Pandora looked at me gave me strength.

'That's right. We're human,' Pandora said. My eyebrows shot up under my hairline. Did she just lie for me? Damn. That's smart. These guys clearly used my kind for shooting practice. And we needed to stay alive long enough to get out of this mess.

'That's – yeah. Right. So by the old rules, shooting us would be, well, murder. So like, you'd better not,' I said.

There was a pause while the two goons looked at the boss man, unsure what to do. Then they all burst out laughing, a laugh filled with snorting and phlegm.

'Did you hear that? The old rules. This kid done cracked me up.' The leader lowered his gun, but the goons were still on us, so Pandora and I kept our hands in the air. 'That's a good one. The old rules. Whatcha gonna do, call a safety bot on us?'

'If-if we need to. Then yes.' Pandora's voice was barely a squeak.

I winced. She knew as well as I did that there wasn't enough juice to run bots out here, and these bozos were clearly locals. And, just as I thought, we set the three musketeers back off laughing again. One of them laughed so much, he had to stop to spit on the marble floor. His saliva was as black as his teeth.

'There ain't no way these two are human. I mean, look at 'em! They're like a living, breathing fashion billboard. You know what, darling? Just for giving me such a good laugh, I'm gonna let you see the merch before I kill ya,' the boss said, and all three of them stopped laughing, weapons raised.

The bottom of my stomach dropped out, like I was on a virtual-reality roller coaster. Shit. They were going to kill us. Well, they were going to kill me. As for P . . . a shudder ran down my spine and I felt sure I was going to vomit. This was bad. For a second, the scene in front of me faded away and my imaginary bearded friend appeared. *This is not a drill. This is what the drills were for*, he said. I bit my lip hard until he faded away. I was getting good at getting him to bug off. *Not now, creepy old guy. Especially when you only speak in riddles.*

'Look, fellas. I'll make you a deal. You get me, and you let her go.' What was I saying? I was throwing myself to the wolves. The slightly less mutated wolves. I shot a look at Pandora, who was crying, pleading, shaking her head as a violent *no way*.

But I couldn't let her down. My fate would be quick, but hers? She would be alone. And I knew how lousy it was to be alone.

'And why the heck would we do that?' the boss man asked.

'Because I'm valuable,' I said. I was really winging it now, but I managed to keep my voice steady. 'You said it yourself. You couldn't even tell we were human, with our fancy threads and shizzle. We got plenty more fancy stuff where this all came from. I can show you where our stash is before you kill me.'

My mouth ran dry as I spoke, but it was the only thing I could think of. I looked at Pandora again and she was sobbing. I wished I could take her hand, one last time.

'There *is* that trader out near the highwaymen's outpost. He always says he's looking for good stuff. Maybe he knows where some working electronics are. Kid might have a point.' It was the guy on the left, the one with the rifle, that addressed the boss man.

Christ, how many of these humans were there? I can't believe I had been awake three years – possibly a hundred – and never come across any. Why were they all so far from the city? Didn't they know it was safer there? It didn't look much better out here. These dudes had guns, but they looked dead on their feet.

'True,' the boss man said. He chewed the inside of his cheek.

He was considering my offer. He was going to let Pandora go. Me? I would be OK. I'd wait till they were asleep, then I'd make a run for it. I could take them. Right?

'OK,' the boss man said eventually. 'Sandy, you take the kid, and me and Skye will have fun with the girly. We'll let you have a go when you get back from the outpost.'

I had read in books about when blood ran cold, but my CPU kept my insides at a constant temperature, so I had never felt it before. But there it was. The blood went icy in my veins as the three men stepped towards us. *Idiot.* I was such a fucking idiot. I had given them the both of us on a platter.

'No!' Pandora screamed, and she stepped in front of me, like I was the one that needed protecting. Maybe I was. I'd never been shot before. I threaded my fingers through hers and pulled her closer, trying to position my body in front of hers, just in case bullets started to fly.

'What on Earth do you think you are doing?'

OK, I had officially lost my mind. Three new voices in one day was one thing, but now there was a fourth? On top of creepy-inside-my-head dude? And this one was female, an older voice that spoke with authority that boss man could only dream of. I was right, because at the sound of it, they immediately lowered their weapons and dropped to their knees, like they were bowing or something.

P and I looked over their heads and spotted our rescuers, a group of people dressed in camo gear similar to the dead soldiers we had seen down the road. There were at least a dozen of them, and in the middle, a woman with a severe haircut and matching expression. She brought up a fist and the platoon stopped in their tracks, weapons raised.

'And who,' the woman said, 'on God's dry earth, are you?'

14

'Who are we?' Echo spat, his hand curling into a fist under my fingers. 'Are you serious? Who are we? I'll give you a hint, my man. We're not the ones pointing guns at anyone.'

'I'll kindly remind you that we just saved you with these guns, boy,' the woman shot back. Her eyes narrowed. 'Do you want me to regret that decision?'

'OK, hang on. I think we got off on the wrong foot here.' I squeezed Echo's hand until the tension released, like squeezing an orange loose of its juices. He shot me a look, but let me talk. 'We are very grateful to you. Are these your men? They weren't acting with the most gentlemanly of manners.'

'That's putting it lightly,' Echo muttered.

'Shut your mouth, boy,' the leader hissed from the floor, but he didn't get up. He didn't so much as look at us. Whoever this woman was, she had complete authority, and that meant Echo and I had to play nice. For now.

'I am sorry about that. We thought you were bots, rogues from the city,' the woman said. Her expression smoothed a fraction, but she only looked at me. 'Sometimes they get lost and end up this far out, but we haven't seen one for years.'

'Well, we're humans. I'm Pandora, and this is Echo,' I said. I craned my neck to look at Echo but his jaw was set, his eyes on the woman in charge. It looked like I was on my own with this one.

'Razor,' the woman nodded. Razor by name, razor by nature. 'And we can see you're human now. The halflings can't hold a conversation like that. They just repeat stupid shit.'

I winced at the slur, but Echo didn't move. I guessed he didn't remember it like I did, being slung around school corridors and in the street. Halflings. Some nasty people about. But I was sure from the look on his face that he knew what it meant. He was just choosing not to react.

'Ms Razor—'

'General Razor, if you want to address me by my full title.'

I sucked in a breath. So she *was* in charge. And better

yet, it seemed like there was some sense of order, despite the lewd and horrific comments of the men earlier.

'Pardon. General Razor,' I said. Echo vibrated with rage next to me, but he still held it in. I had a feeling he would blow if we didn't defuse the situation: us on one side, them on the other. 'General, we seem to be on the same page. I am human. My friend is human. So why don't we get moving? This hardly seems a safe place to continue this conversation.'

Echo squeezed my hand behind my back and I suppressed a smile. I was glad he understood. We needed to stick together, but I couldn't ignore the excitement rising within me. People. Echo had thought there were none left, and yet here they were. I had so many questions, but I had to wait until they trusted us. We had to see where they had come from.

Razor studied us for a moment and whispered something to the man on her right. He nodded. Was he some kind of advisor?

'OK. We're going to need you to come back with us, for now,' Razor said.

Wow, just like that? It couldn't be so easy. I stepped forward, past the men who moments earlier had the upper hand, but something stopped me. Echo. He had hold of my hand and he didn't move.

I looked back over my shoulder. 'Trust me,' I whispered, and he reluctantly came with me. He had gone along with my lie about being human. He had trusted me that far, so he had to follow through.

'How do you like me now?' Echo practically spat at the three men on their knees, and they muttered slurs under their breath in response.

'Enough,' Razor said. She pointed at the kneeling men. 'Back to your posts, if you want to get paid this week. Keep a tight perimeter.'

The men stood, nodded and jogged off into the darker recesses of the mall.

'We have transportation outside,' Razor said. I noticed she only addressed me, not Echo. That was fine for now. She wouldn't let us into her life without some trust.

We followed her, surrounded by the armed guards, back down the rusted escalators and to the smashed entrance Echo and I had come through the day before. He didn't let go of my hand the whole time, a layer of sweat building between our palms. I had to remember that Echo wasn't used to trusting humans. For all he knew, humans just edited the personality out of all his fellow TeenSynths and left him to rot.

I used my free hand to shield my eyes against the morning sun as we crossed the parking lot. There, as if for a strange wedding party, were two sets of horse and cart.

No, that wasn't accurate. There were four horses, one with a growth on its stomach and another with three ears, and each pair was roped up to a makeshift vehicle behind them. They looked like minivans that had been sawn in half lengthways, with the seats still intact.

I followed Razor to the front carriage. She climbed up the metal step where the door used to be and sat behind the 'driver's seat', which now held reins instead of a wheel. She gestured for me to sit next to her and I froze, one foot on the step, Echo's hand still tight in mine.

'Calm down, love. It's only a half-hour ride from here. Loverboy can sit behind you for a little while.' Razor rolled her eyes and hooked her elbow over the edge of the cart, where the window used to be. Waiting.

I looked at Echo, who had been quiet for the longest time since I had known him, and slowly he released my fingers. I moved up the step and two of the guards pushed past me, grabbing Echo by the shoulders and sitting him firmly between them on the long padded seat at the back of the van. I opened my mouth to protest, but Echo shook his head. Probably for the best. He hadn't exactly been as polite as I had towards our rescuers, and we didn't need to raise any suspicion about him.

I took my seat next to Razor and the rest of the guards took theirs across the two carts. The driver of our cart snapped the reins and the horses moved forward, pulling our weight behind them. We sat in silence all the way to the edge of the lot, and I kept craning my head to look at

Echo, but he kept his eyes on the ground. His hands were knitted so tightly together that his knuckles were white.

'So, Pandora is an unusual name,' Razor said, and I jumped because I'd almost forgotten she was there.

The sun was hot. I hadn't realized it was morning, but already the sun was baking, beating down and turning the metal of the seatbelt red-hot against my thigh despite my combat pants. I shuffled in my seat.

'Not that unusual where I'm from.'

'And where exactly is that?' Razor raised an eyebrow before fiddling in her top pocket and bringing out a small burlap pouch. She pulled out papers and related paraphernalia and began to roll a cigarette. 'Smoke?'

'No, thank you,' I said. I tensed up at the mere sight of the stuff. Didn't she know how high cancer rates were? Then we hit a rock in the road as we turned out of the lot and I remembered. She didn't care. The world had been through a hundred years of climate change and nuclear meltdowns and goodness knew what else. Animals had three eyes, or sometimes none. Smoking probably made no difference at all.

'So?' Razor said, lighting the cigarette. I was glad the cart was open-topped.

'What?'

'Where are you from? We never see new people any more. We rarely see bots. You and Romeo back there are the first ones we've seen in years. And certainly the first ones to look so good after living in the wasteland. What's your secret, girl?' She jabbed a finger, indicating her own sagging, pale face and then my own.

I hesitated. I needed to find out where the cryogenic labs were, and these people had appeared right near Gort's indicated search zone. Razor might know where they were. She might even be guarding them.

Another thought crossed my mind, of course. A much darker one. What if my father, and Lexi, and all the others, were woken up too soon? Decades too soon? Razor and her people had clearly had time to build up supplies – how much time? Were they the descendants of the cryogenic labs, or contemporaries?

'We're from the Aurora Tech labs,' I said. No more, no less. I didn't need to tell her who Father was. Not yet. But I did need to know what she knew. And at the end of the day, she had spared our lives. Why keep us alive if it wasn't to help?

'Thought as much. You don't look hungry enough to have been here long.' Razor took a long drag on her cigarette and my mouth dropped open despite the fumes.

'So you know where they are? The cryolabs – you know people from there?' I asked. I was too eager, giving too much away, but I couldn't help myself. I was so close to the one thing I thought I had lost for ever.

'God, no,' Razor laughed, and then choked on her cigarette smoke and took a moment to compose herself. My heart sank. 'I mean, we come across some empty or destroyed pods every now and then. But I never met a live one. You two must have been lucky, surviving a crash like that. Damn lucky.'

'So . . . others were ejected?' I whispered. I think about what Gort told me, about how the ships didn't take off in the end and instead were buried in these special silos underground. Razor's words went round and round in my head. *I never met a live one.* So what happened to everyone else?

Razor finished her cigarette and immediately started rolling another one. 'Yep, there were others ejected here and there. My guess is the earthquakes caused some of the pods to eject. The rest of the pods . . . ?' She shrugged. 'Probably rubble.'

Everything up until the earthquakes matched up with what Echo and Gort had told me. I swallowed hard.

'That can't be true,' I whispered. I slumped forward like a puppet with the strings cut. 'There has to be some . . . someone left.'

'What are we, chopped liver?' Razor spoke through a haze of smoke. '*We're* what's left. The true salt-of-the-earth types, like my grammy. Not the rich folks like you. Most people died out in the droughts, and the freeze, and then there were the flares and the nuclear meltdowns and the massive supervolcanic eruptions, which caused the tidal waves and the tremors. But you don't need to hear about that,' Razor said, with exactly the tone of voice that suggested she wanted to let me know *exactly* about that.

'See, what you see here is the cream of the crop. The very best humanity had to offer. The ones who were tested and came out the other side,' Razor continued. She smiled and her teeth were yellow. My stomach rolled and I prayed to a non-existent God that I wouldn't be sick.

'So . . . there aren't any ships left?' I whispered. 'Everyone's dead?'

Razor surprised me then. She put an arm around my shoulder and squeezed. Her breath smelt like tobacco and rot.

'Cheer up, kid. I mean, we haven't checked *every* centimetre of the continent. There might still be some out there.' She pointed to the endless horizon and I tried not to let panic overwhelm me. Maybe she was right. Maybe Father was still out there somewhere.

The thought of him caught me by surprise. He had been my everything before, my only remaining family. He had worked to save my mother. His job had given me protection, access to the pods, and then . . . what? I had landed on the world alone, and it had been Echo and Gort who had helped me. A world that was scorched and abandoned, full of mutant monsters and sparse colonies. All because of Aurora Tech, the very company that had paid for my whole life. That Father had become so involved in, it was hard to draw the line where the company ended and he began.

I had to find him, but not because I needed him. Because I needed answers.

'There is still something I'm confused about,' I said, as desperate to change the subject as I was for Razor to move away from me. By some miracle she did. The moment had passed. 'Where are your bots? I know the batteries in most things still work, from – from our travels. We even drove a car most of the way out of the city.'

Razor had rolled yet another cigarette, but she didn't light it. Instead, she turned it in her fingers, like she was deciding what to say.

'My people don't trust the bots,' she said eventually. 'We don't use anything beyond radios and lights that use electricity. Our greed for technology was what put us up shit creek in the first place. This place used to be a country. A whole empire. Isn't that wild? There used to be lots of countries, and languages, and accents and everything. Now it's just one big, sandy blob on the globe. Even now, everyone sounds the same. Aurora Tech made sure of that when they combined the ten richest countries in the Western world.' She laughed, but it was hollow. 'And that was before they got so powerful they bought up the rest of the damn planet. Why have a country, and elections, and liberty, when you can just have one giant conglomerate? Ain't that the truth of it.'

I swallowed. I did know the histories of the old country system. They had taught us at school, but of course, it was an Aurora Tech curriculum. We had always learnt that business was the key to earning potential, and money was what made the world go round. It paid for medicine, education, housing. Money was a good thing. Before, everything was based on what was known as 'politics'. Sometimes only two parties, with opposing views, dividing the people. Aurora Tech provided for everyone. It was better. Wasn't it?

Thoughts of the rolling blackouts that never affected me or my father ran through my mind, and I shook my head to clear them.

'W-wow. That's amazing. And you helped your people build a community, then?' I said, trying to still sound like I didn't know any better. Well, it at least explained why the cities were empty. They ran on a whole grid of technology, its very existence as important and ubiquitous as the branches on a tree. It was also where the most pollution was. Hopefully, out in the countryside, the earth had had more of a chance to recover.

At the very least, they had grown tobacco.

'Well, I can't take all the credit. That honour goes to the Chief,' Razor said. She blew smoke rings as she spoke, like the effort of the conversation was boring her.

'The Chief?' I pressed. So Razor was high up, but there was someone else in charge. Hopefully they were a little less aggressive.

'Yep. The Chief is in charge of everything. He gave us food, and family, and he keeps us safe. The Chief is our everything.'

'Can I get an audience with this – this Chief? What's his name?' I pressed, excited again.

Razor shot a look at me and stubbed out her cigarette on the outside of the car before rolling another one. 'You can't just talk to the Chief. And that *is* his name – just the Chief, especially to you. Only his most trusted advisors get to speak with him. It's one of our most sacred rules.'

'Why?' I asked before I could stop myself. I was only making Razor angrier, but I had to know more. I tried to catch Echo's eye from the back seat, but he still just stared at the floor.

'Why? Because we're the last humans standing, so we make the rules. That's why.' Razor regained her composure after another drag on her new cigarette and to my surprise, she smiled. 'You know what, Pandora? I like you. You remind me a little of myself at your age. Curious, like.'

'Really?' I asked. I was embarrassed to admit it, even to

myself, but a sense of pride glowed warm in my chest. As an only child left alone a lot, I always did crave attention from adults. Teachers, staff, Dr Kapoor. I just liked to feel . . . I don't know . . . seen.

'Really.' Razor smiled again and tucked a loose hair behind her ear. 'We girls gotta stick together. Show these men who's boss. We survived the apocalypse, Pandora. That's gotta count for something. You hear me?'

'Right,' I said.

Razor looked out down the road again, lost in thought. A couple of the men nearby rolled their eyes but if she noticed, she didn't care enough to comment.

'Anyway, as I was sayin', Chief's house, Chief's rules,' she said, putting her clunky boots up on the back of the driver's seat. 'Speaking of which, we're here. Home sweet home.' Razor nodded ahead and blew out a long plume of smoke.

Ahead, off to one side of the road, was a low wall with a huge gate. The wall was metallic and glinted in the sun, only rusted at the corners near the hinges of the huge doors. As the cart moved around to face the entrance, I saw distant figures run the length of the wall and towards the opening. With a deafening creak, the doors swung outwards to greet us, revealing several low buildings beyond.

'How did you build such a thing without technology?' I said, marvelling at the sturdy nature of the wall. It would keep mutant coyotes out, that was for sure.

'Our ancestors built it. The Chief, my grammy and the rest. We were out in the wastelands before then, for decades. They made this a safe place where we could put down roots,' said Razor, stubbing out her last cigarette and pocketing her pouch.

'Well, how did they build it?'

'Girl, if you want your time here to be anything less than difficult, you'll learn when question time is over,' Razor snapped, and a couple of her men turned to look at me.

That was the first time she had lost her temper, and I had a feeling it wouldn't be the last. I swallowed and sank down into my seat as the huge gates fully opened to receive our convoy.

The camp itself was incredible, really more of a village. There were at least twenty intact buildings spread out in front of us, each with two storeys of matching windows. The telltale pockmarks of where signage once stood proud against the walls of the buildings remained, but I wasn't surprised. This place probably belonged to Aurora Tech – as most things did – and Razor had made it very clear that everyone who lived under the Chief hated them.

But the best bit was the people. There were tens, maybe hundreds, criss-crossing between buildings holding bundles of wood or meat or cloth. A community. A real, proper community built from the ruins of civilization. Aurora Tech's top scientists had been convinced that no one could survive the climate catastrophe. The climate of Earth was too unstable, they said. That was why they had packed us up with everything we could ever need, like frozen seeds and animal embryos. Yet here humanity was. Thriving.

Beyond the wall was a large paved courtyard, where we were met by a stable boy who came to calm the horses. We stepped out one by one and I was glad to have Echo by my side again, but he was still quiet. He didn't pull away when I reached for his hand, but he didn't squeeze my fingers back, either. I would have to fill him in on everything Razor had told me later.

'Welcome,' Razor said, tucking another cigarette behind her ear. 'To the New Republic of the People.'

'Wow. Catchy name. Real original,' came Echo's sarcastic reply.

15

It was a dump.

Well, maybe that was a little harsh. But dude, it didn't even have en suite showers. And there wasn't even a Rosie here.

There was no TV.

Pandora seemed to think it was the bomb. I couldn't believe it. The chick probably lived in a mansion with servants and shizzle before she got her very expensive golden ticket to the ark, and this was how she wanted to spend the apocalypse?

I didn't get girls.

Captain Ashtray wasn't much fun either. I mean, I got it, shoving me to the back of the bus, but did she have to talk to Pandora the whole trip like I wasn't even there? It was a minibus, not a jumbo jet. I got ears. I got feelings, too.

Pandora tried to hold my hand when we arrived, but I wasn't in the mood. I mean, how had I gone from lying in bed with the girl of my dreams, to getting imprisoned while she rode shotgun with the Queen of Darkness? It was some bullshit. If they had even an inkling of what I really was, I'd be target practice by now. I had to hide in plain sight, and it was already getting on my nerves.

Anyway, things only got worse when Captain Ashtray started showing us around. There were tons of humans here. Even more than all the bots in the city put together. And they had farms and beds and everything. There's even this big wide space – the courtyard, they called it – where they grow stuff on these raised beds, but it didn't look great. I even heard one guy talking about how crappy the latest crop was.

'Toxicity levels are still too high,' he said. Pandora didn't hear, because she was too busy with her new best friend. The dude was holding the saddest and smallest carrot I'd ever seen, and I'd only ever eaten tinned so that's saying something. It was covered in black spots, too. But when he saw me, he quickly hid it behind his back, which I thought was kind of suspicious. This place needed a reality check. Never thought I'd say it, but man, I missed Gort.

Next, Ashtray showed us a big classroom where actual kids were being taught, all a couple of years younger than us. No university programme here then. I tried not to stare, but a couple of them didn't look right, and it took me a minute to notice the missing limbs. They were skinny too. Pandora was all moon-eyed about what a great job they were doing, but I wasn't convinced. A hundred years, and they couldn't even grow a carrot? What did these people eat?

I bet they didn't have strawberry laces, either.

Eventually, they showed us to our room. I say *our* room – Pandora's room, then mine. Apparently boys and girls under eighteen had to sleep separately. I tried telling 'em that we were used to sleeping in the same room, but no dice. Instead, I helped Pandora unpack the little we had brought with us while they got my room ready.

'Did you see the solar panels?' Pandora said, pulling me out of my huff. I was standing by the window, which had a view over the whole compound.

'Yeah, they're really something,' I muttered. There was no TV but they at least had running water and electric lights. I could plug in at night and keep pretending I was human. Great.

I scanned the open areas again. No livestock either, although the HUMANKIND bots in the city told me not to eat any animals because of the toxic waste or whatever. Not that I had needed to. Civilization usually had a supermarket.

'Look, this isn't for ever.' Pandora sensed my mood and came to the window, put a hand on my shoulder. Despite myself, I melted. She had a way of doing that. 'We just need a rest stop, and to learn what they know about the area, and then we can keep searching for the ship. They can't have checked everywhere.'

I bit my lip. Hard. I had heard as well as she had what Captain Ashtray said on the way here. But if a little hope was going to get us out of here quicker, then I could kick that truth-can down the road.

'Sure. Sorry. Just sucks having to pretend to be something I'm not. Think I'll feel better in my own crib,' I said, swallowing my mood and turning from the window. I took in the bare framed bed and the small desk in the corner. Yeah, this place was a dump.

And it was obvious why. Cheap manufacturing. They had tried to remove most of it, but I still recognized some. The sun-faded varnish around where the metal wheel cut-out had been. On every door and wall and even the desks. The spinning wheel that was etched on to the back of my neck, so tiny it blended into the barcode. This was an old Aurora Tech site, although what they made here, I couldn't quite work out. Obviously some boring research centre or something.

Pandora smiled. 'You have such a way with words,' she teased, and then she stepped forward and gave me a light peck on the lips that sent my heart into overdrive.

Not long after, one of the goons came back and showed me to my own room, on the other side of the building. I left Pandora to it because what I really needed to do was charge my batteries. The disturbance in the night, plus staying up late to keep watch at the mall, meant I had only got to half charge before we were so rudely interrupted.

The room was a mirror image of Pandora's so I dumped my stuff on the desk and kicked back on the scratchy sheets of the bed with my charging cable. There was a socket next to the bedside table and I plugged in, ready to relax for a half hour and get a bit more juice before the day began. I closed my eyes.

Something overhead flickered, bright enough to light up pink behind my eyelids. My eyes flew open in time to catch the overhead light flicker on and off, and then the ominous sound of a metal ping.

Crap. The solar panels were old, sure, but I didn't realize I would literally overload the system. The lights weren't even on because it was daytime, and the sun was out in force. Yet I'd still managed to suck all the power. Everyone was out at work now but there was no way people wouldn't notice that on overnight charges. Houston, we had a problem.

'Knock knock,' Pandora said as she knocked on my

door, but I still scrambled to unplug myself like she was a stranger. Another problem. My room didn't have a lock.

'Hey.' I tried to sound casual and not at all spooked when she opened the door and smiled at me. 'What's cooking, good-looking?'

'What?' P laughed, and I cringed internally. What did I just say? Clearly playing it cool wasn't one of my strengths.

'Shit, I don't know. You make me nervous.'

'*I* make *you* nervous? Really? I thought I was the only one.' Pandora sank down on to the bed next to me. Her fingers brushed mine and it felt like 50,000 volts left my body.

'Hold up. For real? But you're always like, I dunno, making the first move and stuff.' I said the last part as fast as I could because this was sort of embarrassing.

Pandora leant down to catch my eye. Man, her eyes were beautiful.

'That's only because you never make the first move,' she laughed.

'Well, that's because I was trying to be a gentleman. No pressure.'

'Yes, I worked that one out.'

'And I didn't know if you had a frozen popsicle boyfriend in your ship thing with you, and that would really harsh my vibe, you know?'

She laughed again. 'I think I know what you mean. But

no, no frozen significant other. It's just me. I haven't actually . . . I've never felt like this before.'

'Me neither.'

I sat up and looked at her then, really drank her in. The way her nose scrunched up when she laughed. The freckles that had come out across her cheeks, the ones that reminded me of when we slept under the stars, all constellations and light. Her blue eyes that I really could drown in. The way her blonde hair fell across those long eyelashes.

'Maybe you could be my non-frozen boyfriend?' Pandora asked, her voice so quiet it was almost a whisper.

'Thought you'd never ask,' I said.

I didn't wait for her to make the first move this time. I leant in and cupped her chin in my hands, my lips finding hers. Her hands were in my hair and she was pulling me down, on to the bed. I opened my mouth and something in my brain exploded. Man, is this how I could have been feeling the whole time if I just got my E-Mote chip fixed?

We fumbled but then seemed to know exactly what to do, her legs wrapped around mine, my hands around her waist. Fireworks went off in my brain as I moved down her jaw, kissing every centimetre of it. The noise she made when I got to her neck nearly ended me.

A door slammed in the corridor and the fireworks fizzled out in a second. It probably was getting a little *too* hot and heavy. There wasn't even a lock on the door. We both took a second to straighten our clothes and hair but when I looked at Pandora again, I wasn't embarrassed any more. I just wanted to sink into that smile for ever.

'So . . . did you want to go somewhere? I could, uh, I could eat,' I said. *First date with my new girl*, I said in my head and not out loud. I wasn't *that* chilled in front of her yet.

'Right, sure. Actually, me too. But someone just told me we have to go and register for a workstation first, then we can go get some breakfast. Seems fair enough. I thought we could go together?' P's eyes were pleading because she knew I wouldn't exactly be jumping for joy over signing up to work in this dump. But she hadn't said anything about the lights, and she had at least ignored how weird I was being when she walked in, so I went with it.

'Sure. Let's go sign our lives away,' I said, only half joking.

I left my stuff and we wandered through the building until we were back at the entrance. Pandora seemed to know where she was going, so I just followed her, dragging my feet a little. Volunteering for work wasn't exactly what I was used to. In the city, the bots do everything for you. Why did people choose to live like this if they didn't have to?

Oh yeah, right. They hated bots like me.

We walked across the yard to another squat concrete building with no signage. Everything was the same here. Inside was a small reception desk on a grey carpet. It's like they literally repelled anything colourful. I adjusted my lime-green baseball hat so the brim fully covered my neck. I stood out like a sore thumb and didn't need any more reasons for these people to hate me.

'You're the new recruits?' A woman with stringy hair spoke to us from the reception desk. Pandora stepped forward and I hovered like a bad smell in the doorway.

'That's us.' P beamed at the woman, all polite. Crazy to think that a few days ago she was telling me how embarrassed she was to even talk to me, never mind strangers. And now look at her. I sighed. I had to give this a shot. Even when we left here, we were going to live with some people somewhere. And if I could learn to live with these numbnuts, I could learn to live with anyone.

I crossed the lobby and stood next to P at the desk. The receptionist looked at me over the top of her glasses – two different frames that had been taped together at the bridge – before she passed us two pieces of paper and two biro pens.

'Fill these out. I'm gonna need to know what skills you're bringing to the community so we can place you in the best jobs. Or if you don't know anything, I can just put you on farming duty. What will it be, ladies?' The woman folded her arms and sat back in her office chair, which was missing the left armrest.

'Wow. A sexist joke. So funny, so fresh.' I spoke through gritted teeth and Pandora put a hand on my arm as a warning.

'Whatever, maggot. Just give me your names and you can have your overalls.' The woman blew out a pink bubble and let it burst before Pandora spoke again.

'Oh, of course,' she said politely, as if this lady deserved anything other than a kick up the backside. I dug my nails into my palms and kept quiet. Just a few more days of this and we could get going to where Pandora's real people were. Hope they had a TV. 'I'm Pandora and this is Echo.'

'Echo? What kind of a name is Echo?' the woman spluttered and turned to me. Two camo goons in the lobby, ones that looked just like those with Razor, joined in laughing.

'The kind of name that does what it says on the tin. Shout it loud enough and it will smack you right back in the face,' I said, my hands just fists of fury at that point.

'What Echo means to say is that it's a very common name where we come from. A good, solid name,' P interjected before I went full metal jacket on this bozo.

I relaxed my hands. 'That's right. A good, solid name from the twenty-first. No wonder you haven't heard of it,' I said. Pandora smiled at me from under her gold hair.

'I don't need your life story. Just the name,' the woman said, like she hadn't asked the question in the first place. She at least had the decency to stay quiet while she got out two sets of beige overalls. Not optimal. They deffo wouldn't go with my high-tops.

'Hey, kid.' One of the goons that had been watching called over to us and I ignored him. P and I picked up our overalls and turned to leave. 'Kid in the goofy hat. Hey, I'm talking to you.'

Pandora looked at me as we crossed the lobby and I kept my eyes locked on hers, only hers. *Be cool. Just ignore the gorilla in uniform.*

But I couldn't ignore him, because the next thing I knew I felt a soft blow to the back of my head and my cap tumbled in front of my vision and landed on the floor.

Mother. Fluffer.

I threw my overalls on the ground and turned to face the goons. There they were, all smug-faced and yellow-toothed, patting each other on the back and laughing at me. Why did they hate me so much? I'd barely said a word since I got here. I curled one hand into a fist.

'Echo, your hat.' Pandora spoke through gritted teeth, not even worried that I was about to get into a fistfight with a soldier. She bent down and grabbed the hat from under my dropped overalls.

And that's when the penny dropped. My barcode. My

charging port. Without the hat, both were on show. I'd always kept a fly do by going to the barberbot every month, kept everything trim. Idiot. I should have let it grow out like Kurt Cobain.

'Shit. Right,' I said, dropping to my knees to help her. I snatched the hat from her hands and put it on back to front, pushing the brim as low as it would go over the nape of my neck to hopefully cover my barcode and charge point, then picked up my overalls.

'Hey, leave the rich kids alone. They've never had to carry their own shit before, let alone dress themselves,' the other goon, the one that hadn't gone for me, said, and all three of the idiots in reception burst out laughing. It was enough of a distraction for Pandora and me to hightail it out of there.

Duh. No wonder he picked a fight. These people had nothing, and as far as they knew, P and I had come through the Aurora Tech cryo-programme. And those tickets cost a lot of money. They thought we were born – well, defrosted – yesterday, and we had to let them think they were right.

'I dunno how much longer I can do this, P,' I sighed, following her across the yard and back to our bunkhouse. 'I can't keep pretending. It's not really who I am, you know?'

'I know.' Pandora spoke quietly and didn't look at me.

'I didn't think about how difficult this would be for you. I'm so sorry, Echo. I have no idea why they're picking on you so much. It's not right.'

Relief seeped through me. My girl got it, she understood. That should motivate her to get us out of here quicker.

'I'm going to try and speak to the Chief at breakfast. Do you remember, the one General Razor said was in charge? If anyone knows where the labs are, it will be him,' Pandora said. It was like she read my mind.

'Good idea. The quicker we work that out, the better. This place gives me the creeps.'

'If you mean it's a little odd, then yes, I concur,' Pandora said, a frown creasing her perfect forehead. 'Let's get dressed and meet outside the mess hall. There has to be someone here that knows something.'

I sure hoped so, my dude. I sure did.

16

Echo was still a little quiet when we got to the food hall, but that was to be expected. It was all very new to him, being around so many people. And some of them were sort of rude, but maybe that was just fear talking. We were new, an unknown quantity. It would just take them some time.

And then there was Razor. Sure, she was a little rough around the edges, and the smoking was a bit intense, but there was something about her. The way people looked to her reminded me of the way people used to look to my father. It was power. She just commanded the room – literally, in her capacity as a general. There was something so effortlessly nonchalant about her that I envied. She really didn't care what anyone thought of her, and that was the exact opposite of Lexi, and Dad, and even I had been in my past life. And it was impressive to see a woman heading up the military presence.

Although the technophobia left a little to be desired, that was for sure. Perhaps, with time, we could win her round.

I squeezed Echo's hand once and joined the queue for a tray. The dining hall was vast, almost a whole building dedicated to the cafeteria. It reminded me of my old school dining hall at Aurora Prep, with long benches set out for communal dining and people milling about with water jugs and plastic pots of tapioca.

The smell was different, though. As we moved down the line, I could see serving trays filled with vegetables and meat, but the meat was in better condition than the veg. The tray labelled 'pork' had large, round steaks of perfectly cooked meat, just faded pink, whereas all the vegetables needed a spoon for serving. Creamed spinach. Creamed corn. Mashed carrots.

'What can I get ya?' A man with a hairnet addressed me from behind the serving table.

'Um . . . creamed corn and mashed carrots please,' I said, trying to raise a smile. OK, so they weren't the gourmet chefs I was used to at the house or school. Maybe I could teach them something before we left. I'd always been a dab hand at cooking.

'Sorry about that. Nothing in season right now. We're working off tinned stock.' The man slopped two scoops of each mashed product on to my plate, sending waves of stale veggie smell up to my nose. I held my breath.

'The pork is freshly butchered though. Want some of that?'

'Oh, I'm sorry, I'm a vegetarian.' I shrugged apologetically and the man snorted.

'Suit yourself,' he said. He turned to Echo. 'And for you, sunshine?'

I looked at Echo and gripped my tray so hard I thought the plastic would crack.

'Echo? Do you want anything to eat?'

'Well,' Echo began. His nose curled up at the smell of the food and the chef's face darkened. Echo wasn't exactly making friends fast, but he was also right. Something about everyone we had met so far seemed a little off, no matter how hard I tried to see the positives. Then again, Echo wasn't used to having to fit in, like I was. It was always going to be an adjustment.

'I'm not hungry. Think I'll just skip straight to dessert.' He dropped his tray on the counter and snatched up a pot of tapioca and a spoon.

'Suit yourselves,' the server muttered. I quickly grabbed up some cutlery and we left the queue to find somewhere to sit.

There was nowhere that wasn't rammed with people, so we perched on the end of a table with some younger-looking members of the dining hall.

'Well, at least they have pudding,' Echo said, licking the lid of his pot.

'The food isn't all bad here,' a voice to our left spoke up, a girl who looked about our age with a boy next to her. She smiled, and I was relieved that someone wasn't sizing us up for once. 'I'm Rebecca. This is my brother Miles,' she said, gesturing at the boy next to her.

I was about to introduce myself in response when something moved under a limp bit of greenery on Miles's plate. My jaw went slack as a small creature emerged from under the leaf. It was about the size and furriness of a hamster, but somehow it was . . . lizard-shaped? That was it. A small, hairy, brown and white lizard.

'Oh, sorry. And this is Rex,' Miles said. He picked up the lizard thing – Rex – and pushed his long tail into the top pocket of his overalls before sliding the rest of him in. Rex seemed content enough, his tiny claws gripped on the edge of Miles's pocket. On further inspection, he had just one yellow eye in the middle of his furry head.

'How . . . cute,' I said. I wondered if I would ever get used to these mutants. I guessed the real animals were all being used for livestock.

'Rad,' said Echo. He pretended not to be impressed but

I saw him eye up the creature.

'Nice to meet you, Rex. Pandora, Echo,' I said, pointing from myself to Echo. Echo gave a half-hearted wave before carrying on with his dessert.

'The newbies! We haven't had new people in . . . how long, Miles?' Rebecca asked him. She squirmed in her seat with an excitement that had her sit on her hands. I smiled. At least someone was happy to see us.

'My momma says she doesn't remember anyone coming in from the desert since Big Ron, when she was a baby,' said Miles. He pointed at a tiny ginger fellow sat at the next table who didn't suit the name Big Ron at all.

'If she was a baby, how does she remember him?' Echo muttered, and I kicked him under the table. 'Ow.'

'Don't be rude,' I hissed, then turned back to Rebecca, all smiles. 'So, you were saying about the food?'

'Oh, yes. The crops aren't much to sing about this season, so the Elders are relying on canned goods. But the meat is always good. Didn't you get any?' Rebecca held up one slice of many from her plate.

'I'm vegetarian.'

'What's vegetarian?' Miles asked.

'Oh. It's where you don't eat meat?' I said uncertainly, like I didn't already know the answer myself. No vegetarians here? I'd have to find a way to avoid meat. I hadn't eaten it for a long time.

'Sounds weird. Must be an outsider thing.' Rebecca shrugged and shoved more pork into her mouth. The juice dripped down her chin.

'This stuff is nearly as grey as the walls,' Echo muttered, poking at my plate.

'I have ears, you know,' said Miles. He pointed a fork at Echo. 'Just because we don't got fancy paint or carpets, don't mean we ain't happy. We live a simple life here. We work, we eat, we're happy.'

'Clearly you've never seen a candy machine,' Echo said, so quietly this time only I could hear. I shot him a look.

'What was that?' Miles narrowed his eyes.

'Sorry, just a quick question. You said something about Elders,' Echo said, changing the subject. He turned to Rebecca. 'Are they the people in charge? Do they help out this Chief guy?'

'Sure do,' said Rebecca. 'Hail to the Chief.' She saluted and Miles followed suit. They didn't look at anyone in particular, but Echo and I still looked around.

'Is the Chief here?' I asked, butterflies in my stomach. The sooner I could speak with him, the sooner I could find my father.

'Hail to the Chief.' Rebecca and Miles repeated the phrase and salute before answering. I exchanged a look with Echo. 'No. The Chief doesn't have time to eat up here with us, silly. He's too important.' Rebecca shook her head and smiled like I had asked a stupid question. My cheeks flushed.

Echo rolled his eyes. 'And let me guess. Every time we say Chief, you say—'

'Hail to the Chief.' Rebecca and Miles were right on Echo's cue.

'If someone else is talking about our great and powerful leader, we must respect his title.' Miles scowled at Echo. 'I'd appreciate it if you didn't use his name so often. It should be reserved for special occasions.'

'Special occasions. Of course,' Echo muttered, but he still seemed interested. 'So the Elders and the – the leader, they make the rules around here?'

'That's right,' Miles said. 'I'm hoping that with my schooling, I can be an Elder someday. They get to work with the animals. Not that Rex ain't enough, but it sure would be nice to find him some furry friends.'

In response, Rex yawned and tucked fully down into Miles's pocket, out of view.

'You keep dreaming that dream, Miles,' Echo said, and I kicked him again.

I needn't have bothered, though, because Miles smiled a grin of missing teeth. I tried to hide my grimace. I had nightmares about losing my teeth. Did they not have toothpaste here? And everyone I had seen so far was very thin. Maybe that was just how people looked a hundred years after I was born. Maybe this was evolution.

'So, you like animals?' I said, changing the subject.

Miles nodded. 'Oh, sure. I'd love to see the pigs and the dowgies – that's cows – and the sheeps and chickens. But I know the rules. They have to ration who goes in there.'

'Who goes in where?' I asked, and Echo perked up again.

'To the farm building, o' course.' Rebecca spoke up this time. 'Can't just let anyone in, and gotta keep the animals inside, or they'll catch diseases. And they're the only animals left in the whole wide world, 'cept the mutants, so they're precious.' She nodded solemnly and Miles copied her.

I shot a look at Echo. He raised an eyebrow at me, which at least told me it wasn't just me that thought it was weird.

'I think – don't animals need some sort of sunlight?' I asked tentatively.

I realized immediately that I had overstepped. Miles's expression darkened.

'Battery farming is the only way we have to feed over two thousand people. That's how many the Elders have kept alive, for three generations. How many people have you kept alive? Huh?'

'Miles, she's new, cool it,' Rebecca said. She put a hand on Miles's arm and he stopped, sighed and went back to his food.

'I'm sorry. I didn't mean to question your methods. I'm just interested in how everything works here,' I said. Besides, Miles had a point. The very reason I became vegetarian was because of the need to battery-farm on a planet with a population reaching eleven billion.

'It's fine,' Rebecca said, although it was clearly not fine from the way Miles aggressively skewered his portion of pork.

'I'm surprised the Ch— I mean, the fearless leader, has time to farm meat as well as run the whole base,' Echo said. I narrowed my eyes at him, waiting for the sarcastic remark, but again he seemed genuinely interested.

'I know. Our fearless leader is amazing,' Rebecca said. 'And have you met General Razor? Some say she's the only one lucky enough to speak to the leader in person. Isn't that amazing? When I grow up, I want to be just like her. You know, the leader set up this whole base. He helped build the walls and everything. Found the people who were left and led them to this place. It's a miracle really.'

'Sorry. The leader did all that? How old is this dude anyway? He must be, like, a hundred, right?' Echo choked on his pudding and I glared at him. It was a valid question, but we clearly were not going to get a valid answer. Sure, some people did live to well over one hundred before the Big Freeze, but they usually had money and a 3D printer for organs. They didn't live like this. So it was possible, but likely? No, not likely.

'He is not, how you said, a *dude.* He is our spiritual leader. We do not question age here. Everyone is useful, no matter who they are. That's what our fearless leader says.' Rebecca pushed her jaw forward and I could tell Echo had offended her. 'Besides, no one has seen him for years. He decided a long time ago, before me and Miles were even born, to dedicate himself to our food production. He leaves day-to-day running of the Republic to the Elders.'

'What, not *ever*? Is that really—'

'Of course. I'm so sorry, we only woke up a few days ago. Please excuse us. We're not quite in our right minds yet. We certainly don't mean to be rude.' I cut Echo off and he glared at me, but he stopped talking. With a bit of luck and a smile from me, Rebecca's expression softened.

'That's quite all right. Must be a shock for you folks, going from a world of brain-melting technology to a more wholesome existence,' Rebecca said.

'More wholesome, huh?' Echo said, his voice dripping with sarcasm. I held my breath.

Luckily, Rebecca didn't seem to notice. 'Exactly. In time you will learn the fearless leader's teachings about the evils of technology. And of course, the most evil of them all. The HUMANKIND bots.'

'Oh, do tell me more,' Echo said through gritted teeth.

Miles seemed to take a particular pleasure in explaining

that one. 'The HUMANKIND bots are the culmination of everything bad Aurora Tech ever did. The leader tells us that the HUMANKIND bots are tricksy, they lie, and they are not to be trusted. Shoot them on sight, that's what he says. Not that they're dumb enough to come around here no more.' Miles finished and scraped the last of the pudding from his cup.

Next to me, Echo vibrated with rage. I placed a hand on his knee; *not in front of them*.

'Technology is what got us into this mess in the first place. Made our ancestors lazy. Why, there weren't even any human farmers left by the middle of the twenty-first century.'

'That's right. We're grateful to be here at all,' Miles said, his voice whistling through his missing teeth. 'My grand-pappy is always telling us stories of what it was like after the bad storms, when the weather was wild. Most folks didn't survive, and until the Chief took over here, they wasn't farming. They was fighting for every scrap of food. It wasn't until the Chief had us all work together that we started living again. Eating together instead of apart.'

Miles looked almost as angry as Echo, and I immediately felt a little embarrassed. Who was I to judge what was happening here after less than a day? People certainly weren't fighting. They seemed content to line up for dinner, no pushing. Maybe this was life, now.

'Anyway, that reminds me. Miles and I are due on farmin' duties this morning.' Rebecca stood up and picked up her tray, and Miles followed suit.

'Nice t'meet y'all,' she beamed as she turned away with her tray.

'Wish I could say the same,' Echo grunted.

I decided it was best to stay quiet until they had basically left the building, which was when I took my hand off Echo's knee.

'Ow. You're pretty strong, you know that?' he said, massaging his leg.

'Oh, sorry. And I really am sorry. I had no idea people here would hold such . . . old-fashioned views,' I said, my cheeks burning again. I had hated not saying anything, but we were on thin ice. Perhaps, in time, we could persuade these people around to our way of thinking. Perhaps.

'So, are we gonna talk about the Helter Skelter vibe, or not?' Echo said, pushing his pudding around with his spoon.

'The what?'

'The fact that this place is clearly a cult,' he said.

'I think maybe that's a little harsh,' I said. Echo was a city boy in the way I was a pampered girl. We just weren't used to . . . communal living. But even I had to admit, a secretive, elderly leader that lived his life inside with the only reliable food source didn't sound exactly like a healthy set-up. And the technophobia was very much over the top, too. But maybe that was how things had to be, to keep the peace. We had to give the place a chance, at least.

'You think I was a little harsh? I wasn't the one spouting all that technophobic garbage,' Echo said, his voice barely a whisper any more.

'I'm sorry. And you're right, but maybe we shouldn't talk about it here?' I whispered and gently gestured at the other people in the room.

Echo puffed out his chest. 'Fine. Let's clear these plates and get outta here.'

'Good idea,' I said, standing up. 'We'll probably be on the rota for jobs starting tomorrow. Don't want to waste the last of our free time for a while.'

'Right,' Echo muttered.

The New Republic of the People wasn't exactly what I had envisioned. And I had that gnawing feeling in the pit of my stomach, the one I had at school with Lexi or with Father or when I saw the mounting homeless population asleep on the streets. Was that guilt about how harshly I judged the place? I knew I should speak up, but something stopped me every time. Well, not just something. My anxiety. It wasn't an excuse, but it was a reason. It was why I had been working so hard with Dr Kapoor before . . . before all this. When did I stop being brave? I used to go out to protests with Mother all the time. I was young, but

I still remember how powerful it made me feel, even then. Before boarding school, I'd always spoken up when I saw an injustice. Was it puberty, or her death, or being ripped away from Father and left on my own that had stopped that?

We walked back to our rooms in silence. Everyone we passed had thin, gaunt faces that didn't seem to match their pot bellies, their cheekbones prominent under sunken eyes. And at least half the people we saw wore the telltale sign of a missing limb; some with an empty shirt sleeve, some with a tied-off trouser leg.

We had learnt about the pollution sickness in school. Some scientists had even compared it to radiation sickness, especially the birth defects and their comparable rates in the city centres. A few years before SpindleSleep, the birth rate of healthy babies living past the first few days dropped to under 0.5. The population was dropping, although it had been for years. That was why the ChildSynth programme had been established, so that those who couldn't have children, could. Well, those who could afford it.

These people reminded me of the pictures from my textbook. The hunched backs, the missing limbs. There was an ever-present cough everywhere we went, from the dormitories to the raised farm beds.

'You hear it too, huh?' Echo said, reading my mind.

I unconsciously stepped back as a man nearby broke down in a splutter of coughing. He bent double, close to the ground, and a woman with patchy dark hair went to rub his back.

'The cough? Yeah. Do you think it's pollution poisoning? Even out here?'

Echo chewed his lip. 'No. I think it's more likely the lack of fresh grub. I mean, I've been eating canned crap for a while, but my biological system is propped up with mad electronic skills. So I'm fine.'

'And these people are descended from generations that lived through the end of the world. Those gene pools could be damaged by pollution sickness, or even radiation if the nuclear plants weren't shut down in time.' I brought my voice to a whisper and quickened my step to move away from the farm we were passing.

Farm was a bit of an exaggeration. There were no green shoots coming from any of the raised beds. If anything, the 'farmers' seemed to throw more away than they kept, judging from the overflowing sacks marked 'COMPOST' at each corner of the makeshift allotments.

'But hey, they're still here, right? And they are at least eating something. A mostly meat diet isn't all it's cracked up to be, although I guess you're veggie so don't know the pure goodness of a cheeseburger. I once ate fifty chicken nuggets all in one meal and I couldn't poop for a week.'

Echo bit his lip after that last sentence. 'And yep, TMI. Point is, I learnt the value of a balanced diet.'

'Do you think it's safe now? The food, the environment?' I asked him. Suddenly, the air felt less fresh, less breathable. I studied the back of my hand. Was my skin dry and scaly, like Rebecca's? Would I end up with no teeth, like Miles?

'I think so,' Echo said. 'I know I'm totally rad and can live through anything, but I have thought about it before. When I realized how long it had been since the Big Sleep, I did some digging. You guys were supposed to wake up around now, according to estimates from the bigwigs on how long it would take for Earth to recover. Plus, Gort told me that the air was all tasty and fresh now, and that was in the city. They must be super close to getting some crops out by now. We'll live on the tinned stuff, I'll take the meat, and soon we'll be chowing down on a Waldorf salad. So I think your theory is probably on fleek.'

'I'll assume that's a good thing,' I said. I lowered my hands. Echo was right, one hundred years was chosen as the best scientific estimate of how long the Earth needed to recover versus how long human biology could withstand being held in stasis. Earth would keep improving, especially with a decimated population, but the human body couldn't really take much longer in cryogenic hibernation. I swallowed hard.

It was better being here, with some food, than out there with none at all. And while people looked tired, as Echo pointed out, they weren't dead. Just because it wasn't the five-course dinners I was used to at home, or the designer clothes and white plastic smiles, didn't mean it was all bad. It would just take some getting used to, that's all. Everyone seemed to know each other, calling out and waving hello. One boy helped a woman with one arm carry a basket of washing down the front steps of an outbuilding. Another girl ran up to her dad, arms out, and laughed as he spun her around. Simple pleasures. Out there, there was nothing. In here, there was life.

'Do you think Razor is right? About the cryolab ships being destroyed?' I asked Echo. I knew he had heard our conversation on the open-topped cart, but this was the first time I had brought it up. The general had said some pretty hurtful things about Echo, things I hoped he didn't hear but knew he did, deep down. Another time I hadn't spoken up for him.

'I dunno,' Echo replied. We sat down on a worn bench outside one of the squat buildings. 'It's possible, for sure. But even an Elder as mighty and wise as Captain Ashtray can't know everything.'

'Is that what you call her? Come on, Echo,' I said.

'What?'

'Call her by her title. Don't be sexist.'

'I'm not! I'd find her equally as aggy if she was a dude. And she hates me just because I'm part bot, so I think social niceties have gone out the window.'

'She doesn't— Never mind.' I trailed off because at the end of the day, she was a little . . . offensive sometimes. We had to lead by example, but it wasn't me getting dirty looks every time I set foot outside.

Echo was right about one thing, though. The general didn't know everything. If only we could get an audience with the Chief. If he really was as old as Miles suggested, he was more likely to know about the labs than anyone. The next oldest person I had seen here had to be in his fifties, max. Maybe it was a good thing he was shut up in his indoor farm, after all.

'Whatever. I'm cool,' Echo said. He smiled, but it didn't quite reach his eyes.

'Then why don't you look "cool"?' I asked. He looked away, the tips of his ears turning pink. 'Hey, you can talk to me, you know. Plus, I think I know what it is.'

'You do?' he said. He turned back to me, his eyes wide.

My heart broke for him. 'You heard what General— What Ashtray, as you call her, said about you on the cart. And the way Rebecca and Miles spoke about you, plus those brutes in the mall that used the "H" word. You know that that's not how I see you, right? I'm so sorry, Echo. I should have said something. They're just ignorant, but I know better. I shouldn't excuse it.'

'No, you shouldn't. But you're totally right, we just have to keep our heads down until we speak to this Chief guy. Hey, I know this stuff is hard for you too. I gotta work on my temper, then maybe I could say something they'll actually listen to,' Echo said.

'No, I was wrong. Next time, I will try and say something. I need to be braver, for both of us,' I said, and I squeezed his hand. There was that goofy grin again, the one that melted me every time I saw it. 'We can show them they're wrong. But these people, they don't have the same experience we do, and that doesn't make them evil. It makes them ignorant, to people like you. And maybe we're ignorant of, what did Rebecca call it? A simple life? I know it's not what we're used to, but it's people. Living. It's families and friends and siblings. I really think we have to give it a go, not just give up because it seems hard. What do you say?'

Echo sighed. 'All right. I can give it a shot. At least for a few days. Maybe the creepy *Wicker Man* vibes will calm down. Plus, it's not like we can't just leave if it gets too weird, right?'

While Echo went off to his room, I hung out in mine, trying to read an old book on my bedside table – but the lamp kept flickering and the sky was so overcast outside it was hard to read without it. It was so difficult being alone, but I couldn't cling to Echo all the time. Instead, I busied myself with the map I had been given and trying on the overalls, which were even worse than I thought they would be. Then I tried to nap, but I couldn't do that either – thoughts of my father, the rich people like me in the pods and the people who struggled out here spinning round in my head. Could the world ever offer a clean slate – a way to live together again?

A knock on the door saved me from my thoughts and Echo walked in.

'Hey, where have you been? You've been gone for hours,' I asked. We had missed lunch, but I couldn't say I was exactly looking forward to it. It was closer to dinner by now.

'Sorry. Just getting some charging in before the solar panels pack up for the night. Must have fallen asleep,' Echo said. He turned from the door and wrung his hands before pacing the room. 'And then on the way here . . . I dunno, man. I think I just felt like everyone was staring. At me. Like they know.'

'Oh, Echo,' I said. My heart hammered in my chest and I closed the space between us, cupped his face with my hands and stopped him in his tracks. 'They don't know. They can't. Most of them haven't even seen a bot before, they're just afraid of what they don't know. It's me and you. We'll get through this.'

Why was it so much easier to be brave with Echo than when I was on my own, or with other people? Why couldn't I take that courage and carry it with me, tell people what I really thought?

'I mean, maybe if we did a little digging of our own?'

'Echo, no. I mean it. We have to give these people a chance, and trust is earned. It's a two-way street. Promise me you won't do anything crazy; at least can we talk about this in a week or so?'

'I'd be discreet . . .'

'Echo!'

'All right. Fine. I promise. I'll just suck it up, I guess.'

Echo stared down at me, no trace of his usual humour on his face. I hadn't seen him like this before, so fired-up and worried. I felt awful, but we had to get people onside, and the way to do that was not to barge in and start questioning the way they'd lived for a century. I'd get justice for Echo, a good life. Eventually.

I held the sides of his face. 'Come on. We don't need to investigate anyone, because we have each other. Me and you. OK?'

'Me and you,' he whispered eventually, and he leant down to kiss me. He was gentle at first, barely a peck, and then he pushed harder, his lips pressed hard against mine, his hands in my hair. I reciprocated, the smell of him intoxicating, the burn of his stubble on my skin sending me deeper. I didn't want to think any more, and neither did he.

We staggered back until I bumped into the bed and dropped backwards, and he was on top of me, forcing the air from my lungs and causing me to gasp.

'Sorry,' Echo said, breathing hard. I could feel the frantic beat of his heart against my own.

'It's OK. It's more than OK,' I said. I leant in again, but he pulled away slightly, broke eye contact.

'I think . . . I don't want to move too fast. Maybe we can just . . . lie together. For a while.' Echo moved off me and to the left side of the bed.

I pressed myself into the contour of his body, the little spoon. He wrapped an arm around me and I listened to his breathing slow, still, in time with my own. It didn't take me long to fall asleep.

17

As soon as I was sure Pandora was asleep, I made my move.

I moved my arm as carefully as I could from around her waist, and her hand dropped limply to her side. Good. I wasn't surprised at how tired she was, after the last few days. Clearly a hundred years of beauty sleep wasn't enough for her.

I slid my weight to the end of the bed and then tiptoed to the door. I took one last look at her before I creaked the door open. She really was beautiful, even when she was asleep.

I wasn't stupid. I knew where those moves had been going. The rush of blood to the pit of my stomach had made my head spin, but it wasn't right. I just couldn't do it. I can't have our first . . . you know, be here. Not before I had spoken to this Chief guy myself.

I squeezed into the corridor and closed the door as gently as I could, then froze. No sound of movement from inside, even after a few seconds. Perfect.

I started down the empty corridor but stopped in my tracks. Stood in the corridor, looking real as heck but obviously not really there, was bearded dude. The guy from my malfunctioning brain. *Man, he's clearer than ever*, I thought.

Then he started to speak. *Echo, I need you to get into the basement. Hide where I showed you. Go!*

My imaginary frenemy yelled at me like we were in an action movie.

'Buzz off,' I muttered as I walked through him. He turned to smoke in front of my eyes and when I looked back, he was gone. I needed to talk about this dude to Pandora . . . but not now.

OK, back to it. The most important part of my mission involved avoiding Captain Ashtray and her goons, which was going to be difficult. It was nearly dark now and I could see the shadows of people packing up tools ready for parlour games or human sacrifices or whatever these people did for fun in their downtime.

Ashtray and her minions could be anywhere.

To be fair, I wasn't expecting to bump into the good

captain herself. Running around guarding secretive goings-on seemed more like grunt work to me. But if I was right, then the building I was headed to was going to be crawling with people in that whacko camo uniform.

I headed out the front door of the dorm building and into the courtyard. I considered running, but that would seem weird with everyone else slowly limping along to their next activity, so I slowed to a walk that was the opposite pace of my heart in my chest.

I felt bad about lying to Pandora . . . but I had to know the truth.

I moved behind the farms, waving to a middle-aged dude who responded by spitting at my feet.

'Always nice to meet a fan,' I muttered.

Luckily, he hated me so much that he didn't even think it was weird that I was moving in the opposite direction to everyone else. In fact, people actively swerved to avoid me. Well, being the Most Hated Man in the People's Republic of Shit All certainly had its perks.

Pandora and I had circled the compound at least twice that day, so I knew most of the buildings, and there weren't more than thirty altogether. The only place we hadn't really explored was the outskirts, so I assumed that was where my target was. I rounded the last concrete block and peeped out into the ever-approaching darkness.

Bingo. At the edge of the compound, right next to the

fence, was yet another concrete structure. This one was lower than the prison-block dorms, though, and only had narrow slits for windows. But the biggest difference with this one was the amount of Ashtray goons that were loitering outside, and the floodlights lighting up the area all around.

I crouched down by my building, a good ten or so metres away. There was only a string of lights over the walkways and I was well away from those. The goons wouldn't be able to spot me in the shadows. I watched as one camo goon approached the front door and waved something in front of it – a pass, maybe? After a second, the entrance slid open, nice and smooth like a lift.

Interesting. Nowhere else in the compound had locked doors, never mind a swish metal job that looked downright impenetrable. As I watched, another group of grunts appeared, these ones on horseback.

Another thing that didn't add up. The horses were responsible for pulling the transport here at the Old Republic of the Idiots, but they weren't kept with the other animals. I saw them tied up near the gates, in the courtyard. There were makeshift stables and everything. If they're willing to do that for the horses, why hide the other animals away? Miles said some shit about it being a privilege to work with animals. So what were the horses?

Nah. Something was going on.

The horses were led to a different building once the goons had dismounted. I watched one goon slap another on the back, then he laughed. Couldn't hear them though. Probably needed to get closer.

I ran across the gap between two buildings, hugging the shadows. The goons were too busy gassing to notice little old me.

I spotted a small nook to hide in, right opposite the guarded building. When I slid into the gap, I noticed the metal perimeter wall was dented, and a sliver of moonlight shone through from the other side. A whole person could squeeze through there, no problem. Or a mutant coyote. Shoddy workmanship from a shoddy human cult.

From my new vantage point, I could hear what the new goons were saying, the ones that had ridden in on the horses.

'How did the shipment go at dinner?' Goon One asked. He had a clipboard and seemed to be counting something off in his head.

'Good. Compliments to the chef. It tasted different to yesterday, I think the different cuts are helping,' Goon Two replied.

'What did we say today? I need to change it up for tomorrow. Was it beef?' Goon One asked. He pointed his pencil to his clipboard.

'Nah, pork. So you could do beef tomorrow, but we

had beef on Monday. Maybe something different. Mutton?' Goon Two shrugged.

'What's mutton?' Goon One asked.

I raised an eyebrow. Shouldn't the idiots in charge of killing the animals at least know which was which?

'Uh. I'm not sure. Goat, I think,' Goon Two suggested.

One shook his head. 'We can't just introduce goats now. We've never had goat before. Where did we find it? The petting zoo? Use your head, soldier.' One tapped the eraser end of his pencil and Two laughed before brushing him off, which nearly knocked him off balance. Come to think of it, a couple of the goons didn't seem all there, laughing a little too loud and stumbling around. Not exactly the behaviour of the disciples of a 'spiritual leader'.

'I don't give a shit if we say it came from outer space. Whatever. Go with beef.' Two steadied himself and pressed a finger to One's lapel. 'Now, where's my pay? Not going in there without my medicine.'

'I think you've had enough *medicine*,' One said, and I could hear the air quotes around the word. Dude did seem pretty wasted, which was only proved by how angry he got.

Two brought up a fist and grabbed hold of One's lapel, slamming him into the wall. The laughter from the other goons stopped abruptly.

'I don't want to have to remember a damn thing.

D'you hear me? I don't want to remember a fucking second of it,' Two said. Another goon had got hold of his shoulders, and I was embarrassed to hear a sob escape from Two's throat. Carefully, the other goons pulled him off and put an arm around him as he cried out whatever it was he was so upset about.

Damn. What was the Chief making them do in there?

Goon One smoothed down his faded uniform and set his clipboard on a nearby crate. 'OK, OK. I understand. We'll keep this time off the books. Mitch?' One gestured to a goon next to the crates, who pulled out a small glass bottle of clear liquid.

Two, who had got a hold of himself, snatched the bottle from the goon's hands and drank it in three huge gulps. The bottle was unlabelled, and most of the stores we had seen nearby were picked clean. Stuff was probably moonshine, and plenty of it. My stomach turned over at the thought of knocking back so much all at once.

Satisfied, Two threw the bottle on the floor and it smashed into a thousand angry shards. One shook his head but he didn't do anything to punish him, which surprised me. Glass bottles were probably pretty tough to make at the end of the world, yet these morons just chucked them around like they were nothing?

Without another word, Two marched towards the metal door, and I watched as the goon there let him through. I was right about the key card, at least. The goon held up a small plastic card from a lanyard on his neck and the door slid open. Goon Two disappeared inside, head held high, and a swoosh of air signalled the door closing behind him.

That's another thing. Captain Ashtray had been going nuts about electronics, to the point that people like me weren't welcome here. That was a direct order from the mighty Chief himself. And yet they had a building with a keypad-operated door? Where was the electricity for all this stuff coming from? The floodlights would be taking up a lot of juice on their own.

I ducked down to a crouching position and held a hand to the dry earth. When I closed my eyes, I concentrated, listened for the same buzzing sensation that I sensed on the electric cars and the generators at the school.

There. My electronic circuits fell into sync with the buzz of electricity all around me, but there was more than just the last quarter battery of an electric car. The power I could sense running under the ground almost deafened me now I was tuned into it, the usual buzzing of the odd live wire building into a crescendo that nearly knocked me backwards.

There wasn't just enough power for floodlights, or string lights, or even electric doors. There was more than enough to light every dorm room and then some. I had never felt so much power, not in the buildings in the city, not even in the server room I found for my movies. The closeness of such a huge energy source sent butterflies skittering in my stomach and put every fibre-optic nerve length in my body on end. I felt the hair on the back of my neck stand up, like I had rubbed my scalp with a balloon.

Freaky. And freaky meant something was definitely going down. That power source could run my batteries for the rest of my human lifespan, and that was saying something. Yet when I plugged in, all I got were the same stupid solar panels that lit the hallways? What gives? Was it something to do with the Chief's secret farming technique?

I opened my eyes and looked at the building. I was no expert, but no way did it look big enough from outside to house herds of livestock. And then there was all that power *underground*. This wasn't a surface farm – it was in some sort of . . . bunker. *The* bunker? Couldn't be . . . right?

Goon One had moved away from the crates nearest to me and was talking to the goon on the door. The soldier boy who had been guarding the crates of booze had moved to pick up some of the glass on the floor, and immediately cut himself because clearly brains are not a requirement to be part of the Chief's team.

'Shit,' the goon said, sucking the finger on his left hand. Blood dripped out of his mouth.

Goon One looked up from his clipboard and sighed. 'Go to the medical bay and get that checked out. You can clear this up later. It's nearly time for shift change anyway.'

'Roger, boss,' the goon said. He stood up and walked into the darkness, towards one of the other buildings.

I looked back at the crates. Something shiny and darker than the glass shards around it had caught my bionic eye. I narrowed my eyelids, concentrating, trying to work out if it was worth the risk.

It was. The shiny thing was a key card. Whether it was from Two or the lumbering moron with the glass, I wasn't sure, but somehow it had come off in the idiotic aerobics of the evening. I flicked my eyes up towards One, who was busy with his clipboard again.

Jackpot. Goon One wasn't wearing a key card. All the other goons had one – a bright piece of red material that hung around their necks, the cards dangling like medallions at the end, but not One. It had to be his card, and seeing as he was in charge, his card had to grant access to the door, didn't it?

I had to at least test the theory. This was my chance to speak to the Chief, or at least work out how dangerous he really was.

With the others temporarily distracted, and the goons avoiding the crates because of the glass, I crept along the building I was next to and slipped into the shadow against the perimeter wall. None of those morons so much as blinked as I crossed from one building to the other, always hugging the wall, and crept up behind the booze crates.

There. It was just past the edge of the crate I was hiding behind, half covered in sand and dry dirt. It had clearly hit the ground hard, probably ripped off when the hammered Goon Two had grabbed One and shoved him against the wall. All I had to do was hold my breath, reach out and grab it. And hope I didn't get caught.

I hesitated. What happened after I had the card? I had thought I would wait for the change of guards, then somehow use it to slip inside and find out what was up with this weird leader dude and crazy power supply. And if they caught me, I'd be recycled for parts.

But what about Pandora? She thought that this place was the answer to saving her fam. She'd begged me to go along with it – even if just for a week. Besides, from what Miles said, whatever was going on was something that the rest of the Chief's good republic didn't know about. They had lived here for nearly a century. They weren't exactly thriving, but they were alive. Who was I to mess this up?

Then again, something *was* going on. And Pandora wasn't going to do any digging, which meant I had to. I had to know the truth before we trusted these people. The cult vibes, and the secret electric bunker, and the booze addiction . . . *I don't want to have to remember a damn thing* . . . it had to be bad, right?

Decision made. I strained my ears to listen for the goons. They were still talking, but the sound of their voices was quiet and they seemed further away. I just had to do this fast, like ripping off a band-aid. I counted to three in my head, held my breath and shot out my hand into the light.

My fingers grasped the corner of the plastic and pulled the card back into my chest, faster than a coiled spring unravelling. I still didn't breathe, sure the goons must have noticed, but they just kept talking. No sirens went off. The card's sharp edges were cutting into the palm of my hand.

'My precious,' I whispered, clutching the lanyard to my chest.

Wasn't out of the woods yet. The goons had said it was nearly the end of their shift, but they didn't say how long the wait was. In video games, guard patrols were always lighter at night. Was that how it worked in real life? I had no idea how I was going to get anywhere near the door, never mind be able to use the key card. I would need a disguise, a uniform of my own. It was a small community, but there were over 2,000 people here. That's what the creepy twins said in the cafeteria. They surely didn't know absolutely everyone, did they?

I moved my feet, the pins and needles already setting

in. How much longer would I have to wait? Maybe I should go back to Pandora's room, wait until it was darker, later. Then again, I ran the risk of waking her up, and without proof I didn't know what I would tell her. I just had to wait it out and hope nobody checked the crates.

A hand came down on my shoulder so hard I nearly screamed, until another hand clamped over my mouth.

'And what the hell do you think you're doing?' my captor hissed in my ear.

I spun round. *Great.* It was Tweedle-Dee and Tweedle-Ugh, otherwise known as Rebecca and Miles. Even Rex had betrayed me, sat up in the kid's pocket with his beady little eye on me. *Et tu, Brute?* Us hybrids gotta stick together.

'Keep your voice down,' I hissed at Miles.

'Why should we keep our voices down?' Rebecca asked, arms tightly crossed. She seemed mad as hell, but she did keep her voice to a high whisper. She turned to me. 'I thought you and Pandora understood that the Chief's headquarters were out of bounds.'

I licked my lips nervously. 'Uh, I was just, I, um . . . hey, I think we were all here doing the same thing,' I said, my mouth playing catch-up with the idea forming in my mind. 'We wanted to see the animals. I assume that's the only reason you two would find yourselves out here, at the edge of the compound? I know you said you so wanted to work with them after all, Miles.' I forced my brightest smile at them, the one I usually reserved for Pandora.

There was a moment of silence while Rebecca and Miles chewed over my lie. *Stay strong, Echo.* This was a game of confidence. And no one was more confident than the dude who wears lime-green high-tops to a fashion-averse cult.

'Well, you might have busted us there,' Rebecca said eventually, and Miles glared at her. 'Miles, own up. We all just got caught out. Your obsession with these chickens and whatnot will be the death of us if you ain't more careful.'

It was all I could do not to whoop out loud. Hook, line and sinker.

'Well he were doing it too,' Miles muttered. He turned his glare to the dirt. Rex turned and dug back into Miles's pocket, defeated.

I tried not to let out too much of the massive sigh of relief that was building up in my chest. 'Well, no harm done. If we're quick, we can get back to the dorms before anyone has noticed we bounced.'

Rebecca looked a little confused, but she caught my gist. 'Well, uh, Miles and I are actually running a little late for kitchen duty. That's why I came out here to find him. He's always hanging around, waiting for a sneak peek of one of the animals,' Rebecca said, and the tips of Miles's ears turned pink. She placed an arm around his shoulder. 'So we better get going. But, uh, Echo? This will be our little secret, right? The Chief doesn't like us getting side-tracked from our duties, and my brother means well, he just gets a little excited sometimes.'

Rebecca pleaded with me with her eyes and Miles still couldn't even look up from the ground. A guilty feeling prowled my stomach despite how mad I was at getting caught.

'Of course. Our secret,' I said, flashing another grin.

I wasn't dumb though. Kitchen duties? In the middle of the night? Pull the other one, Bex.

And with that, Rebecca frogmarched Miles around the back of the building, in the opposite direction to the canteen.

18

I woke up to my bedroom door being slammed by an out-of-breath Echo.

'Echo, my goodness, you scared me,' I said, sitting bolt upright and waiting for my heartbeat to soothe.

In the few seconds I took to truly wake up, I remembered that Echo was supposed to be sleeping next to me.

'Mind telling me where you've been? And why you look so guilty about it?' I asked.

Echo looked over his shoulder, like whoever he was running from could see through locked doors.

'Keep your voice down.' Echo motioned with his hands, palm down, and looked back at the door. 'The walls have ears.'

'The walls have . . . ? Don't be absurd,' I said, rolling my eyes. I lowered my voice all the same. If I wanted to get him to talk to me, clearly I had to do that quietly.

'I'm absurd? Well, check this out.' Echo pulled something out of his pocket and threw it at me.

It was a key card. A key card covered in dust and with a bright-red lanyard attached. On the front it had a photograph of a balding, serious-looking man dressed in a white lab coat. It read:

AURORA TECHNOLOGIES
PROFESSOR JOHN PICKARD

And then under that, a series of serial numbers and barcodes. The lamination was peeling at the edges, and the pass looked old and stained under the plastic coating.

I felt my heart rate rise – and not in a good way, this time. Blood rushed to my cheeks. 'So you stole someone's ID? Nice one, Echo. You *promised* me. You said you wouldn't snoop. You just ignored my wishes and did it anyway.' I turned the ID over, and on the back was a hologram of a spinning wheel.

'OK, so I told a little teeny white lie, but—'

'No buts, Echo. You lied to me.' I was furious, and tears threatened to spill down my cheeks, but I held them in. There were more pressing concerns, like getting the ID back before someone found out we stole it.

'I'm sorry, P. OK? I'm sorry. But there's something

going on here. I don't have proof yet, but I will. I just need more time.'

'No, you won't get proof, because you aren't keeping that pass. You have to give this back, first thing in the morning.'

'Give it back to who? To Professor Pickard?' Echo said. He paced the room, nervous energy emanating from his whole being.

'I guess so, yes.'

'Well that would be hard, seeing as he's dead,' Echo said.

I raised an eyebrow at him.

He punched a balled-up fist into his palm and stopped pacing. 'Don't you get it? The dude who was wearing this was not Professor Pickard. Look how old that thing is. At a guess, I might say, a hundred years?'

I blinked at Echo, then looked back at the pass in my hands. It *was* old. The plastic had kept it nearly intact, so it was possible that it had lasted that long. 'What exactly are you saying?'

'I'm saying that those "Elders" or whatever they wanna call themselves are hiding something. Something to do with the Chief. They say they hate Aurora Tech, but they built their base here. Why?'

'Because Aurora Tech buildings were built to withstand extreme weather? Seems sensible to me. And they ripped down all the signage. It's symbolic. You've been watching too much TV,' I said. I didn't miss a beat, but my heart did. My head searched for the logical explanation while my heart sided with Echo. Something didn't feel right, but was that enough reason to go snooping in other people's business? It certainly wasn't going to earn us any brownie points with the Chief. At this rate, I'd never get to ask him where the labs were.

'I've been watching . . . ? Hmm. OK, then. Well, if they hate technology so much, why keep a pass to the only fully powered building in the compound? And why have it so heavily guarded, if it's just a place to battery-farm chickens and livestock? I felt it, P. I felt the energy coming out of the ground. They're hiding something, I know it.'

'No, you don't know it,' I said. I threw the lanyard across the room and it landed on my bed. 'That's the problem, Echo. You don't *know* anything. These people have taken us in. They've given us food, and a roof over our heads. I know they're a little . . . unorthodox, but they're the only lead I have on finding my father. Why do you feel the need to question that? And waiting until I fell asleep? That's not just going behind their backs, it's going behind mine, too.' It was my turn to pace now, the churning in my stomach moving into my restless legs.

I knew he was right. There were some things that didn't add up, but so what? We didn't have to know every little detail right on day one.

'Oh come on, Pandora. I had to. I knew you would never approve and I didn't want to drop you in it. I needed to know. It's easy when they're so nice to you, that's it, right? Try being the guy that if they really knew, they would throw out on his ass. Try being the guy that everyone assumes is the bad one, all the time.' Echo raised his voice. He wasn't worried about anyone hearing him any more. He threw his hands up in the air then perched at the end of my bed, his head in his hands.

'Look, I know they're a little backward here, but we just have to play the game for a while, and then—'

'Play the game? A little backward? Well, maybe I don't want to play their game, Pandora. Maybe I don't want to just have to deal with lying about myself every damn day. Maybe I'm sick of that shit already.' Echo stood up again and crossed the space between us in two long steps. His face softened, and he lowered his voice: 'Please, Pandora. Something isn't right. I don't think we're safe here. We can use that pass to see what's really going on. I got it from that little weird building, the one Miles said had the Chief and the animals and everything, but I knew something was sus. Or we can just leave. We were fine on our own, just you and me. This wasn't for ever anyway, you said that. If you don't want to look into it, fine, let's just go. Please.'

His eyes pleaded with me and his hands found my

hands, then travelled up my wrists and arms to my face. We stood like that for a little while, him holding me, me deciding what to say.

This wasn't fair on Echo. I couldn't possibly understand because it wasn't me who was being mistreated. If this is how agitated he was after one day, then how would he be in a week? A month? How long did I really want to stay here? At least long enough to find out whether my people were alive or dead. But then what? I had been so excited at the prospect of people and civilization I hadn't even thought about how we would live. I was used to being around people. Echo only had me.

I took his hands.

'OK. I'm listening. Let's talk this through and then tomorrow, we can decide what we want to do. Together. I understand where you're coming from, but I can't abandon this place yet, Echo. It could be my only chance of finding my father, and the rest of the people in the labs. I can't break their rules and lose their trust, and I can't just leave, especially without speaking to the Chief. One more day won't hurt.'

Echo's gaze dropped to the floor and he lowered his hands from my face.

'I'll try, but I'm not making any promises,' he said, his voice barely a whisper.

I caught his chin with my hand, tried to lift his face to

mine, but he wouldn't budge. 'What do you mean? I know this has been hard, I know, but I'm just asking for one day, one more day. Please. It's not much to ask, is it?'

'It's not much to . . . are you serious?' Echo backed away from me, his eyes narrowed. 'I left the city for you, Pandora. That was my home. I left everything I had ever known, for you. When you got sick, I looked after you, even when I was worried my battery wouldn't make it. When you crashed, I risked the mutants for you. And now you're asking for this, too? Why is staying this *small thing* that I apparently won't do? The only thing I've asked you to do is listen or leave. And it looks like you won't do either.' Echo pinched the bridge of his nose, like the conversation was taking it out of him.

I hugged my arms in front of my chest. I had sensed his temper, especially when we were cornered, but he had never directed it at me before. 'Echo, I think that's a little unfair. I am listening. Look, can't we talk about this in the morning, when we've both had a chance to sleep on it? I just don't think we should be making any split-second decisions right now.'

'You're really not getting this, are you? I am not safe here. We are not safe here. You know how cults get you? They use secretive leaders like the Chief. Until we know more about this dude, I'd rather take my chances with the coyotes. Christ, P, you sound like you've been brainwashed already. Either help me to find out what's really going on here, or we leave. Simple as.' Echo picked up his bag from the door and looked at me expectantly, palm extended.

I hesitated. He made a lot of good points, but were we really any better out on the road, back where we started? Wasn't this partly my decision, too?

'I don't do well with ultimatums,' I said. I left his hand hanging in the air.

Echo let it drop to his side, then he licked his lips. 'OK. Well, I've done all right on my own so far. You'll see. I'm right about this.' He readjusted his pack and put his hand on the handle. 'I'll show you that we'd be better out there than in here.'

'Echo, don't be so dramatic. Stop, OK? Just stop.' I ran to the door, put my hand over his on the handle. Our faces were close enough for me to see the tears in his eyes. He must have seen the tears that were in mine. Why did this feel so final?

'I'm not being dramatic. I just think it's best that we get some breathing space, so you can see that I'm right, and I get a chance to prove that I am.' He sniffed and turned away from me just as another tear rolled down my cheek. 'Please move.'

'Echo, come on. We've been through more together in one week than I have with anyone in my whole life. I've learnt more these last few days than I have in fourteen years of the best schooling money can buy. We need to stick together, but you can't just go off on your own, not now. We need each other.'

'And that's exactly why I'm doing this.' Echo let go of the door and leant back next to the frame. His eyes were dark and cold, his jaw set. 'I know you're used to knowing all the answers, and trusting people to tell you stuff when they're ready, but, well, welcome to the apocalypse. You can't just shrink my head and hope everything will be OK. Life's unfair. You are not, were not and will never be a therapist. That world has gone. The best you can hope for is that you hold on long enough for someone to actually grow a shitty carrot out on one of those shitty farms before you die.'

I took a step back, stunned. 'How can you say that?' I whispered. The tears stopped coming. Echo stared at me for a full minute, but neither of us said anything.

'I . . . I didn't mean . . .' He pinched the bridge of his nose again. 'I . . . I'll fix this. You'll see.' And with that, he was gone.

I didn't move for what felt like a long time after he left. In all honesty, I kept expecting him to come back, to say he was sorry and to hold me and to talk to me about what was going on, but he didn't. His footsteps echoed away and then there was silence, only silence.

I crept to the edge of my bed and lay in the foetal

position, willing myself to cry, but I had nothing left. He didn't mean it. That was the one thought that went around and around in my head, as I willed it to be true. He didn't mean it. He was hurting. The end of the world was tough on everyone, even those who were left behind.

I hadn't felt so cripplingly alone since before the Big Sleep, as Echo always called it. I didn't even close my curtains because I knew I wouldn't sleep, I just lay for hours as the sky turned from black to pink to bright blue. Another sunny day in paradise. Around the time of sunrise, a small part of me wanted to get up, to find Echo and just leave the overalls and the Chief and the responsibility of saving everyone behind. To go back to our car and feel the breeze in my hair as we sped down the highway. To laugh at bad clothes and the way Gort spoke, and watch movies together on the giant flat screen, and ask Rosie to play old theme songs that Echo would know all the words to.

But then Echo's words would rattle around my head and dispel any thoughts of that. The old world was gone for ever. This was our life now. He'd have to get used to it, too.

Sunrise came and went. I didn't even go to the window. I would go to breakfast, and speak to someone, perhaps General Razor, and work out my next steps. She seemed like a woman with a plan for every situation. Echo could go on his crusade for all I cared. I had people relying on me. As long as he didn't do anything too stupid, he would be fine. He wasn't a child. This was a small place, I would see him around once he calmed down. I would wait until he came to me.

I tucked my chin deeper into my chest. Getting up was going to be harder than I thought. I was officially on my own.

19

Well, that went well.

I probably sounded a little, you know, conspiracy nut, and giving her that dumb ultimatum wasn't my finest moment, but my points all still stood. Something fishy was going on, and I was going to get to the bottom of it whether P liked it or not. I think.

I shouldn't have said that stuff about shrinking my head, though. That was a low blow after everything she had confided in me after the university. Man, that felt like a million years ago. She was right, we had done more together in this short time than I had the entire apocalypse. Maybe I should go apologize. *No, wait.* I needed evidence first, evidence of what the Chief was up to. Kissing and making up could happen later.

Then why did I already miss her?

I was pacing my room like a cliché in a movie when I heard him.

'Knock knock.' A camo-dressed goon knocked on my door and then immediately opened it without waiting for an answer. Rude as well as suspicious. Good to know. 'The general would like to see you, *Echo.*' He said the last part like it was some sort of joke.

I sighed. 'Fine,' I muttered, following the soldier out. 'So, I've got a hot date with the general herself, then?' I asked. The soldier didn't look at me, just straight ahead as we turned left and right through the building.

'Something like that,' he said eventually.

The hairs on my neck prickled. Something wasn't right, but I couldn't let them know I was on to them. If I kicked off now, with no idea where I even was, they would have even more reason to question my humanity. I pulled my cap as low as I could over my barcode.

Finally, we stopped outside an office two floors below my room, which if I was right, meant we were in the basement. Soldier boy held open the door for me and I gave him one last look before going in.

It was Captain Ashtray's office, all right. Inside was a concrete windowless box with a chest of drawers, a metal desk and a grumpy old lady sat back in her office chair, smoking what looked and smelt like a fat doobie. Awesome.

'Take a seat, Echo.' Ashtray pointed through the cloud of smoke to the chair opposite.

I heard the door slam shut behind me and tried not to jump. I wouldn't give her the satisfaction.

'Am I in trouble, miss?' I smirked as I dropped my bag on to the floor, looking her dead in the eye.

She smiled. 'You could see it that way. However, I'm more of a glass half full kind of person. I'd say there's an opportunity here, and you should really think about taking advantage of it.' She blew out another cloud of smoke and my vision swam. Contact high, no doubt. I'd smoked before, but the stuff was so old it barely touched the sides. The stuff Ashtray smoked was lethal.

I hesitated, trying to keep my thoughts straight through the drug haze. I was locked in, with no way out. There was no point trying to run, no matter how much I wanted to. And besides, what about P? And the Chief? I'd have to hear Ashtray out. At least then I would have the evidence I needed to persuade Pandora we were safer with the mutant coyotes than the smoking ones.

'I'm listening, Captain,' I said, spreading my legs and sitting back on my chair.

That annoyed her. 'General,' she corrected me.

I smirked. 'Oh yeah. Sorry, easy mistake to make. Go on.'

Ashtray stubbed out the end of her blunt and walked round the edge of the table. She sighed, bringing the last of the smoke to the back of her throat before she had to go a few minutes with just fresh air. The horror.

'Listen, kid. I actually don't mind the halflings. Heck, most of you seem pretty harmless to me. I mean, those of you I've met out there.' My heart dropped into my stomach. She knew? 'Don't look so down, robo-boy. I had my suspicions. The lights only flickered when you were in your quarters. And once my men saw that barcode, it was game over. You were gonna get caught eventually. The Chief was especially impressed with my detective skills.'

The goons at the labour-registration place. They had gone for me for seemingly no reason. And that was after the lights thing. I should have been more careful. Now I knew why they had it in for me, at least.

She perched on the edge of the desk and lifted her camo jacket to reveal a handgun, which she stroked. My mouth dried out in an instant, and not because of the smoke. When she said the ones she had met were harmless, she meant HUMANKINDs. There was no reason for many of them to come far from the city, like the pervy weirdos said back at the mall, but the odd one must drift out here. That was why they thought P and I were bots. And HUMANKINDs didn't fight back.

And Ashtray was telling me she saw me as target practice.

'But I'm afraid the Chief isn't as open-minded as me,'

Ashtray continued. 'There are a lot of people here that blame Aurora Tech for what happened. And you really do just *reek* of Aurora Tech.' Ashtray wrinkled her nose.

Yeah, like she still had any sense of smell left.

'I see you're happy enough to live in their buildings, though,' I shot back, pointing at the faded mark in the enamel at the corner of her desk. I could even still make out the spokes of the spinning wheel.

'We only took what was owed to us,' Ashtray hissed.

She had a shorter fuse than I thought. But as quickly as she lost it, she straightened up and pulled yet another cigarette from behind her ear. If I were as mad as her all the time, I would take up smoking too.

'Anyway, it doesn't matter what you think,' Ashtray continued. She lit her cigarette with a gold zippo lighter and inhaled deeply. 'Because you won't be here for long.'

'Wasn't planning to be,' I said.

'I think you'll be here even less time than you think,' Ashtray said.

I raised an eyebrow at her.

'Look, Echo, whatever you want to be called. The people, they're talking. You've been here a day and you've already disrupted the carefully planned routine of my camp. The rules we all live by here are simple. No Aurora Tech. And especially, no bots. You have to go.'

I licked my dry lips, which just tasted like ash. *Damn.*

Pandora wasn't going to be happy, but what choice did we have? 'All right. We'll leave. Just let me break the news to Pandora.'

'We?' Ashtray smiled. 'Oh no, halfling. Pandora won't be going anywhere. You're going to leave that girl, and that dirty little perversion of yours, at my front gate.'

'What?' I said, annoyed to hear my voice break. I sat forward on my chair, anger coursing through me, setting my nerve endings on fire. 'Say that again?'

'Do you really think she loves you?' Ashtray asked. She almost laughed.

I leant back a little. Love was strong. We'd only known each other what, ten days? But she liked me. She really liked me. We kissed. She told me stuff. She was my first, and only, friend. You don't do that with someone you don't like, right?

'Oh lord, you *do* think she loves you.' Ashtray sighed and rested her cigarette on the edge of the desk. She leant forward, hands clasped, like a Bond villain about to monologue. 'Listen, Echo. Pandora is human. You know what humans used the technology that powers your brain for? Because it wasn't just sad old spinsters that wanted kids. You were made to be used, Echo. You're a commodity. Sex bots? Same positronic chip set. HUMANKINDs? Mindless idiots designed just to help humans. Don't you see? You're a blip. A mistake. Or as little miss Pandora sees you, a shiny new toy.'

I sat very still. She was still a bitch, but the bitch was right. I knew about the positronic chip sets and what they were used for. I had seen the articles in the library. But P and I covered that at the university, right? We worked all that out?

Didn't we?

'You're wrong. She's not like that.' Damn, that shake in my voice wouldn't shift. But maybe if I said it enough, I would believe it. I sure as hell wasn't taking the word of some psycho I just met over my only friend in the world.

'Honey, a rich girl from the twenty-first? They're all like that,' Ashtray said. She didn't budge, and the corner of her mouth twitched. A shit-eating grin was hiding under there. She knew she had me.

'Pandora's different,' I said. I looked at the ground, and my dusty high-tops.

'If you really believe that, then you really have to go,' Ashtray said. Her voice was different. She had changed tack. I couldn't let her sway me, not now. I was totally right about that cult thing. The Chief had taught her well. I took a deep breath and looked her in the eye again.

She smiled wider, showing off those nasty teeth of hers. 'Stare me out all you want. You saw how excited she was to get here. What's out there for her, a girl used to people and community and family? The world is dead. There is nothing left, but this.'

When I thought about it logically, she was probably right. Even in the city I had felt the earthquakes – the ships were probably rubble, like Ashtray had said. Pandora's survival was basically a miracle.

'If you tell her you're going, she may well follow you. And then what? Two, three years down the line, drinking down her fiftieth can of peaches, she starts to resent you? What happens in ten years, when she's clearly much older than you? When her adult brain has developed? You are stuck, halfling. You can't age, you can't develop any further. You will only hold her back. Is that what you want her to remember you as? As the one who ruined her life?'

It wasn't stuff I hadn't thought about, but it was the first time hearing my innermost fears out loud. *Damn.* Ashtray was smarter than she looked, for someone intent on filling their lungs with tar. I really liked Pandora, and she was good for me. She fixed my E-Mote chip without even trying, which still made no sense to me. I needed her.

But did she need me? She needed me that time in the park against the wolf freak. And again, to drive the car, and at the school. That said, she was the one that talked us out of getting shot at the mall. When every fibre of my being wanted to run and fight, she had stayed calm. And we were still alive because of it.

And the ageing thing really sucked. As far as I could

tell, there were no programmers at the Chief's school for technophobes. I didn't really care much about my memory any more, but I did care about the whole Living-My-Life-in-the-Body-of-a-Man-Child-For-Ever thing. That didn't sound great for our relationship.

I sank back in my chair. I wasn't robot enough for the city. I wasn't human enough for Pandora and the rest of the last humans on Earth. I didn't fit. The very thought made me ball my fists until my knuckles went white, but Ashtray was right. Pandora was better off without me.

'Can I tell her?' I asked. I felt broken, like when my battery was low, but my HUD told me it was still at a healthy eighty-six per cent.

'It would be better if you didn't. Pandora is a sensitive girl. If she thinks you just left her, she'll learn to hate you eventually. And that way she won't go looking for you on her own in that vast wilderness,' Ashtray said. She picked up her cigarette, relit it, and took another drag. This speech sounded memorized. She had got what she wanted. She had won, and I had lost.

Story of my life.

'The Chief and I expect you to be gone before sunrise.' Ashtray waved a hand and the door clicked open behind me. A single soldier was waiting for me at the glass panel, no doubt. My humiliation was complete, then. I stood up to leave.

‘Hey, kid.’ Ashtray caught my attention before I trudged out the door. I stopped, but I didn’t turn around. ‘You’re doing the right thing. You leave now and you’ll be a distant memory once Pandora gets settled into life here. We keep our charges busy. And hey. Hail to the Chief, right?’

I set my jaw and didn’t give her the satisfaction of an answer.

Soldier boy led me back to my room, through the maze of corridors and staircases, then left me blissfully alone. It crossed my mind to ignore Ashtray, to go and find Pandora and tell her what had happened, but dammit if Ashtray wasn’t right. P would come with me, and hadn’t we just argued about that? We ran into trouble after barely a week out there. What if she came after me and got lost? What if the coyotes got her?

No. It had to be me. I had to go alone.

After I’d packed my stuff, I followed the string of bare light bulbs to find the gap in the fence I’d seen earlier. Like hell I was going out the front gate. If I had control over anything, it would be that the Chief and his disciples didn’t get to see which way I went.

I found the hole quickly enough. The only people I had to avoid were Ashtray’s goons, still guarding the entrance to their fearless leader’s bunker. It killed me that

I'd never know what was going on there, but deep down I knew. Just some old dude wielding way too much power. He'd get what was coming to him someday. I hoped it would be Pandora who gave it to him.

On the other side of the fence there was nothing but the moonlight. In the distance, I could see the street lights along the main road we had come in on.

Now what? Did I go back to the city, with my tail between my legs? Maybe that's where Gort had gone. I could at least try and look for him now. I could walk back to the car – it was only a few kilometres away. I had a full tank, so I could make it, even if it took till morning. Then I could drive home.

'Hasta la vista, baby,' I whispered, saluting at the silent wall. At Pandora.

I sighed. Shortest relationship in human–android history.

I walked until I hit the highway, then took one last look back at the camp. At Pandora's new home. Tinges of pink started to appear in the sky. It should have been pretty, but the place still looked like a prison to me. I took a deep breath and turned away.

I walked for an hour and watched as the sun rose and started to move across the sky. Pandora was probably waking up now, if she'd even slept. Would she be sad?

Would she even care? She was so mad last night. Now I thought about it, I had said some pretty shitty things, but it was better this way. This way, she could forget.

I wished I could forget. Forget like Gort and all the other bots. Just have one job, like cleaning the lobby floor or alphabetizing books. Not think about other people. About her. Every time my mind wandered to her face, her baby-blue eyes, the way her hair smelt, something hurt in my chest. A malfunction, maybe? But my E-Mote chip was still registered as working. Maybe this was what heart-break felt like.

I was surprised when I reached the mall. Maybe I had been walking longer than I thought. The sun was up but I was still in shadow, cast by the dunes and rocky hills either side of the highway. I stopped at the welcome sign, took in the scene in front of the doors. This was our downfall. Should never have stopped here. The mall had sucked, anyway.

'Well, wouldn't you believe it? Look who it ain't,' a familiar voice spoke behind me, and I closed my eyes and sighed.

Of course. Razor's desert boys were back.

20

Eventually, I managed to get up. I splashed water on my face at the vanity in the corner of the room and leant on the edge of the sink, resisting the urge to be sick. In the cracked mirror, my face was pale and drawn.

I drew in a deep breath and tried to think about what Dr Kapoor would say. *Be kind to yourself today. Don't forget your breathing. You can be the person to help yourself. In, one-two-three-four. Out, seven-and-eight.* She was right. I could still do this. Echo was hurting right now, he needed time. That didn't have to affect me. I could use this time to concentrate on my own goals. On finding out what happened to my father and everyone else from the twenty-first.

The heavy feeling on my chest lifted just enough for

me to get dressed and drag a brush through my hair. I could do this. Just one step at a time.

I headed out of my room and down the steps, making my way towards the cafeteria. It was early, but the people rose with the sun. Already the compound was buzzing with activity, with people sleepily making their way to breakfast.

In the dining hall, I held my head up as I collected a tray and lined up for food. Today there were more tinned veggies, and this time an offering of bacon. My mouth watered. Bacon was the one thing I had missed the most since turning vegetarian. It smelt delicious, so salty and fatty that it took all my energy not to take an extra-large helping of the stuff. It was a funny shape, round instead of long and streaky, but then again I'd only ever had factory-made bacon. Maybe this was the more rustic version.

'Just spinach and powdered egg for me, please,' I said, my stomach rumbling as the server dished up the food.

When I turned to the tables, my heart sank. I couldn't help but look for Echo, and he wasn't there. Made sense. He'd have to turn up for his work assignment, though. But for now, where would I sit? Before I had a partner. Now I was on my own.

I shook my head. I was being ridiculous. I could find my own friends; I had done it before and I could do it now. I would be best pushing Echo out of my head for the rest of the day. Too distracting.

To my relief, I saw a hand pop up and wave at me from a far table. Rebecca and Miles. I smiled and walked over to them quickly. At least there would be no Echo today to—*Stop. Stop thinking about him, Pandora.*

'Hi, you two,' I said, plastering on my biggest grin and hoping the smile spread to my insides. 'What's up?'

'Hi, Pandora. Nothing much. Say, maybe we can work together today. It would be nice to have a new person on duty with us, right Miles?'

Miles kept eating. He shared every other mouthful with Rex, who shot his tongue out over ten centimetres to grab each morsel before pulling it back to his mouth just as fast.

'She can't work with us,' Miles said eventually. He spoke without looking up from his food. 'We're on duty with that crater today. Beyond the fence. No way she'll be trusted beyond the fence yet. Hasn't had training.'

'Oh, right.' Rebecca pushed out her bottom lip. 'Sorry, Pandora. I forgot.'

'That's OK. If Miles says I need training, maybe I'll get to go next time,' I said.

'Where's your friend?' Miles asked.

I shrugged. 'Not sure. We aren't joined at the hip, you know.' I hoped I sounded less worried than I felt. Echo had barely eaten yesterday, and now he was skipping breakfast? *Get a grip, Pandora.* He had survived on his own for years before I turned up. I needed to snap out of it.

'So, what's the crater that you're working on?' I asked, changing the subject.

'It's the hole where the spaceship came out of,' Miles said, scooping a last piece of bacon into his mouth.

I froze and my fork clattered on to my plate. 'I'm sorry. Did you say . . . did you say spaceship?'

Rebecca folded her arms. 'Miles swears it was a spaceship. I think it was just an earthquake.'

'At the same time as that thing in the sky?' Miles asked, pointing his fork at her accusingly.

'It's possible it was a storm, and the thunder was so loud it felt like an earthquake. We've had those before.'

'Bull. Lightning doesn't leave a trail through the sky. It was a spaceship,' Miles said, placing his knife and fork together on the plate.

'Sorry, but what did you say? A trail through the sky? And a hole?' My mind was spinning and the creamed spinach threatened to repeat on me. 'Where is this hole?'

'Just beyond the fence. Maybe a half mile or so? But don't listen to Miles, he's always got his head in the clouds. The Chief himself, *Hail to the Chief*, said it was a lightning strike, and the shakin' we felt was probably just a small tremor. It's really just making somethin' of nothin'.'

'So this . . . lightning strike,' I said. My mouth was so dry it was hard to get the words out. 'When was this?'

'Maybe a week ago. Maybe more. Anyway, we best ship out. Bex, you comin'? I wanna see if there's any shrapnel,' Miles said, standing with his plate. Rex retreated to the safety of his pocket now feeding time was over.

'Any . . . ? Honestly, Miles. You're incorrigible. There ain't no shrapnel where there ain't been a spaceship. Besides, you know the Chief had the general's men fill most of it in already. We're just there to pat the topsoil solid,' Rebecca said. She stood and smiled at me. 'See you later, Pandora.'

'Yeah, bye,' I whispered, my thoughts a blur. Even though Rebecca had been so sure, reports of a spaceship from around the same time I crashed in the city were some coincidence.

I didn't eat another bite. After emptying my tray, I headed straight for the gates at the front of the compound.

'Not happening, girl. Sorry,' the guard on the wall said when I asked to leave. 'Too dangerous out there. You'll be needing a note from the good Chief himself, *Hail to the Chief*, if you want out any time soon.'

'Can't I just come up there and have a look at something?' I shouted up. The wall was at least three metres tall, and the desert was flat as a pancake, so I could get a good look at the hole from up there at least. 'Please. It's important.'

'So's my job. And I won't have it for much longer if I let

every Tom, Dick and Harry climb up here for a jolly. Now scram. Find some work of your own to do.'

The guard chuckled with his friend as I walked back across the courtyard. There had to be some way to get a look at this thing. I stared at the far wall, trying to bore a window through it with my mind, but unsurprisingly the concrete didn't budge.

There was nothing for it. I had to speak to General Razor, or even the Chief himself.

'Hey, do you know where General Razor's office is?' I asked a nearby man pulling weeds from the farming beds.

After he gave me detailed directions, I walked with purpose to the building he pointed out on the opposite side of the compound, and soon saw two Elders dressed in army fatigues guarding the front door.

'Good morning, gentlemen,' I said, forcing my sweetest smile on them. 'I believe I have an appointment with the general?'

'First we've heard of it,' the first guard grunted. 'Besides, the general isn't in. Important business to attend to, you know.'

'I did not know,' I said. My heart sank. 'She really doesn't have a minute? I haven't even been assigned a specific work activity.'

'Well, can you see the workers all around ya?' the second guard asked, pointing to the farmers in the courtyard.

I nodded.

'Pick up a trowel and use some initiative,' he growled, and the two of them started laughing too. Laughed at twice and it had only just gone breakfast. Quite the achievement.

I dragged my feet around to the side of the building, where I paused to coax the heat from my cheeks. This was humiliating.

'Hey, Pandora.' I had been sulking on a bench near the farms for at least ten minutes when I heard Rebecca's voice. 'You OK?'

I looked up. Miles was with her, and he was carrying a bag of tools slung over one shoulder.

'I thought you had to help with the . . . with that hole today. Did you see it? What was it like?' I sat up, aware that they might be the very people that could help me.

'Naw. All that work was finished yesterday. It looks great, you'd never even know the spaceship was there,' Miles said, and Rebecca glared at him.

My heart sank.

'Miles, what have I said about that spaceship nonsense? You get that out of your head for farming duty. You coming, Pandora? Looks like we can work together after all.' Rebecca smiled at me with those crooked teeth and I sighed.

'Yes, all right. It would be nice to do something useful.

Lead the way,' I said. The hole was gone. I couldn't see it even if I wanted to. I would have to wait until the general was back and request an audience with the Chief.

I wished I could talk to Echo. He would find a way to see this hole if it was the last thing he did.

Miles handed me a trowel from his pack and the three of us walked over to the nearest raised bed of spindly green sprouts. Rebecca showed me what to do; how to take clippings of the sad-looking plants – cabbages, apparently – and save them in a small bag attached to our overalls so that the Chief and his Elders could inspect them later for signs of positive growth.

'The crops haven't been doing too well this year,' Rebecca explained. I stared at the cutting in my hands, which was riddled with black spots.

'Doesn't that worry you? What about last year's crops?' I asked, anxiety pooling in my stomach at the thought of more canned goods.

Rebecca shrugged. 'The Chief always provides for us. I do wish there was more for Miles, I hate to see him so tired all the time. All this meat ain't good for him or Rex. Well, maybe not so much Rex. Mutants seem to be damn near the only things that do OK out here. We've had bad harvests for pretty much as long as I can remember. But we have the farm animals, and the old cans of food. We get by, and one day hopefully we'll thrive. *Hail to the Chief.*'

'Indeed,' I murmured.

Miles soon left us to talk to some friends of his at the next plot, and I took the opportunity to talk to Rebecca one on one. I had looked, but still no sign of Echo. He must have asked to change work assignments so he didn't have to see me, and I wanted to keep my mind off it.

'So, Rebecca. How do you find it here? Do you live in the family quarters?' I asked, only half invested in the answer.

'Oh, no. Our parents died in a flu outbreak when we were only small. Miles and I just have each other now.' She spoke with the sort of cheer one would use to order an ice cream cone.

'I'm so sorry to hear that,' I said. 'My . . . my mother died too, when I was small. And I don't know where my father is.'

'It's rough, but we get by. Say, I meant to ask, where is that fancy accent from?' Rebecca asked, moving her topsoil over the cuttings she had already taken.

I blushed. Was it that obvious? 'Oh, erm, well. As I'm sure you've worked out, we . . . Echo and I are from a malfunctioning pod. We . . . we bought tickets for the cryogenic freezing programme in the twenty-first.' I didn't like lying to her, but argument or not, I had to protect Echo's true identity.

'Yeah, I thought as much. So that means you were alive

way back when. What was it like? The late twenty-first?' Rebecca's eyes shone with curiosity.

I smiled. 'It was lovely, some of the time. It was also sad, and scary near the end. I do miss my Rosie though. That was my digital personal assistant. She did everything. Woke me up for school, suggested outfits, told me jokes. Sometimes I think I miss her more than my school chums.' Well, at least that was true.

'And Rosie was a bot? Weren't you worried she was gonna, you know . . . how did you trust her?' Rebecca wasn't even pretending to work now.

'No, Rosie was just an automated system. Voice controlled. But we had lots of bots, yes. Most of them didn't have thinking brains like the HUMANKINDs do. There were bots for everything. Some cleaned, some cooked. There were police bots and information bots. They were always very good and polite, because we programmed them to be. To be honest, seeing it from the outside like this, it felt a little like slavery. I think the world is better without those types of bots, because the way they were programmed to do everything for us just encouraged people to be rude to the HUMANKINDs, too. It really was the other humans you had to watch out for.' I gave Rebecca a sideways glance. She was completely rapt.

'What do you mean?' she asked.

'Well, it wasn't the bots' fault that the Earth was

warming up, or the crops were failing. That was down to the people. Especially the greedy billionaires behind Aurora Tech.' My stomach turned over at how close to the wind I was sailing, but I wouldn't let the image of my father stop me now.

Rebecca nodded sagely. 'Exactly. And Aurora Tech was in charge of the technology. That's why our fearless leader shuns all that. Those humans were thinking too much about making more robots, and not enough about crops.'

'Well, that's partly true, but sort of missing the point,' I said. 'It was never about the bots. You could trust them. The people were to blame.'

Rebecca gave me a sidelong glance. 'I didn't come down in the last dust storm, Pandora. Echo's a HUMANKIND, ain't he?'

I blink at her. Either Rebecca was more observant than I thought, or Echo's true identity was obvious. I pushed down the stab of fear I felt at the idea. 'How did you guess?'

'Had a hunch, then saw the hole on the back of his neck. You should tell him to be more careful. Folks round here hate HUMANKINDs,' Rebecca said.

I studied her face but there was no sign of malice there. She was simply warning me.

'He's . . . he's not quite a HUMANKIND. He's different. He was made to be a ChildSynth and then, when he got older, a TeenSynth. Those bots were made for people who couldn't have kids – infertility was a lot more common in my time. They're almost completely organic – and they have thoughts, feelings, family and friends, just like you and me. But cloning humans never quite worked out to full term, so the synthetics parts of them, their positronic brains, were created to keep them alive. It also means they can't grow organically, which is why after a hundred years of not being frozen Echo still looks young.'

'So what about the HUMANKIND thingies, then?' She put down her trowel, tilted her head at me.

'OK. So, HUMANKIND programming was a late-stage emergency protocol, a computer virus originally invented to infect all bots in case of a mass extinction event. They didn't have time to create new purpose-built robots like they wanted to, so the coders decided to just infect the TeenSynths, the bots left behind that had decision-making capabilities. They wiped their memories and personalities and replaced these with the program. The aim was to make sure these robotic humans could release us from our cryochambers, once they had determined it was safe for humans to return to living on Earth's surface.'

'But it didn't work, right? Your pods, they all broke up in the earthquakes.'

'That's right,' I said. I couldn't correct her, tell her my

suspicions of what I thought created the true crater Miles was so obsessed with. I had no proof. Yet.

'And what about the . . . what did you call them . . . TeenSynths? Seems kinda cruel to just wipe their memories and personalities like that,' Rebecca said.

She was drawing sketches in the dry dirt with her finger. I half smiled as I used my trowel to dig over the earth, so we wouldn't get in too much trouble for falling behind with chores. She was feeling *sorry* for the synths, for people like Echo.

'I agree. Perhaps their memory chips couldn't hold both sets of information, human and HUMANKIND. Perhaps people . . . I don't know, worried the bots would forget about them if they were able to hold on to their humanity. But it was cruel. It was like they killed them and made them into slaves.'

'Why didn't that work on Echo?'

Pandora shrugged. 'I don't know. He doesn't know either.'

'Seems kinda lonely to me. If anything, I'd say that name is a little ironic. He's just been an Echo for so long, he don't know how to respond to anyone but himself.'

I felt a lump in the back of my throat. *Echo, where are you?*

'That's . . . I never really thought of it like that. You're pretty smart, Rebecca,' I said.

'I've been called a lot of things before, but never smart.' After a thoughtful pause, she asked, 'Well, what about the – what did you call them? ChildSynths? Were they younger than the teen ones? I ain't seen any little HUMANKINDs in the fearless leader's teachings.' Her eyes were huge, two saucers in a pale face. She *was* smart. Why did they keep her on vegetable duty? She was capable of so much more.

'The ChildSynths were . . . decommissioned.' I was surprised to see a single tear escape down her cheek.

She believed me.

'That's awful. I can't believe that humans in your time would do something so rotten and cruel,' Rebecca said. I reached out and squeezed her knee. She sniffed, her eyes distant as she took in what I said. 'So, the HUMANKIND bots are just mindless, like those cleaning doohickeys and the like? Then why is the fearless leader always telling us they're evil?'

'That, Rebecca, is the right question to ask,' I said, my mouth set in a thin line.

Another worker signalled that it was time for lunch and we packed up in silence, Rebecca's eyes still faraway and lost in thought. This so-called Chief had a lot to answer for. Echo was right, the lack of free thought and the abundance of lies did make it feel like a cult. Where was he?

As we walked over to the cafeteria, my eyes wandered to the low building on the other side of the compound, the one with the electric door. The one that Echo had stolen a key card for.

But no. That key was still in my room, and Echo said he was going to be more careful. He wouldn't.

Would he?

21

'Hello . . . what was your name again? Something imaginative like Sandy or Skye or something?' I spun round to meet the boss man head on. I should have realized he would still be hanging around like a morning fart.

He was flanked by his goon friends again. They pointed their weapons at me. Déjà vu.

'Name's Rocky.' Boss man looked a little confused for a minute, like he hadn't expected to be introducing himself.

I shook my head. 'Rocky. Course it is. Seems legit. Did it take your mom a long time to think of that?' I shifted my weight to my front foot, staring them out. I was outnumbered. I was outgunned. Resistance was futile, but I wasn't going down without a fight.

Boss man – or Rocky, as he so eloquently put it –

narrowed his eyes and clicked the safety off his gun. 'Shut your mouth, halfling. At least I had a mother. You're just an abomination.'

Shit. How did *they* know about me? Was I really that bad at pretending to be human?

'Touché, really got me there,' I said, deadpan. My eyes dropped to the gun in Boss Man Rocky's hand. It looked old, older than the ones in my video games. Did it even still work? And for all he knew, I was still under the protection of Captain Ashtray, and they were shit-scared of her. I turned and carried on down the road.

'Where do you think you're going?' Sandy-or-Skye shouted.

'Anywhere I want. It's a free country,' I shot back, quoting the phrase I'd heard people use on TV. Back when countries were a thing.

A shot hit the dirt in front of me and I dropped to my knees. My ears rang with the noise and the breath was knocked from my lungs.

'You're not going anywhere, halfling,' Boss Man Rocky said. Now I was on my knees, he walked round to talk to me face to face. He pointed the gun at me again, which was still smoking, and I raised my hands above my head.

'Listen, guys. The good general won't be happy if I don't make it back in time for mashed swede tonight,' I said. I stared at the dirt as I spoke, partly to avoid enraging the big dudes with guns even more, and partly so it would be harder to tell I was lying.

'The good general? Is that what you're calling her?' Rocky laughed, which was more of a deep cough than a laugh, before continuing. 'Who do ya think told us where you would be?'

I bit my lip so hard that I tasted blood. Of course. Of course Captain Ashtray sold me down the river. She couldn't risk me changing my mind, coming back. She didn't even give me that much credit.

'And we know just how valuable a proper, working halfling like you is, so we had to come take a looksie,' Sandy-or-Skye grinned.

Idiot. I was a grade-A moron. Maybe if I hadn't given in so easily to Ashtray, she wouldn't have told these goons of hers that I was an android. She'd have never given up getting rid of me though, even if it meant chucking out Pandora too. And would I do it again, knowing Pandora was safe and warm and would soon be happy, once she forgot all about me? The sad truth was, yeah. In a mechanical heartbeat.

'On your feet, halfling,' Rocky spat, dragging my ass up. 'Move.'

They forced me to walk in front of them, hands behind my head, three guns pressed into my spine. We headed towards the mall at first, but took a right turn before the entrance and bypassed the parking lot until we reached the far side. Nobody talked.

Sweat built up between my palms and the charge port on my neck. I was heartbroken, sure, but that didn't mean I wanted to die. And the situation was bad. Really bad. I had to find a way out, but I was fast running out of options. Beyond the mall, a small town had once stood, but now it was more of a dusty criss-cross of roads with mostly crumbling houses. We dropped down into the basin and walked until we hit the first intact house, a two-storey villa that was probably nice once, but now had dead grass in the front yard and boards over the windows.

'This is your stop, halfling,' Sandy-or-Skye said.

Rocky walked up to the front door and gave the wood a rap with his bony knuckles. Almost immediately, the door opened a crack, stopped by the chain across the frame. I was too far away to hear what was said, but I could guess. The door closed and then opened fully, this time revealing a dude in a white coat, coke-bottle-thick glasses, and wild hair. He looked like the closest thing I had seen to a mad professor, but, like, in real life.

The professor dude handed over a heavy-looking sack to Rocky, who checked the contents and grinned a toothless smile. He stalked back over to us and gestured to the bag.

'Our work's done here, boys,' Rocky said. I felt a gun

press into my back again, forcing me forwards, towards the house. 'Let's ride.'

'I'd say I'll miss ya, halfling, but that would be a lie,' Sandy-or-Skye said, pushing me again.

He didn't follow and I turned around, considered running, vaulting the crumbling fence and taking my chances. But there was no point. I couldn't outrun a bullet.

'And I'll miss our witty wordplay,' I muttered, walking towards the house.

Einstein stepped out of the way once I was at the door. He was tall, but skinny, like most of the humans we had met out here. I could take him. Once the goons were gone, and the guns were gone, I could still get out of this alive. I stepped inside and the door whooshed shut behind me.

The inside of the house was nothing like I expected from the outside. The place looked like it had been pretty swish once, so I thought it might look a little like my apartment, but any signs that this place had ever been a family home were long gone. There were no chairs, or sofas, or even beanbags to sit on. All the windows were boarded up, and the only light was the artificial glow from a huge bank of half a dozen computer screens.

In the centre of the room was a metal table with a pile of wires and metal parts and microchips, plus some other shit that I couldn't even begin to guess at. The things that sent my heart racing, though, were the distinctive metal cuffs attached to the surface, the ones that looked just right to strap down a person and hold them still, like something out of a James Bond movie.

'So, is it true?' Einstein spoke for the first time and I nearly jumped clean outta my high-tops. He moved into the dim glow of a screen and I could see he was wringing his hands, like . . . he was nervous? He was acting like a dude on a blind date.

'I guess we're over the introductions then?' I said. My gaze slid to the left of Einstein and on to the desk beyond. In the glint of the half-light, a penknife stuck out from a pile of wires. Bingo.

'I don't see the point of names. I haven't spoken mine in years. Don't get many visitors.' Einstein tried to smile, which looked like it caused him pain, and a shiver went down my spine. Dude wasn't just weird, he was certifiable.

'Seems legit,' I said. I took a step sideways, moving in a semicircle towards the desk. As I hoped he would, Einstein moved in the opposite direction, keeping the distance between us. Away from the desk. Perfect.

'Curious. You don't even use the set language sequences,' Einstein said. He pulled a tablet from the pocket of his lab coat and tapped something on to the screen. In the brief moment when his eyes were down, I closed the gap with the desk and backed into the pile of wires.

'You mean, I don't talk like a robot,' I said. Keep him busy, that was the key. My hands reached behind my back and my fingers closed around the cool plastic handle of the knife.

'Precisely.' Einstein stopped tapping and slid the tablet back into his pocket. He adjusted his glasses and looked at me. 'But before you try and butcher me with that knife, I would like you to hear me out, Echo Zero-One-Three-Five.'

I blinked. Maybe he had seen me grab the knife? If he had, he had almost led me to it. It had been too easy. And he knew my name – that tablet must have had a scanning port. *Damn*. This was a trap for sure, but I couldn't see any way he could get the drop on me. Maybe he was bluffing. I brought the knife forward and jabbed it like a tiny lightsabre.

'I don't want to cut you, but if you stand in my way, I will,' I said. Sweat built up between my palm and the handle of the knife, which sort of contradicted what I was saying, but Einstein didn't have to know that. 'I've got places to be.'

'Do you, Echo?' Einstein said.

He was the picture of calm, so much so that it was really grinding my gears. Couldn't he see that it was over?

I had the only weapon. And yet I still hadn't stabbed the guy. It wasn't because I'm a pacifist. I'd do it if I needed to. But the dude knew my name. He knew something about me he couldn't just by looking at me. What was it?

'Please, Echo. I'm just so excited to meet you. I'm sorry about my men, they really weren't meant to frighten you.'

'I wasn't scared,' I said. Another lie wasn't going to hurt.

'OK. Well, that's because you are brave. Just like your father was.'

'OK, say what now?'

'Well, I think I know more about you than you realize,' Einstein said. 'Allow me to explain. I'm sure you have guessed by now that I pay those men to find robotic parts for me. When Mr Rocky told me about you a couple of days ago, I was curious to say the least. At the time, they were under the impression you were human. But earlier today, they returned with news from the general. They told me you were a synth.

'When they described you and your humanlike behaviour, I knew immediately who you were. I know all the TeenSynths in the database, but you're special. Very special. I've been looking for you for quite some time.'

'Nothing special about me, bud. I don't even remember if I had a dad. You got the wrong guy.' I still had the knife, but my heart was fighting hard with my head. Heart wanted to know more about my lost past. Head wanted to get the heck out of dodge. Damn E-Mote chip, always trying to kill me. Definitely made better decisions when I had a swinging brick in my chest instead of a fully working set of positronic chips.

I took a step to the left, towards the door, but I could see from here that it was locked with some sort of screen. Maybe fingerprint recognition? I hadn't watched Einstein close the door, but I could force him to open it with the knife. Right?

'On the contrary. You, Mr Echo Zero-One-Three-Five, have a very unusual entry in the HUMANKIND database,' Einstein said, holding his hands out once he saw I was headed for the door.

I stared at him, waiting for him to continue. Einstein lowered his hands. He knew he had my attention. 'You see, the database for the HUMANKIND program was created by your father, along with my grandfather.'

'So . . . you're saying my dad, the dude who picked me out of a magazine and brought me home, was a coder?' Wow. The irony was biting. You'd think he'd at least have taught me a thing or two so I could have fixed myself. Maybe he did – not like I remembered him anyway.

'Precisely. In fact, your father and my grandfather were friends. They both wanted to see the HUMANKIND project through, but never got the chance. Now we can perhaps rectify that mistake. Together.'

'How do you . . . what do you . . . talk faster, doc!' I said. My hand with the knife wavered. Three years I had spent looking for answers inside my useless, biological, positronic brain. Three years I had seen the HUMANKIND chip, known it was there, worthless, lodged in my brain like a bullet or inoperable tumour. Three years I had asked Gort why it was there, what made mine broken and his complete. Three years with no answers and up rocks this dude with everything I've ever asked. 'Seems a bit of a convenient coincidence if you ask me.'

'I prefer serendipity. It took the best part of ten years, and the life's work of my father, but we finally hacked into the database mainframe. After all, Grandfather created it. It's in our blood. Well, and also our brilliant minds,' Einstein said.

Well, at least he's modest.

'No offence, my man, but cut to the chase. What do you want with me?'

'I believe, if I can access your memories, I can find out who made it on to the SpindleSleep programme and where they are. Then I can have my family back. My father, he died waiting to find out. I will succeed where he failed.'

OK, I thought, *a bit creepy.* But also, the poor guy seemed genuine. He hadn't hurt me yet, hadn't tried anything. And I knew too well what years of loneliness could do to you – but the guy seemed to make about as much sense as I did, which was pretty much a minor miracle. Maybe he had coasted through watching TV too. Plus, he seemed pretty confident that I wasn't going to cut him. Which if I needed to, I would. I would totally do that. There was only one knife-wielding psycho in the room and it wasn't him.

But there was one problem. 'But didn't all the cryogenic ships get destroyed in the quakes?' I asked.

Einstein frowned. 'Who told you that?' But he didn't wait for the answer. 'Those ships were built to withstand space or a climate emergency. They're practically indestructible.'

It was my turn to frown. So . . . had General Ashtray been lying? Or didn't she know? Whatever. I didn't have time to think about what this meant right now. 'There's something else. I don't know how to break this to you, my man but . . . ah . . . I don't remember anything. Nada. Zilch. Memory chip is damaged, so I'm totally wiped.'

'To be expected after so long. All I need is a few minutes of your time. I can hook you up to one of my monitors, replay your lost memories, and then we're done.'

I glanced at the table. The cuffs made sense now.

'Just a precaution,' said Einstein, reading my mind. 'For your protection as much as my own. One crossed wire and you could break a rib with a carefully aimed punch. The whole process is painless, trust me.'

We watched each other for a few seconds. Einstein was the calmest I'd seen him yet. He knew I was thinking about it. I kept coming back to the same word, though.

Painless. All I've felt recently is pain. Sure, the love bit was great . . . *the love bit.*

I *had* loved Pandora, I realized. Still did. It was a big word, but I meant it.

It had been the best thing that ever happened to me. But the rejection bit? This . . . wasn't so great.

What was I supposed to do – just go back to the city, knowing Pandora was out there? Dealing with the pain every single day?

I couldn't do it.

'Can you . . . when you're done, can you wipe *all* my memories, even the recent ones? And can you like, turn off my E-Mote chip? Thing's been driving me up the wall.' I tried to laugh but it was hollow. Now I'd said it, there was nothing I wanted more. The idea of just . . . switching off, like a TV. That soft buzz before standby. Anything would be better than this.

'So, you want me to make you into a HUMANKIND?' Einstein asked. He sucked his teeth.

'No, I just want my memory erased and my E-Mote chip switched off.'

'Doing both those things would kill the human part

of you, essentially letting the machine side take over. I might as well finish the transition by uploading the HUMANKIND code at that point. It's my grandfather's – and your father's – legacy, after all. It would be my honour to continue the project. It would give you, the shell of you that is left, purpose.'

Now that? That spoke to me. I wasn't human. I wasn't robot. But I was also both, and it was tearing me apart. Gort seemed happy. Maybe I would be too, if I let the doc fix me up. I could forget about Pandora like she would forget about me.

'You can make me a HUMANKIND?' I asked Einstein. I lowered the knife. 'You can make these damn chips work, and I won't be . . . in this limbo any more?'

Einstein nodded slowly.

A true purpose, no memories, no emotions holding me back. That's what I wanted, right? I could just fade away, maybe help this dude at the same time, save some lives. I couldn't survive another heartbreak. At least this way, my life had some meaning. The robot part of me had a purpose. The human part was tearing me up from the inside out.

Goodbye, Pandora.

22

I couldn't stomach lunch. Not just because it was canned vegetables again. I couldn't stop thinking about how agitated Echo was last night, how obsessed with speaking to the Chief. And now I was supposed to think it was a coincidence that he had disappeared? No. Something had happened to him – or more likely, he had got himself into trouble.

'You all right, Pandora?' Rebecca asked that afternoon when we were back in the makeshift fields. 'You ain't said much since this morning.'

'Sorry. Just thinking about . . . something,' I said. I so wanted to tell her how I was feeling, but I couldn't risk exposing Echo.

'I've been thinking too. About what you said, the

half— the robots. Is it really true?' Rebecca asked me a question that pulled me out of my dark thoughts. 'That they were just like us, I mean?'

I blinked at her. 'What motive would I have to lie to you, Rebecca?' I asked her.

She chewed her lip. 'That's what I thought. The Chief – *Hail to the Chief* – is the only other person I know who was alive during the robot times, and I don't got a chance to ask him. I was wondering, maybe, if you wouldn't mind, if we could go and talk to him? About what you said. I just can't stand the thought of those lonely robots out there, and what if some of 'em *have* remembered how to feel? I would hate to be all alone. Maybe they could help us and we could help them, seeing as those smart Aurora Tech guys programmed them to help humans. I was wondering if maybe they knew something about why our crops won't grow.'

My breath caught in my throat. It was clear as day that Rebecca was caring, and thoughtful. She happily introduced herself to strangers and chastised Miles whenever he was rude. But what I hadn't banked on was how smart she was. Even she had worked out that perhaps it wasn't so easy to turn off someone's humanity, robot or not.

I smiled. 'That is a wonderful idea. I would be honoured to speak to the Chief with you – oh, erm, *Hail to the Chief*.' Rebecca grinned and I responded with a frown. 'But I thought it was quite difficult to get an audience with him? Miles especially said you have to work your way up to Elder to spend any time with the fearless leader.'

Rebecca's face fell. 'And he'd be right. I ain't ever even seen him. Big Ron says he has, but I think he's just fibbing. Do you think maybe the general could help us?'

'I already tried that this morning. She's apparently busy today,' I muttered, turning to glare at the guards that still stood outside her building on the other side of the courtyard.

'Then we might just have to wait until tomorrow,' Rebecca sighed and turned over another layer of topsoil.

'I don't think I can wait that long.' I bit my lip. 'I haven't seen Echo at all today. I'm worried he might be in some sort of trouble.'

'Is that because we saw him loitering around outside the Chief's – *Hail to the Chief* – quarters yesterday?' Rebecca stuck her trowel in the earth and gave me her full attention. 'Because we really didn't tell nobody, but you know what my grammy used to say when she was still alive? *Curiosity killed the cat.* He has to be more careful.'

I blinked at her. So that's why Echo was so spooked yesterday – he had been caught out. But Rebecca seemed sincere enough – would he really hide and assume she told the authorities here about his activities? If I could get her to understand, maybe I could persuade Echo to come out of hiding.

Wherever that was.

'Yes, I think it could have something to do with all that. I'm worried he took it upon himself to seek out the fearless leader on his own and maybe he stepped on a few toes to do so.' It wasn't a lie, and it wasn't exposing him either. Before the Big Sleep, I never would have got involved in something like this, at least not after Mother died. But I had to speak up. I cared about Echo, argument or no argument. His fight was my fight.

'I think I see what you mean,' Rebecca replied after a few seconds of silence. She frowned. 'But . . . the fearless leader stays in his bunker with the animals. There's a special door and everything. I don't think Echo would've gotten far.'

Bunker! She called it a bunker. I tried not to let the klaxon going off in my brain show on my face. 'Echo is very good with technology. If he wanted to, he would find a way,' I said. Again, not strictly a lie.

Rebecca nodded. 'If he got into the bunker, he'll be in big trouble. And if you cause trouble here, you answer to the general, and she gets creative with punishments.'

I didn't even want to think about what that meant.

'Rebecca, does that mean you'll help me? I'm asking you as my only friend here. Please.'

Rebecca tried hard not to grin. 'Really? We're friends? I mean, I got Miles, but he's my brother. There ain't no other girls really like me here. They're my age, sure. But I just . . . don't fit in.'

'Me neither,' I said, truthfully. Lexi had been the closest thing, and she treated me horribly. Not that I really gave her much either, except lifts to school and concert tickets.

'What do you need me to do?' Rebecca asked, the frown returning.

'Nothing that will get you into trouble, I promise. I need to sneak into the bunker to figure out what happened to Echo. I have an idea for how but I'll need a little time,' I said, thinking of the lanyard Echo had left in my room. 'So, I just need you to cover for me at dinner. They must take a register of who turns up, even just to keep an eye on food supplies.'

'That's right. You're smart too, for a girl from the twenty-first,' Rebecca said. She sighed, but her smile returned. 'All right. I'll say you got sick and decided to quarantine. People are mighty suspicious of new folk, and we ain't ever had any from the pods. To be truthful, I thought the pods were a myth my grammy made up. So you should be good, they won't go and check on you till at least the morning.'

'Perfect. Thank you so much, Rebecca,' I said, and I pulled her in for a hug. She seemed surprised at first and stiffened up, but after a second or two, she laid her arms gingerly across my back.

'No problem. I have no idea how you're getting into that thing, but good luck,' Rebecca said after she pulled away.

'Thank you,' I said again, and gave her hand a small squeeze.

It was nearly the end of our shift anyway, so Rebecca said I should go before anyone really noticed me and started to ask questions. There were butterflies in my stomach as I put away my farming equipment. Partly nerves, partly gratitude to my new friend. She was risking a lot for me. I had to be right about this.

Once I'd gotten changed out of my work clothes, I hung the key card around my neck and tucked the battered plastic under the material of my shirt. I knew which building it was. I walked back out into the corridor, feeling like I had a flashing sign over my head, the key card burning a hole in my chest. Surely, everyone who so much as looked at me would know.

But, strangely, they didn't. I walked across the courtyard and no one noticed. I walked through an alleyway between two buildings, and no one so much as looked at me. Most of them were stragglers making their way to dinner, anyway. There was one Elder standing guard outside the bunker. He was holding a large gun and standing directly in front of the entrance, which appeared to be a sliding door – the only sliding door I had seen in the whole compound.

'Miss, you can't go any further. This area is restricted to Elders only,' the Elder said, holding out his hand like a traffic warden.

I came to a stop and smiled. 'Oh, sorry. I'm the new girl, and I just haven't got my bearings yet. Do you know where the, uh, the tobacco plants are kept?'

'What? The general keeps her own stash, but I think it's just a house plant. Not for you to worry your pretty little head about.' The Elder grinned, revealing several missing teeth, and something about his confidence sent a shiver down my spine.

I kept smiling, though. 'Oh, I see. Just I heard something about a fire, and apparently the general is away, something about her tobacco going up?'

The Elder's smile faded. 'Shit. Really? That's the last of it . . . shit, OK, well, get back to work. And don't even try and go in there. That's reinforced steel.' The Elder holstered his gun and sped towards the general's quarters on the other side of the compound.

Perfect. It made sense that it was so easy – the door was locked after all, and I'm just a harmless little girl, right? I couldn't stop smiling as I checked both ways before raising the key card to the panel beside the door. I stepped inside and turned around, as if it were a lift, to check no one saw me. To my relief, the doors closed immediately on an empty scene.

Now I was really alone, I surveyed the area. The crates that had been outside had been brought in, and I peeped into the nearest one, which had the top loosened. Bottles upon bottles of a clear liquid. From the smell, it was either a powerful disinfectant or a potent liquor. It probably doubled as both. Strange.

That was the only thing in there, save for a small, rusted bench and a lift at the other end of the room. Whatever farming went on in here, it wasn't on this level. I rocked back and forth on my heels. There was nothing left to do but take the lift, and then what? The building was little more than single-storey from the outside. That lift wasn't going up. It was only going down.

It's the hole where the spaceship came out of. That's what Miles had said. And Rebecca had said it wasn't far from here, just outside the wall. The bunker was next to the wall, maybe in the same direction. It couldn't be a coincidence. There was nowhere else for Echo to go, and he didn't even hear about the hole. There was too much riding on what was at the bottom of that lift to turn back now.

I pressed the call button and the lift dinged instantly,

the doors sliding open to reveal a typical mirrored interior. I stepped inside, the need to see what was waiting for me more urgent and pressing than the fear that made my legs shake.

There were no buttons in the lift. Instead, as soon as the doors closed, it started to descend at speed, so fast that my ears popped and my feet felt heavy, like they had weights attached. Even more off-putting was the lift music, which crackled from the old overhead speaker like light jazz in a bar. Within a minute, the lift dinged again, and the doors slid open on my destination.

It shouldn't have been a surprise, what I walked out to, and yet I still finally succumbed to my sour powdered eggs and let what little lunch I had inside me spew out, straight on to the concrete floor. Because as I looked out at the hundreds – if not thousands – of artificially lit rows, I knew exactly what I was looking at. And it was obvious now what Echo had meant, when he said he could feel a huge amount of energy under the ground. I knew from the preparation talks that the project needed to be run on nuclear power, a new and condensed version of a fast neutron reactor that would be able to operate on its own for a century, and then for longer once the inhabitants it kept alive woke up.

Around me, stretching as high as a skyscraper on each side, were rows and rows of cryogenic pods. Each one was twice the height of an adult, and wider than it was tall. Each one was awaiting launch, probably by the huge red and white rocket that sat dormant in the centre of the room, the whole thing reminiscent of a missile silo. Each one also had a small propellant system of its own, two rocket-fuelled exhausts underneath, in case something went wrong on board the ship.

I had found it. The cryolab where I had come from, where somehow my pod had entered emergency launch mode. Miles was right. He had seen a spaceship. And somewhere in this room was my father.

'Pandora. I expected you eventually, but hoped you wouldn't find us this quickly. A pity.' The voice echoed around the concrete chamber, so I couldn't tell where it was coming from.

I knew who it belonged to, though.

'Hello, General Razor. I think we need to talk,' I said, hoping my voice sounded steadier than I felt.

23

An hour later I was laid out on the table, the creepy one with the cuffs set into the surface, the cuffs Einstein had assured me were for my own safety.

I was staring at the ceiling and trying not to look at all the drills and saws and a whole lot of other scary shit that the good doc was laying out along his workbench.

Einstein locked each of my limbs into the cuffs, and then tightened them until it felt like he was cutting into my skin. Not that it would matter soon. Nothing would, except for my directive. I wouldn't feel pain, inside or out. Maybe Gort would even want to be buds. You know, if he knew what buds were. If I did.

But feeling nothing was better than feeling broken, right? Without her, there was nothing else.

'Now, Echo, I need you to count backwards for me from ten.' Einstein pulled out his tablet and started typing something into it.

'Um, OK? Ten, nine, eight, seven . . .'

'Echo, I need you to get into the basement. Now. Hide where I showed you. Go.'

I groaned. I was laid out on the couch, watching TV. It was the finale of my show and I hadn't set it to record, so I would miss it if I left.

'Daaaad.' I drew out the word so he could tell how mad I was. 'Is this another drill? Because if it is, can't we do it—'

'This is not a drill. This is what the drills were for.' My dad came back into the room from the kitchen. He looked old suddenly, the hair greying at his temples and his eyes sunken under layers of loose skin. In his left hand he brandished a flat metal data drive.

My heart dropped into my stomach. He really was serious.

'I'll get the shutters,' I said, leaping off the couch. Dad nodded and threw open the door under the stairs, the one that led to the basement.

I started upstairs, racing from room to room, slamming the metal safety shutters on the bright sunshine of the day. Before I shut the one in my room, I hesitated, looking out at the hills dotted with sheep and the trees and the wren that hopped across the garden.

This was the last time I would see anything like this.

I shut the last window up and repeated the process downstairs, then ran to the basement.

'How long do we have?' I asked Dad, sealing the door and pulling across all five locking mechanisms.

'Not long. They just stormed the president's house. It's already happening,' Dad said. He was sitting at his desk, his fingers a blur over the keyboard. 'I have to upload this before I lose satellite access— Shit.'

'You lost satellite access,' I said. I bit my lip hard. This was worst-case scenario and I knew it. 'What are we going to do? Is there another way to finish HUMANKIND?'

'I've been developing one other way. Just in case the satellites went down. A fail-safe, if you like.' Dad spun round in his desk chair and held something up. The data drive.

'Um, why are you looking at me like that?' I said, holding my hands up. Mock surrender.

'Echo. You know I see you as my son. I have protected you from the conversion program, I kept you hidden and safe. You know I would never hurt you.'

'Why does this feel like an apology speech?' I said. I perched on the edge of the workbench, ready to listen.

Dad sighed. 'I was horrified when Aurora Tech decided it would be cheaper to convert the TeenSynths for the HUMANKIND project than simply make new androids. The ChildSynths are too little, and the PLEASUREBOTs are inappropriate for a variety of reasons. And your generation would have been the first to graduate to full AdultSynths but . . . it wasn't meant to be. Too many protests. Too little time.'

'I know. That's why we had to move here. You kept me safe,' I said. I thought about our old house, with its rolling gardens and cinema room. I missed my old room with surround-sound speakers, sure, but at least in this dump we were safe. And Dad's skills meant he had easily hacked into his old work account. We had been keeping an eye on the HUMANKIND project ever since we first heard chatter of the catastrophic climate event.

I guessed I just didn't think it would come so soon.

'It occurred to me that solar events might affect our satellite signal. And I've been watching the progress on the project. I don't want to blow my own trumpet, but without me, Aurora Tech are very much lagging behind current events.'

I smiled. If there was anything Dad loved more than programming, it was blowing his own trumpet. 'Get to the point, Dad. I know something is up. You're doing that thing with your beard.'

'What? Oh.' He stopped pulling at the end of a grey hair that shot out of his chin and folded his hands in his lap. 'Sorry. So, here it is. I knew they weren't going to finish the HUMANKIND project in time before . . . before the end. The conversion rate is too slow, and most of the synths don't even have co-ordinates for the cryolabs, because they were late building those too. The Aurora Tech idiots had an idea to beam the co-ords to every synth simultaneously, via satellite, but as we can now see, that won't work either.

'I've come up with a solution. We finish one HUMANKIND, fully, with all the information they need. Then after . . . after they wake up, after the climate event, that HUMANKIND will be able to find other synths and download the necessary data to them, using short-range wireless. Then that synth can spread it to more synths, and so on. Sort of like a computer virus, but this one is good for everyone.'

'Well, that sounds like a workaround. Have you finished the project?'

'Yes. I downloaded everything I needed from the servers and have all the information – timings, locations of cryolabs, everything – right here on this drive. I would just give it to the lab, but all my old contacts are gone. If Aurora Tech so much as caught a whiff of where we were, they'd kill us instantly. They won't trust what I have here, and it would take too long to show them. All I need is a HUMANKIND to install it on, and we can finish in time.'

'Well, where are we going to find one of those?' I asked.

Dad looked at me for a long time. He knew I knew what he was getting at. But he needed me to say it, to choose what he was saying.

'I don't want you to be on your own,' Dad said. A tear streaked down his cheek. 'And you know I won't survive the climate catastrophe without one of Aurora Tech's magic tickets. I need you to carry on. And I won't wipe you like those monsters at Aurora Tech. I've found a way to install the HUMANKIND

information, and keep your identity intact. You'll remember everything. You'll remember me. Your humanity is your most precious resource, Echo. Remember that.'

It took me a minute to realize I was crying too. I had known this was coming, deep down. Without Dad, I wouldn't be able to upgrade to a full AdultSynth. Well, the option probably went out the window along with the house and the money. We were fugitives. The options were die with the rest, or embrace my robotic side and survive. Without Dad.

'How long does the conversion take?' I asked, wiping the tears from my cheeks.

Dad came across and hugged me tightly. 'That's my boy. My hero, saving the world.' He stood back and looked into my eyes, which he had selected to match his, a deep brown colour. 'It will take several days to upload all the information correctly. If we are to have a chance of finishing, we must start now.'

'Well, I guess the world can't wait. I am a hero after all,' I muttered, but I managed a smile.

I had been worked on by Dad before. Just small tweaks and updates that he managed to pirate through his illegal channels from Aurora Tech. I walked over to the dentist's chair that we had salvaged from a skip and made myself as comfortable as I could.

'This is going to be the last time I see you, isn't it?' I asked. More tears pricked at the back of my eyes.

Dad stood to the right of the chair and nodded. 'If the

information I downloaded from Aurora Tech is right, then those of us without tickets to Aurora Tech's arks don't have much time left. We'll be lucky to get the download finished in time.'

'So we're feeling optimistic, then?' I said, and we both laughed through the tears. 'What happens if you don't finish?'

'I'm not sure,' Dad said honestly, shrugging his shoulders. 'I'll keep your lifeline functions active at all times, and I'm hopeful the shutters and basement will protect you from the worst of the catastrophic events. There will be days so cold you won't feel your toes, some so hot you'd die of thirst in minutes if you stepped outside. Hurricanes. Tornadoes. I'll be working in close quarters with your E-Mote chip and your memory bank, because it's the only space that will maintain both your humanity and your new HUMANKIND functions. They might even malfunction with all that going on. I'm just not sure.'

'Well, don't sugar the pill doc, tell me what you really think.'

'Always making jokes, even at the worst of times. I'd say you get that from me, but I think it is uniquely you,' said Dad.

He fiddled with something on the table and held up a tablet. 'Ready? We must begin. I don't know how long the door will hold if the news about riots is true.'

'Ready to say goodbye to my dad? Never.' I reached out and squeezed his free hand. He squeezed back and looked up, avoiding more tears. 'But ready to save the world? Has a cool ring to it. Let's go.'

I swallowed back my own tears as he tapped on the screen.

'OK, my son. You know the drill. Count backwards from ten.'

'OK,' I said. I was still holding his hand as I looked into his eyes. My eyes. 'Ten, nine, eight, seven . . .'

Stop.

It was a single thought in my mind, but it grew, like a whisper changing into a shout.

STOP!

The beardy guy. Dad. I never really forgot him. All along, he was trying to give me this message. That I'm important, that I matter. Dad had protected me in that basement, even if I zonked out for ninety-seven years in between. And my chips had malfunctioned, just like he was so worried about. But I fixed them. Hey, my dad *was* a bio-tech engineer, after all.

Pandora helped me remember, too. I never saw Dad before she showed up and helped me to feel again. Without her, I never would have remembered him in the first place, and now I'd spent so long telling him to go away and not telling anyone what was going on, I was about to ruin everything.

I tried to open my eyes but it was hard. My eyelids were so heavy. I needed to open them though, to stop the man poking around inside my head. Dad? No, not Dad. Dad was kind, and gentle. He didn't tie me down. And he tried to make it work, but he just ran out of time.

Your humanity is your most precious resource, Echo. Remember that.

That was one of the last things he ever said to me. Dad wanted me to embrace every part of myself, human and robot. The man with his hands in my brain just wanted my metal parts.

My humanity. It hurt sometimes, but it was important. Friends. Love. Pandora. Dad.

I had to wake up.

'Stop.' My eyes stayed closed but my mouth moved that time. I even heard the words come out. I let the feelings of my returning memories wash over me, send my E-Mote chip into overdrive. Aurora Tech throwing Dad to the wolves. Having to hide. Losing everything. Losing Dad. Losing Pandora. Remembering my true purpose.

Caution. E-Mote overheating.

I saw the message in the top left of my HUD and grinned, a real grin that reached my face.

'Ow!' Einstein yelped as he burnt his fingers against the chip in my head.

He dropped whatever tool was keeping me still and my eyes shot open. I was still pinned to the table, and the left half of my vision was obscured by my left ear, which really freaked me out until I realized why it was there. Einstein had accessed my positronic brain through the side of my face, lifting my cheek panel to get in further.

'Stop,' I said again, louder this time.

Around the edge of my cheek, Einstein came into view, rubbing his burnt hand.

'How did you—? You shouldn't be awake. Let me put you back under. We don't have the location we need yet. You haven't shown me Grandfather.' Einstein pulled out the tablet and tapped at the screen.

I felt myself slipping under again. My eyelids were heavy. 'No. Please. Stop. I've changed my mind. I want to live. Stop.' My vision was blurry. I couldn't keep this up.

'I think Echo Zero-One-Three-Five has asked you to stop.'

That voice. It couldn't be.

'Gort?' I asked. I slurred like I was drunk. 'Is that you?'

'Affirmative,' Gort said.

'What are you doing up? Defective, the lot of you. I should have left you on the scrapheap I found you on. Leave us.'

'Echo Zero-One-Three-Five, are you in danger?' I heard Gort through the mists of unconsciousness trying to pull me under.

'Hell yeah. He won't get out of my head. Help me, Gort, please.'

With a huge push of strength, I forced my eyes open again just in time to see Gort holding Einstein by the neck. The tablet dropped to the floor and smashed and the heaviness on my eyelids faded away. Gort let go of Einstein and he dropped to the floor like a sack of potatoes.

'I thought you couldn't harm humans?' I said, straining to see where Einstein had gone.

'Affirmative. There is no lasting damage to human. I merely disabled him temporarily to achieve my primary objective.' Gort made quick work of the cuffs holding me down and even clicked my cheek flap shut so I wouldn't have to do it myself.

'How did you . . . what are you doing here? Why didn't you say anything earlier, when I got here?'

'When I first arrived, the strange man asked me to be quiet and not disturb him. I had to follow his human directive. This is the first time Echo Zero-One-Three-Five has been in distress. This is the first time he has asked for my help. If asked, a HUMANKIND must do their best to assist.'

I blinked at him. 'Gort, did you just say that you care about me?'

'Negative. I do not care. I was merely following directive.'

'Could have sugared the pill just a little, there, bud.' I sat up, rubbing at the places where the cuffs had cut into my skin. I could see the soft rise and fall of Einstein's chest. No murders here. 'Well, thanks, Gort. But, uh, we thought you had abandoned us. Or worse. We were so . . . just . . . oh,

God, come here, big guy.'

I leant forward on the table and clasped Gort into a bear hug. It was weird. Different to hugging Pandora, like, *duh*, but still kinda nice. I knew you could have too much of a good thing, though, so after a few seconds I pulled away and slapped him on the shoulder. Manly.

'I am sorry, Echo Zero-One-Three-Five. I would never knowingly abandon human Pandora. Apologies for getting waylaid.'

'Of course – you had to check on Pandora and ignore me,' I muttered. 'But that still doesn't explain how you got in *here*.'

'Humans found me in the car and took me here. The doctor tried to look inside my head. Then he received a call about Echo Zero-One-Three-Five on his radio device, and left me under the stairs with the other HUMANKINDs.'

Gort grabbed a surgical light from overhead and tilted the adjustable neck towards the stairs. I couldn't see them in the gloom before, but underneath there was a pile of what looked like dead bodies. I thought I was gonna hurl until one of them moved one single eye staring out at me from under an armpit. Then I thought I was gonna hurl even more.

'Jesus – are they all HUMANKINDs?'

'Affirmative,' said Gort. 'We were waiting for the next

human directive.' He tried to smile but his eyes dropped and he stumbled sideways like he was drunk again.

'Woah there, buddy. You OK?'

I reached out and steadied him and as soon as I touched the thin material of his nerdy T-shirt, I knew what was wrong. There should be a strong pulse, an electrical buzz that only fully charged bots have. But Gort's was barely there, like a low hum in another room. He hadn't been charged in days.

'Any bots the doctor did not like, he put to one side to keep for spare parts,' said Gort. He was rasping, the electrical current in his body struggling to inflate his lab-grown lungs. 'The strange man didn't let me charge up overnight. And as he is human, we were powerless to repel his wishes. Until Echo, half human, half bot, was in trouble of course.'

'How long have you been here?' I say, easing him into a sitting position on the creepy surgical table.

'259,412 seconds. Or three days if you prefer, Echo Zero-One-Three-Five.'

I stared at the pile of barely moving limbs and faces, like dolls piled up in a toy factory. 'And . . . the others?'

'Some have no charge at all. I was the only one capable of complying with Echo Zero-One-Three-Five's request for rescue.'

'I mean, it wasn't a rescue, as such. I would have had it

if you gave me a few more seconds,' I muttered. 'All right, I guess we have to . . . charge these ones and see who wakes up. Can't leave them here with . . . that,' I said, waving my hand at Einstein's body. There it was again. The sour taste of imminent vomit that I had to swallow down. Why they gave TeenSynths a human stomach, I will never understand.

Gort and I made short work of the pile of . . . *collectables* wedged under the stairs, mostly because Gort didn't find anything creepy about pulling severed arms away from intact bodies and sorting out who was still in one piece. I shuddered as I put another loose foot in the discard pile. Synths were weird. If we're alive, synthetic hearts still beating, we bleed. But once you let us run out of juice . . . the synthetic blood just solidifies and turns blue. Dried blue gunk hung from every body part, which made the job even worse.

Eventually, we were left with three intact synths.

'Aren't they a little . . . small?' I said, crossing my arms. All three were wedged up against the staircase, folded legs keeping them from falling to the floor. Their eyes were all closed but there were two girls and a boy, all with dark hair and big features.

'They're ChildSynths, Echo Zero-One-Three-Five. They are meant to be small.'

I pulled a face. ChildSynths? I read in the library once

that when they started work on the HUMANKIND project, they said they would decommission the poor little guys. Their positronic brains weren't really made for the end of the world. Not that mine was, but I had a feeling that all the shit that had happened to me so far would be *waaaay* worse if I had the brain of a ten-year-old.

'Where did he find them?' I asked.

'Unsure, Echo Zero-One-Three-Five. They had been discharged for a long time when I got here. The good news is these are all later models. Triplets, I believe. They should all be fully charged in around ten minutes.'

And as usual, Gort was right. We plugged them in and ten minutes later, three sort of adorable pairs of eyes sleepily opened for me. Gort even managed to get some charge back into his tired circuits.

'Aww, they're sort of cute,' I said. I'd never seen a little kid in real life before. They really were kinda sweet, in a living doll sort of way. I wondered if their parents had protected them from the decommissioning, hidden them away somewhere Aurora Tech couldn't find them. Maybe that's how they'd survived.

All three kids looked at me for a few seconds, then smiled in unison.

'You are our daddy.' They spoke in one voice, one creepy, perfectly pitched voice. Like a tiny a cappella group.

'Oh God.' I turned to Gort. 'They've been out so long they don't remember anything. How do we make them stop, set them up properly or whatever?'

All three children turned their heads in unison to Gort, still smiling. Christ, no one told me kids could go from cute to creepy so fast. 'You are our daddy, too?'

'No, no no no. We are not a couple – we are not your daddies.' I waggled a finger at them like I knew anything about what I was doing.

The children turned back to me.

'You are our—'

'All right, you want a family? Sure. Me, friend. Gort, big brother. Happy now?'

'Big brother Gort?' the world's freakiest triplets said.

'That's right. So that's Gort, I'm Gort's best friend and handsome, debonair companion, Echo, and you can be called' – I pointed to them each in turn, as they were sat: boy, girl, boy – 'Zort, Cort and Mort. Yeah, your parents weren't the sharpest crayons in the box, but they were very nice. They wanted you to stay together, that's right. And Gort is gonna look after you little rascals, so if you need anything, ask him. OK?'

I dunno what possessed me to come up with the backstory, but despite their clearly possessed demon-head movements, they were just kids. Maybe thinking someone cares about them would help.

'Echo Zero-One-Three-Five, I cannot possibly—'

'Listen, Gort,' I said. I turned him away from the kids because I couldn't bear their eyes boring into me. They really needed to practise blinking. I brought my voice down low before continuing. 'Look, I get it. They're not exactly functioning at super-computer levels right now. Maybe they were damaged, who knows. But we're all they've got now. You up for a challenge?'

Gort looked over his shoulder and into the darling angels' creepy, unmoving faces. 'I guess it would be good to help develop the HUMANKIND program. Perhaps these children have traces of the code, too, and that is why the strange man kept them. Perhaps they can help locate the bunker.'

'You know what? Not a bad theory, but I think we might have a solution to that once I have a second to think,' I said. 'Now listen, Gort. These kids. I'm not feeding them, or toilet training them, or talking them for walks. The Three Stooges are your responsibility now. *Comprende?*'

'I did not know Echo Zero-One-Three-Five knew Spanish,' Gort said.

I rolled my eyes.

'*Comprendo. Los cuidaré*,' Gort said.

'I'm gonna assume that's a yes. Good man, Gort. You just became a family man.' I slapped him on the back and turned back to the kids. 'So . . . what now?' I asked them.

'That is up to you, Echo Zero-One-Three-Five. You have much to teach us. I await the information from your update.' Gort held out his hand like a businessman striking a deal.

It all came flooding back to me at once. The memory. My dad – I had a dad, one that cared enough for me that he literally evaded the law to keep me safe. My hand went up to my cheek. I had his eyes, I knew that now. I was loved once. And even more, I was loved enough to be given a purpose. Possibly the most important purpose in the world.

I couldn't explain it, but I knew what to do. I grasped Gort's hand and waited.

The download took less than a minute. It was almost physical, the feeling of the information downloading from my brain, travelling along fibre-optic nerves, then jumping across to Gort's hand. Dad had done well. My update had taken days, but the virus was compact enough to quickly upload to the new host.

When the download was finished, Gort let go of my hand. The kids were just as still and terrifying as ever, but one of the boys was blinking now. Progress.

'Well? He's alive,' I said to Gort, more to break the tension than anything, hands raised like Dr Frankenstein.

Gort just looked at me. *Right.*

'So, you knew I had the update? You sensed it?' I asked, moving past his still-inferior knowledge of anything cultural.

Gort nodded. 'Something like that, dude.'

I burst out laughing. *Dude* was certainly not in Gort's vocabulary, not before anyway. Part of the update must have tapped into my learnt speech or something. Maybe a little goodbye present from Dad. My heart swelled. Gort might even watch *Back to the Future* with me. But just the first two. Always the first two.

'We can totally help too, my man,' the kids all said in unison.

Woah. I hadn't even tried to upload it to them, but it looked like it worked just by being near me. Interesting.

'Yeah, we'll work on all your lingo,' I replied. And I had something else I needed to say. 'Uh, look, Gort. I'm sorry I, you know, left you alone in the car by the airport and let you get kidnapped by morons. But I knew you'd make it out, right? Although, yeah, now I say it, that's not an excuse. So, like, I'm sorry. Really. You saved my life.'

'Do not apologize, Echo Zero-One-Three-Five. I do not feel emotions or pain. You could say that if you and human Pandora had not left me behind, these human "morons" as you call them would not have found me, which would mean I was never kidnapped, and then would not have been here to save you. In reality, it appears you did yourself a favour.'

'Yeah. Not really sure that logic works, but I'll go with it. Thanks for understanding, buddy.' I slapped Gort on the back, relieved he couldn't feel anything.

'Of course, Echo Zero-One-Three-Five. Now, if it is agreeable, I am wondering whether we can go and wake the first cryogenic lab. I believe it is nearby, word,' Gort said.

I nearly smiled at how he said it, then paused. I could see the location in my head too. And I didn't like what I saw.

'Let's roll,' I said to Gort.

'Let's roll,' the kids chanted, springing up. They were a little wobbly on their feet, but they seemed OK for three tots that had been put to sleep for a century.

'I am sensing the coagulants in the children's bloodstreams will not break down for a few hours yet, Echo Zero-One-Three-Five. It will make them a little stiff, but also less prone to harm. Less blood means sixty-eight per cent less chance of injury.'

'Superkids. Good to know. Not incredibly weird at all,' I said.

We made short work of the locks now there was no one watching us, and the last one ticked open after we dragged Einstein across the floor and laid his palm to the touchpad.

'Mmmmhmmm.'

Uh oh. That was Einstein. And was it just me or were his eyes twitching?

'Say, Gort. Before we go, did you say that old Einstein here locked you under the stairs?'

'Some of the time, Echo Zero-One-Three-Five. But he brought us out when working on new projects, like when he worked on you, for possible spare parts. I am ninety-four per cent certain that he did not think we would attempt to save you. He did not see us as a threat.'

I snorted. 'Big mistake,' I said.

I nodded my head back to the understairs cupboard and Gort helped drag Einstein inside. As I clicked the lock shut, I peered at him through the shutter on the cupboard door just as the good doctor himself blinked his eyes open.

'Seriously? Huge mistake.'

We didn't look back.

After around half an hour of walking, the gates of the republic came into view. Luckily the sprogs didn't slow us down too much – they couldn't feel pain, like Gort, so they didn't get tired, even with their gross coagulated limbs. I scanned the landscape. There weren't any guards on the wall – weird – so we ran straight towards the hole I'd left through.

We climbed inside the perimeter and peered around

the low building nearby, but there was no point – the buildings were deserted. The hairs around the charge point on the back of my neck stood up. Something was going on.

I led my new creepy adopted family through the barrels and boxes at the entrance to what – thanks to the HUMANKIND tech flowing through my terminals – I now knew was an elevator. Under our feet was a bunker. And beyond that? People.

We slowed down at the boxes and I signalled for the others to be quiet – surely the goons would still be guarding the doorway, right?

The person standing there wasn't a goon.

'Rebecca?' I hissed.

She turned around. Yep, it was her all right. I'd know that slapped-with-a-wet-fish face anywhere. 'What the hell are you doing here? Wait, why are you hiding?'

She was crouched in the exact same position that I'd been in when I was snooping the other day.

'Why are you hiding?' The triplets peered around me and spoke in unison.

Rebecca looked like she had seen three identical creepy ghosts.

'Guys, let me handle this. And I'm looking at you, Gort. Keep the kids under control.' I narrowed my eyes at Gort and he nodded. Then I turned my attention back to

Rebecca. 'Well? Spit it out, dude. What's going on? Why are you here, where is everyone? Where's Pandora? We need to show her – well, everyone really – something super important.'

'Does it have anything to do with that door?' Rebecca finally started talking. 'Because Pandora asked me to cover for her so she could go down there, and she's been gone for over an hour. I've been keeping watch but no luck. I'm starting to get worried.'

My heart sped up. 'Anyone else go down?'

'Uh, yeah, actually. I saw General Razor head down there with a bunch of guards around the same time Pandora did. She excused herself from dinner and everything. There were some guards left up here, but I got Miles to show them Rex. They all love that little guy – weird, right? When they have access to the animal pen right there?' Rebecca bit her lip. 'Something ain't right, Echo. I cleared the guards so I could sneak in, but Pandora must have swiped a pass or something because I can't get past that door. So I've just been watching.'

I blinked at her. *Wow.* So Rebecca was . . . useful now?

'I think we can help there,' I said. I held out my palm. 'As long as you don't mind getting into bed with a bunch of child robots. Wait. That came out wrong, that sounded weird.'

I recoiled in horror at what I said and gestured for Gort

to go open the door. He waved his hand once across the keypad and the door slid open.

'Holy—You did it. Wow.' Rebecca turned back to me. 'And for what it's worth, Echo, I'm real sorry. Pandora explained a few things, about you synths and HUMANKIND and why you were made and whatnot. I get it now. General Razor and the chief – *not* hailing that guy any more – were wrong. I think Pandora could be the key to bringing us all together for a brighter future. Not just for us, but everyone. I have my brother to think about. He needs more than canned spinach and a furry lizard, you know?'

Double wow. Maybe Pandora didn't hate my guts after all. Just another reason to get moving.

Plus, I had to agree that Miles, poor kid, really needed a dog or something. Although the lizard is rad. Maybe he could live at Chez Echo when this was all over.

'All right, so we all go. Maybe, Rebecca, you can talk some sense into General Razor. Anyone ever tell you you have a way with words?' All six of us walked through into a short hallway, the only exit another set of double doors. The real entrance to what I knew was below: the bunker.

Yeah, probably had to warn poor Rebecca about that before we got down there.

'Thanks, Echo. So, these guys are adorable. I didn't realize you had a husband and kids? You seem so young?'

Rebecca stroked Cort's hair. The triplets turned their heads just a fraction too far to the left to smile at her, and she recoiled slightly. Fair. Had to teach them not to do that.

'Uh, I'm not married. But they're sort of Gort's kids. You know what? I have a feeling this thing will take a while to go down. I'll just explain the bare basics on the way,' I said as Gort pressed the elevator's call button. It was in the shape of a spinning wheel.

Can't say these guys didn't have a great marketing department.

The doors slid open, and we stepped inside to start our descent.

24

'You want to talk to me? So you're calling the shots now? That's rich, even for a pretty little rich girl,' Razor scoffed. She was flanked, as always, by a whole team of Elders, at least ten or more. One of them swayed on his feet slightly, like he was drunk.

'General, all I meant was—'

'Shut up!' Razor screamed. The shout startled the man who was already swaying and he almost dropped his gun. 'Shut. Up. It's our turn now. God, your privilege extends even to the end of the world, doesn't it?'

I kept my mouth clamped shut. I didn't know everything about people, and Echo was correct in that I had barely begun to train in the human mind, but even I knew not to argue with guns. I tried hard to remember this place, this huge cavern where I had spent the last hundred years, but I just drew a blank. The last thing I remembered was being evacuated from home. After passing out, there was nothing. Which made sense – the sort of drugs they would have had to use to knock us out would have been powerful. It's possible they gave them to us before transporting us underground.

My eyes fell back on Razor.

'That's better. God, you're giving me a headache.' The general pinched the bridge of her nose and perched on a nearby cryopod, an empty one. Obviously the poor soul that bought that ticket didn't make it in time.

'I need to speak with the Chief,' I said, not bothering to add the catchphrase Rebecca always did. Was that why the other Elders were laughing? Because they were laughing, the drunk-looking one was even struggling to stand up. 'What's funny about that? I'm serious, General. I have something important to ask him.'

'Then ask.' General Razor spread her arms wide and the Elders laughed even more.

I looked around. Was one of these men really the great and powerful Chief? None of them looked like fearless leaders to me. And why would they all follow the general's orders if that was the case?

That was when the penny dropped.

'There is no Chief. It's just you,' I said.

Razor started a slow clap and the men finally stopped laughing.

'Why? Why not just rule as yourself? Clearly you have the respect of your men,' I asked. I was furious with myself. It seemed so obvious now. No one could even describe what the Chief looked like. Of course he wasn't real.

The men stood to attention when I mentioned them and the general smirked. 'That's true, little Pandora. My men know what's best for them. But the people don't always. I remember the stories my grammy used to tell me, about the infighting and the coups. The leadership of this place changed almost daily when I was a girl.

'And there was a Chief, once. A tyrant that ruled with an iron fist and was as stupid as all the idiots before him. Because to be fair to the moron, before he got here, it was chaos. There was no community. We were starving, and starving people ain't reasonable. It was every woman for herself. We were living off rotten canned food, and running out fast. I begged him to open the vault but he wouldn't even entertain the idea of seeing what was down here, the technology was that frightening to him.

'So ten years back, when he eventually kicked the bucket, like all the idiotic men before him, I was the lucky lady that discovered him. Barely an adult myself, really, but good with a gun, and so I was on his protection team. I took charge and all the other Elders supported me. We told no one that he was dead, dumped his body in the desert for the coyotes to find. And we were finally able to open up the treasure trove that is this place – we told the people the Chief had moved here to perfect his farming technique. It's pretty hard to stage a coup against a man who doesn't exist. We have lived peacefully ever since.'

I blinked at her. She had always oozed authority, and now I knew why. She was ruthless.

'And I suppose that explains the technophobia within these walls?' I asked. 'Why did the Chief come here at all, with all the chaos, when it's a campus for the very institution he hated so much?'

'Look around, sunshine. There aren't as many buildings out here as there are in your precious, educated, rich cities. The bots, they kept everything running, right? Course they did. Digital slaves. There were some here too, I guess to help keep the place all clean and nice until their precious human overlords came back. They were disposed of in the early days. It's not like they were programmed to fight back. And we needed the space, with the weather getting worse. These buildings can withstand hurricanes, extreme temperatures, torrential rain. Aurora Tech knew what to expect when they built them. It's us idiots that were left outside to die.'

Those poor bots. I knew they weren't all like Gort, but

that was no reason to show malice. But the general, she was right. The school's windows had been mostly blown out, not to mention the bodies. And the mall was ransacked by mutants, too. In comparison, the Aurora Tech buildings here in the Republic really *were* quite well maintained, the best we had seen since the university. Living somewhere your worst enemy had built, or dying out in the wilderness . . . well, it was an easy choice.

'I guess the technophobia also helped with the myth of the Chief,' I said. 'Plus, it meant you never had to risk one of your people speaking to a HUMANKIND, who may have then exposed the cryolab you'd been keeping secret.'

'My, that private-school education really has served you well, even in the apocalypse,' the general sighed. 'I suppose you've worked it all out. Well done you. Quicker than Echo was, and he has a positronic brain helping him out.'

My blood ran cold. She'd found out about him – or had she really known all along? Did I really think I was clever enough to fool a woman who had fooled a whole civilization of people? 'Where is he? What did you do with him?'

General Razor rolled her eyes. 'I kicked him out yesterday. When he realized you were better off without him it wasn't really that hard to push him out. I assume the bandits have found him by now – I gave them enough of a clue as to where he would be. He reeked of halfling from day one. Did you really think he wouldn't get found out?'

'You're a monster,' I whispered. I should have trusted my gut. Echo had been in trouble for hours, and I had done nothing. God only knew where he was by now.

And I was trapped nearly a mile underground.

The general looked up from her perch on the cryopod, elbows rested on her raised knees, clearly bored of talking about Echo. 'Pandora. Such an unusual name. Really, I can only think of one other Pandora, the one my grammy told me about. Can you think which Pandora I'm talking about?'

The hairs on the back of my neck stood on end. I knew it. That first day, when she had commented on my name, I knew. Razor knew who I was.

'The president's daughter. She was called Pandora,' I said. I held her gaze, but the guns were always prominent in the corner of my eye. Was this it? She was just waiting for me to find this place and then what? She would shoot me down here? Why not just end me when we met, in the mall?

'Don't you dare use that name,' Razor spat. She stood up from the pod and her eyes went dark, furious as a stormy sea. 'President is a name reserved for leaders. For elected leaders of free, independent countries. Your daddy was a murderous, capitalist pig. He didn't care about anyone but himself. He didn't even care about you. Here he is, in this place, buried in ten thick layers of concrete. And you, in one of the last pods to be filled, right at the top of this godforsaken bunker.'

Razor pointed upwards and I looked at the ceiling, so far away it was shadowed in darkness.

'So that's what happened to me? I was in a pod and it . . . took off? Went into escape mode?' I asked. I was terrified, but she had me right where she wanted me. She knew who I was. If I could at least get to the truth before I died, it was something. At least Echo was free. He would escape the bandits, wouldn't he?

Razor sighed and fell back on to the pod. She looked exhausted, even more skeletal than the other residents of the compound. Her uniform hung off her bones like clothes still on the hanger.

'That's about it. These darn passes get more useless by the day.' Razor pulled her own red lanyard out of her jacket and turned it over in her hands. 'We were trying to defrost someone at the bottom of your column and the top just went off. Straight through the roof, caused a big-ass hole. Took us days to patch it up, lying to the workforce so no one would ask questions. Guess this bunker ain't as strong as it used to be. I wasn't lying about the earthquakes, you know. This whole place has nearly caved in half a dozen times since I've lived here. We're just lucky all these pods failed to launch, until yours took a joyride, or else we'd have a whole bunch of craters and no pods.'

I remembered what Rebecca had said, how calm she was about Miles's claims of a spaceship. A crater. She said it had happened before, and that tallied up with what Razor was saying.

Defrost someone.

What did that mean? Why didn't I listen to Echo's concerns more? Why had I been too afraid to ask more questions?

What was happening here?

'I think the electrics are starting to go to shit,' Razor continued. 'A pity. We need the food, but we'll find something else, I suppose. We always do.'

I stopped breathing. It felt like all the oxygen had been sucked from the room, and I was suddenly and acutely aware of how deep underground we were. I was drowning. Everything came at me at once.

The meat is always fresh. Nothing grows here. The Elders are in charge of the animals. You need a key card to get in. The booze, probably to self-medicate. The guards who can't even stand straight.

'You're eating the people in the pods,' I said, with the last of the air in my lungs. If General Razor was barely an adult when she seized power, they must have been harvesting the pods for, what, twenty years maybe? My stomach churned at the thought. All those living souls, wasted. Dead.

'These aren't people. They are the remnants of a dead empire,' Razor said, her voice measured. 'They were willing to use up this planet until there was nothing left, and then leave us with the mess. Leave us to die. They made their fortunes doing it. An eye for an eye. I just didn't think it would be so literal.' Razor half laughed, but I saw a tear escape down her cheek despite her best efforts to turn away. She pulled something out of her top pocket, a hipflask, and took a swig.

'They are people. You're eating people. That's cannibalism,' I whispered.

I used the general's brief lapse in concentration to turn to one of the Elders. He blinked at me with bloodshot eyes.

'Don't you look at me, traitor.' His voice rose and he raised his weapon. 'I said don't look at me!'

I held my hands up in surrender and stared at the concrete floor, watched as the tears fell from my eyes and splashed against the ground.

'Pete, calm down. Did you hear me, soldier? I said stand down.' The general had composed herself.

I looked up just in time to see him obey her and slowly lower his gun. I looked at the other men, who were all as skinny and unsteady and tired-looking as Pete was. This wasn't a platoon of soldiers. It was a mess.

A mess with bullets, but still a mess.

'How could you do this?' I asked. I stared at the empty pod Razor used so comfortably as a sofa, and realized that the entire row near the entrance was empty. There were thousands, if not tens of thousands, of pods here, but how many were left? How many people could even be woken up?

What about my father?

'You really don't get it, do you?' Razor sighed. She leant forward again. 'Once the cold hit, nothing would grow. And as for the pollution? It rained down acid for years after the factories stopped working. Even the weeds died eventually. The soil was ruined. The animals were so messed-up with birth defects they barely lasted long enough to eat, and those that did made us sick. We were running out of canned food, and no one trusted the cities. They were crawling with Aurora Tech bots. No telling what they would do if they saw one of us.'

'They wouldn't do anything except help you. They were made to serve,' I said. I lowered my hands.

Razor laughed so hard it turned into a cough. She spat on the floor, a black goo that didn't look right.

'Sure. We're just paranoid, right? We should just accept the help that Aurora Tech are offering, even after everything they've done?'

'I never said you were paranoid, I'm just saying that the HUMANKIND project was put in place by Aurora Tech to help humanity survive.'

'They were helping *themselves* survive, like they always did.'

'Why do you keep speaking like we aren't even the same species? Aurora Tech, rich, poor, we're all the same.'

'Oh, is that what you call cryogenic safety pods with space capabilities, the "Great Leveller"?' Razor used air quotes around the words. 'Bullshit. Either you had a billion in dirty notes, or you didn't. You lived, or you died. Us, and them.'

I pursed my lips as her words hit me. Hard. She was right. I always knew it, deep down. Aurora Tech had separated people right until the very end, no matter which way you spun it. And my father was responsible for those decisions. I could count on one hand the number of times in a year he would even be at home, never mind how many times I saw him, but I still could have said something. He was never the same after my mother died, but neither was I. I had gone to therapy, and he had buried himself in work. The man Razor described, the company he embodied, was both familiar and a stranger to me.

Maybe I didn't deserve to live. I hadn't put in the hard work, made the tough decisions. What Razor had done was unforgivable, but what would I have done in the same position? Starved? Let good people like Miles and Rebecca go hungry?

I needed to listen more. Plus, the longer Razor talked, the longer I was kept alive. Maybe we could even come to an understanding. Talking was better than bullets, and I couldn't try to help Echo if I was dead.

'Is that why you're telling me all this? To hurt me?' I asked her.

Razor sneered at me. 'You could never hurt the way we have. Three generations my family has kept alive. Three. But yes, I am glad that you get to see that your precious experiment went wrong. That it's us who are alive and surviving, and not you.'

Inside I was falling apart, but I had to keep it together. Calm. Measured. I had to busy my mind away from the empty pods, and the drunk guards, and the pieces of bacon that had smelt so good that morning.

'How did you find this place?' I asked, breathlessly.

'Easy if you know where to look.' Razor paced in front of me, then smiled and stopped, her face just centimetres from mine.

I didn't dare move. Behind her, one of the Elders hiccoughed and readjusted his gun.

'My grammy had a husband once, in the city. I never met him, of course. He died the day you all went to beddy-byes, decades before I was born. He had a good job.

Gave ten years of his life to those monsters at Aurora Tech – but then again, who else could he possibly work for? And at the end, you just left him there, dead in a pool of his own blood, on the floor of your fancy mansion.'

The pain of the memory was so sharp and sudden it made me gasp. *His skin was pale, his eyes cloudy. My own eyes traced down his body until I saw it. A red bloom of blood, spreading out from under his suit jacket. He opened his mouth, groaned and sank to the floor.*

'Your grandfather was named Scott, wasn't he?' I whispered. I tried to control my breathing but the sobs were desperate to rip out from my chest. 'I'm so sorry.'

'Fairly typical. I thought you might have made the connection when I told you who I was, but you didn't even know his last name was Razor, did you?'

I blinked at her as the truth sank in. I did not know Scott's last name. How had he been my bodyguard for four months, and I didn't know his last name? There were just so many guards that I never stopped to think. It was no excuse, though. The man had died for me.

'Thought so,' said Razor. 'Well, guess what? He knew where the cryolabs were. Couldn't afford a ticket but told Grammy, in case she could barter her way in, which obviously she couldn't. So instead, she told a large group of her friends, one of whom had a kid, and that kid would grow up to be the dear old Chief himself. She said it was easy to get here. But maps were obsolete with satnavs and the internet, and that all went down in the first winter, so we wandered in the wasteland for years before we found this place. The Chief grew up in that wasteland, watching six-eyed coyotes rip apart his mama right before his eyes just before he turned ten. Changes a kid, that sort of horror. My daddy went the other way – Grammy protected him, and he clammed up. Never talked to me about that time. Those first few settlers of the New Republic, they were lost out there for damn near twenty years. This was all way before I was born. She should have known the Chief would be too damaged to make a good leader, but it don't matter. He got what was coming to him in the end.'

Razor sniffed, paused and took another swig from her hipflask. Pete looked on longingly.

'And no one up there knows about . . . this?' I spread my hands.

'When the Chief died – no kids, because no woman would go near him – I made the decision. The Elders – my most trusted men – they all swore themselves to secrecy. For the good of the colony. If the people knew, they'd lose their damn minds. The Chief, he was sorta like a god to these people already. Why not carry on the myth when he wasn't with us no more? Isn't that right, Pete?'

'Yes ma'am,' Pete slurred, still watching the hipflask that Razor waved in the air.

'All right, I'm bored. Pete, shoot her. We can serve her up tomorrow at dinner,' Razor said. She turned away, hands behind her back, and Pete raised his weapon, his aim wobbly as ever.

'Wait,' I half screamed, pleading.

Despite everything, despite the crippling guilt and the horror, I didn't want to die. There had to be a way out of this.

'I'm sorry, Pandora. Did you have some final words?' Razor faced me and crossed her arms.

'Yes. Well, no. At least, I don't want them to be final. Please, have mercy.' I addressed Pete directly this time, and his eyes flicked from Razor, to me and back again. 'I'm awake. I'll struggle, fight to survive. It won't be the same as when you get people out of the pods. Please. Please.' I was crying now, and Pete was too. He looked uncertain.

'Pete. Shoot her. That is an order,' Razor growled.

'Y-yes, ma'am,' Pete said. He clicked the safety off the weapon.

I closed my eyes and waited for the bang. But it never came. Instead, I heard the doors of the lift ping. I opened my eyes carefully.

'Sorry we're late,' Echo said.

He walked out of the lift like he was walking on to the set of a talk show. I was so relieved I let out all the air that had felt trapped in my lungs. I could have kissed him. He smiled at me, but not a big, Echo smile. He could see the guns as well as I could. Inexplicably, he was joined by Gort, who of course didn't seem worried at all by the stand-off. And . . . a set of identical triplets? Nearly identical anyway, two boys and a girl. Lastly, Rebecca stepped out, her mouth set into an 'o' of surprise as she looked around. They looked like the strangest superhero team I had ever seen. I had never been so glad to see anyone in my life.

'What on Earth?' Even Razor was rendered almost speechless.

'Oh, right. Introductions. So obviously I'm Echo, the robot reprobate you hate so much, you know me,' Echo said. He pointed down the line. 'Then we have my robot bestie Gort, and our robot children, Zort, Cort and Mort – Pandora, for the love of God, don't ask – and at the end there is our new pal Rebecca. Think you should know her too. Yep, that's everybody.'

He was stalling for time, the group edging closer towards me with each step, although I wasn't sure what they thought they could do. Our backs were to the lift, and Razor and her men were opposite us, spread out across the walkway. They must know we wouldn't be able to scan our stolen ID card and call the lift before they could shoot us, or they wouldn't let us be so close to the exit. We were still outmanned and outgunned.

'Whatever. Enough of this. Two birds, one stone,' Razor said, her voice deadpan.

Echo and his crew came to a stop next to me.

'Line them up, boys.'

The other Elders around Pete also raised their weapons. Echo put his hands up and nudged Gort, who copied him. They walked sideways towards me, never taking their eyes off the guns.

'Hey,' Echo whispered once I was in earshot. 'Sorry about, uh, getting kidnapped. Long story. Also, Gort is cool now. And he's alive. And we found some creepy kids. Who knew?'

'Only you could still make jokes with half a dozen guns pointed at you,' I whispered back. I was so happy to see him, but I was also still so angry. So much had been said. And yet, if this was the end, he had come back. There was no point dying alone, and furious. I reached my raised hand towards his and interlaced our fingers. And as for the ChildSynths, the ones I thought had all been wiped out? It was a question for after we survived this.

'Adorable. Truly. But I really have had enough of this shit. Elders, do your worst,' Razor said.

'But . . . ain't those kids?' one guard said, pointing the muzzle of his gun at the triplets. 'I ain't never seen a little kid robot before.'

'No, you idiot. The robots want you to think that, but

they're just toasters. Fire!'

The guards exchanged looks.

'Big Brother Gort? What is a toaster?' The three children spoke in unison and if I wasn't so terrified, I might have been more than a little freaked out.

'The angry lady with bad lipstick is referring to a food-making device,' Gort replied.

Razor snarled.

Gort continued. 'But toasters, like us, have electrical components, and cannot feel pain. They do not bleed – do you remember, children, what I told you about your coagulants?'

The three children smiled and turned back to the gunmen.

'Uh, Echo? What's your plan here?' I whispered out of the side of my mouth.

'See? Disgusting robots. No child speaks like that,' Razor raged. 'Shoot. Them.'

The sound of half a dozen safety catches clicking off sent a shiver down my spine. This was it.

'Uh. Well, no real plan. Rebecca told us you were down here, so I knew I had to be down here too. But don't worry. I'm really good at winging it.'

'Echo—'

'Fire!' Razor shouted, and the unsteady men fired their weapons.

I didn't close my eyes this time. I wanted the men to look into them as they killed me. Now all there was left to do was to let the bullets take me.

But I didn't see or feel any bullets. Gort leapt across my vision, like a goalkeeper reaching for a ball, followed by three mini-me shadows. He jumped in front of both of us and we watched as his body convulsed after the first bullet hit him.

'No,' I cried. Gort hit the floor, but his eyes didn't close. He didn't even call out in pain. Only one bloom of blood spread out, from his shoulder. Either the men's aim was put off by their alcohol intake, or they had tried to miss on purpose. Possibly a mixture of both. I could see a couple of bullets had gone into the concrete, taking chunks out of the floor.

Meanwhile, the kids tackled three of the men. They were actually giggling as they climbed up their arms, hugged their waists, sat on their feet and hung on to their legs. Some of the men softened immediately and put their weapons down. Some got angrier and shot at the kids, which sent my heart leaping into my mouth. But the kids didn't stop laughing, and no blood came, like with Gort.

'Still . . . coagulated, human Pandora,' Gort wheezed. He smiled, his teeth covered in blood. 'Toasters . . . don't bleed either. It's rad if you think about it.'

Is Gort malfunctioning, or did he just say rad?

Rebecca, meanwhile, had headed towards two of the other guards, hands up, self-surrender.

'Come on now,' she said, hands still high above her head. 'Little Bobby-Rae? What would your momma say if she knew you were pointing a gun at me? We used to make mud pies together, do you remember that?'

The guard on the left, who I assumed was Bobby-Rae, lowered his gun. Rebecca turned her attention to her next victim.

'And is that Big Bill under all that hair? Listen, I just wanna talk . . .'

Meanwhile, Razor was getting angrier by the moment. She had lost most of her team and now just had three or four trustworthy men left, the ones who didn't even look drunk and held their weapons true. In other words, the ones that didn't need any liquid courage to carry out her gruesome commands. They had been separated by the distractions, but now they were together and making their way through the mayhem, straight towards us.

The scene in front of us was chaos.

Chaos that Echo wasn't willing to waste. 'Run!' he screamed, and he pulled me towards the wall of pods.

25

It was a weird thing, knowing exactly where you were going without having any memory of being there before. But that's what it was like as I half dragged Pandora around the maze of concrete corridors, cut up by row upon row of cryopods. The entire bunker was mapped out in my mind, all 10,650 pods, and the name of each person inside them.

'Bring them back here,' Razor snarled behind us. 'But don't shoot like you did before. If you hit any of those rocket-fuel canisters on the pods, you could blow the whole place sky-high. Just bring them to me.'

We were fast, faster than the skinny, boneheads that Razor sent after us. I checked over my shoulder and saw them bumbling along, but they weren't catching up. Then again, that didn't mean we were out of the woods. We couldn't run for ever.

But in a bunker this large, we could sure as hell hide.

'This way,' I said, pulling Pandora left at the end of the aisle.

I noticed the pods to that side were empty as we sprinted past. Phillipa Reeves, Bob Freeman, Jessica Dorne. All not where they were supposed to be. Their details spread across my mind like a window with too many tabs open. Height, weight, occupation, photographs.

'Why are these empty?' I panted as we ran. We took a right next. I had an idea where we could hide until the coast was clear.

'They . . . they . . . ate them,' Pandora said bluntly.

I stopped running, skidding to a halt in my high-tops. 'What did you just say?'

'Please don't make me say it again,' Pandora whispered. She used the break to catch her breath, her hands on her knees, her chest heaving.

I knew it. I knew there was something going on. That weird-ass meat, and the secrecy around the animals. It made total sense. I was glad I was too busy throwing shade to eat anything last night.

'That's sick,' I said, because there was nothing else to say.

'The people. They don't know,' she panted.

Well, that made sense. Miles even said he wanted to be

an Elder, so he could come and pet the chickens or whatever. Things would be a little different if he knew the truth, and it explained the rampant alcoholism.

At the other end of the row, we heard the muffled footsteps of the Elders.

'Come on, I know a place. We need a plan,' I said.

Pandora took my hand and jogged alongside me. 'How do you know a place? What happened out there? I was so worried about you.'

I tried not to grin. 'No need to worry about old Echo. I always land on my feet. I'll explain when we get there, but it might be a little . . . You'll see.'

It had seemed an obvious place to go at first, but now I was having my doubts. Surely I had access to it too, right? We had no trouble accessing the metal doors now we had the full HUMANKIND upgrade. The HUMANKIND access seemed to have no bounds.

I hoped.

We ran down another row and I strained my neck, looked up at the towering pods that disappeared into the darkness above. It kind of reminded me of the city. All twinkling lights and possibilities. Soon, we got to my destination. Another, much smaller concrete bunker in the centre of the maze of pods. It looked almost identical to the one above ground that was the entrance to this place, with a matching sliding door and no windows.

'Quick, in here,' I said. I scanned my hand against the panel next to the door and it slid open.

'How did you . . . ?' Pandora started to ask, but I shoved her inside.

'I said I'd explain, and I will. Once there is three metres of concrete between us and them,' I said, spotting the first of the army men coming round the corner. We slipped inside and the door sealed silently behind us.

Beyond the door was exactly what I knew there would be. A corridor of concrete that opened up into a sort of cave. On one side was a wall of tiny drawers, each one labelled with a scientific name. On the right, a row of ten pods, each with an undisturbed sleeper inside.

'Is this . . . a seed bank?' Pandora asked. She was fingering the label of each drawer, mesmerized. 'There must be what, hundreds? Thousands?'

'Over two thousand different genera of genetically modified fruits, vegetables and, like, some flowery things,' I said, pulling the data from my HUMANKIND chip so fast I almost surprised myself. 'Listen, P, we're safe for now but I have to explain some things to you—'

'Oh my God,' Pandora interrupted me and ran to the first of the pods to the right.

They were mostly old dudes and dudettes, dressed in the same Aurora Tech onesie I'd found her in, but one of them wore a black number instead, with gold stitching. I didn't need my new chip to tell me who it was, but it helped.

'Yeah. That's Il Presidente, all right. The head honcho of Aurora Tech,' I told her.

'Also known as my father,' Pandora said. A tear slipped down her cheek.

I nearly facepalmed. Of course. The new information from my chip was still settling in my positronic brain, but a part of me always knew. I had seen Pandora's name on the manifest, so I knew her pod had come from here. She was rich, and her home was stormed on the day everything went sideways. Of course she had something to do with Aurora Tech. It made sense now.

'Right,' was all I said. Pandora didn't look at me. 'Hey, if your dad is in the super-duper secret bunker, why aren't you in here with him?'

'I was late. He was already at work. His security service would have sent him down here at the first sign of trouble.' She shrugged, as if her dad leaving her for dead at the end of the world was the same as being grounded. 'He was a complicated man. Especially after my mother died. We were strangers, really.'

'Um, no. You weren't. He was your dad. That's . . . that's messed up, P,' I said. I put my arms around her and held her in a tight hug, and caught a quick glimpse of my potential father-in-law. Lying there, in his jammies, eyes closed, he didn't seem much more special than the dudes either side of him.

'Hey, you wanna hear something cool?' I said. Pandora pulled away from my shirt, now wet with her tears, and looked up at me expectantly. 'I think I remember my own dad.'

'What? How? Echo, what happened out there? That's wonderful, but . . . what happened?' Pandora wiped the tears from her eyes and backed up, waited for me to begin.

I told her everything. About Razor's ultimatum, and Dad, and the HUMANKIND project. About Einstein and Gort and the highwaymen. About the end.

'Oh my God, Echo, I am so sorry. It's all my father's fault. I should have seen it earlier, I should have realized that I didn't even know him at all. That I was blinded by the money and the lies,' Pandora said. And then she was crying again.

'Hey, P. Chill, OK? It was a long time ago. I only just remembered it, but it's weird. My brain can tell it wasn't recent. We aren't our parents, OK? It's not your fault.' How could I blame her for any of it? She was just a kid, like me, when everything went down. Dad didn't mean to leave me unfinished. Pandora didn't want her dad to do all these things. We live and learn. I pulled her back into my arms and we held each other.

'And I'm sorry too. I didn't mean a damn thing that I

said last night. And I shouldn't have left. I just let Razor get into my head. I was a dumbass.'

'I guess we both have things we need to work on,' Pandora said.

I half laughed. 'OK, *now* you're sounding like a shrink.'

'Apologies, Echo Zero-One-Three-Five, for the interruption. But we appear to have a problem.'

The voice that came from the corner of the room made me jump out of my skin.

'Jesus, Gort. How did you get in here? Are you even OK?' I said, as Gort crept out from the end of the row of pods.

Pandora was so happy to see him that she went to hug the guy, then stopped when she saw his shoulder.

'Fear not, human Pandora. I cannot feel pain. And my internal diagnostics assure me it is a superficial wound,' Gort said, poking a finger into the bullet hole. It oozed black blood that made me want to vomit.

'OK, yeah, great, Gort. You don't need to show us, buddy. We believe you. Did you get here faster than us? Have you been here the whole time? What about the sprogs and Rebecca?'

'Human Rebecca and my siblings are well. Human Rebecca persuaded the hostile humans to lay down their weapons, and some are really rather partial to the triplets, bro. I managed to find an alternative route once the deadlier humans chased after you. It seemed logical that you would head to the most defensible part of the lab. I believe I beat you by one point four-five minutes. But I did not have a human weighing me down,' Gort said. Such a charmer, that one. And I never would get used to Gort talking like me. I mean, he just called me bro. So rad.

'Jesus. OK, whatever. Can you tell me what the problem is?'

'Well, Echo Zero-One-Three-Five. As you can see, we appear to be trapped. As you might say, Echo Zero-One-Three-Five, this is a sticky situation.' Gort gestured to the back of the cave where a screen had been set into the wall.

P and I peered over his shoulder. Sure enough, the screen showed footage of the corridor we had just run down, which was filled with Ashtray's loyalist goons. Ashtray herself was holding back, talking into a walkie-talkie.

'That's not good. We can't hide in here for ever, but they can stay camped outside that door,' I said. 'Or try for a "Here's Johnny" entrance.' My heart dropped into my stomach. Idiot. I had trapped us, not saved us.

'I really wish you would stop speaking in riddles,' Pandora snapped. Her eyes were big and pleading. 'Well, what about the pods? We – well, you and Gort – you can just wake everyone up, right?'

'It's too slow,' I said. Her face fell. 'You remember what

it was like when you woke up. It takes some people days to come out of the Big Sleep. Razor will just gun them down where they stand. Or worse, if that's possible . . .' I trailed off and the colour drained from Pandora's cheeks.

'There has to be another way. This can't be the end. We're so close,' she said. She walked away, towards the seed drawers, and traced the writing on a label.

I looked at Gort, who just stared back, empty. Fat lot of use he would be right now. Actually, that was a little unfair. He had stuck his neck out for us – kind of literally.

'Hey, Gort? Even if it was for nothing, uh, thanks. You know, for getting shot and everything.'

'Not a problem, Echo Zero-One-Three-Five. I will not let harm come to human Pandora,' he said.

I clenched my jaw. 'Right, yeah. Well, thanks anyway, I guess.'

Pandora said nothing. She was just staring at the drawers with the same look in her eye that she had when we went shopping at the mall a couple of weeks back.

'I've got it,' she finally said. She pointed to a drawer marked *Solanum lycopersicum*.

'What, is the good general allergic to tomatoes or something?' I asked, my mind pulling the information about the seed straight from my chip.

'No. We use it to bargain,' she said. I raised an eyebrow. 'Listen. I know you hate Razor for what she did, and I'm not saying she should get away with it. But we can't blame all these people for her mistakes. These seeds, they will provide food for these people. There's no way she knows this is here, not without the HUMANKIND technology to open the door. The scientists will have organized enough for thousands, and you said they were genetically modified to survive here. The Elders hate eating the people in the pods, can't you tell? They're sick as dogs over it.'

Damn. Girl was smart. The goons were clearly that, just goons. If we gave them a future, an alternative, they might even stand down.

'And that way, we could even wake the others. Get some healthy, un-irradiated DNA into their current gene pool. I'm not naive, and I know it won't be easy. The people in the pods lived because of how healthy their bank balance was, and that's unfair to the point of cruelty. But we have to give everyone a second chance. It's a question of survival now, and we can deal with the hurt later. You don't blame me for what my father did. We can't blame Miles, and Rebecca, and all the others for Razor. There's wrongs on both sides here.'

'All right. I think you might be on to something there. Gort, open up a line of communication. Uh, you know. Turn the speaker thingy on,' I said, cringing at how much I sounded like a space captain from a bad TV show.

Gort nodded and pressed some things on the screen.

'Go ahead, Echo Zero-One-Three-Five. They can hear you.'

'Right. Erm, yes . . . actually, P, I think you might be better for this one.' I gestured to Pandora and she nodded.

On the screen, the goons and Razor looked up to see where the noise was coming from.

'General Razor. We have a proposition for you. Clearly, you have never had access to this pod and the contents inside, or you would have taken revenge on my father many years ago,' P began. I grinned. Pandora was ballsy, all right. I watched the screen as Razor visibly recoiled.

'Well, I can now tell you that this pod has more than just my father inside. It has food. Genetically modified seeds that can grow effectively, even in poisoned soil,' Pandora continued.

Now the goons were looking up, their guns loose in their hands. I gave her a thumbs up.

'You don't have to keep doing what you were doing. And none of your people need to know what happened here. You can grow healthy, nutritious food, for generations to come. You just have to let Echo and Gort wake the scientists, and release the seeds. You just have to let us go. Forgive us as we want to forgive you. The bloodshed stops here.'

'Nice speech,' I mouthed. Yo, my girl was the *bomb*. I'd been away five minutes and she had got even braver all of a sudden. I knew how difficult it was for her to speak up, and now she was speaking up for the whole damn world. Pride didn't cover it.

The goons reacted first. The system was two-way, so we could hear them as they muttered to each other and holstered their guns. If anything, they looked relieved. No more fighting. No more bodies.

'What are you doing?' Razor screamed. I exchanged a look with Pandora. 'Didn't you hear them? They want to wake up these traitors. The same ones that sooner saw your ancestors dead than alive. And this food that she promises? Is it even real? How can we trust anything made by them? By Aurora Tech.'

A couple of Razor's goons fiddled with their weapons. The tide was turning. I looked at Pandora.

'General, please. This is a peace offering. I understand why you are paranoid, but by opening this door, we are laying our trust in you as we hope you will in us. Please look at your men. They don't want this. I think, deep down, you don't either.' Pandora held her breath, waiting for Razor's reply. We both did.

'Paranoid? We are paranoid now, is that it?' Ashtray's bitter laugh reverberated around the cave. 'Paranoid is what Aurora Tech called climate scientists when they tried to warn us about global warming. And look where that led. You don't know anything about us. You don't know,' Razor spat.

'Well, she might not have you, but she got me,' one of the goons said, the one Ashtray had called Pete. He pulled off his gun and laid it on the ground. 'I'm sorry, ma'am. But I can't do this any more. My boy, I can't keep lying to him. And the meat, it's not even keeping him fed. Makes sense to me that the rich folk would have some special seeds. I wanna see what the kid has.'

'Me too,' said another goon. He dropped his rifle. 'Sorry, boss. This ain't a dictatorship. I'm tired. I can't do this any more.'

'No. This isn't right. Pick up your guns. Pick them up, dammit! That's an order,' Ashtray screamed, but the rest of the goons just dropped their guns too.

'It's over, ma'am. There's a better way. We've spent years trying to get into that box. I'm ready to see what's inside,' said another goon.

Razor threw her head back and screamed, a primal noise that was guttural, like the sound of a dying animal. She finally stopped and ran for one of the guns, which Pete deftly kicked away. Finally, two of the goons grabbed her shoulders and wrestled her to the floor. Then, all six of the goons looked up to the camera.

'I think they're waiting for us,' Pandora said.

I grinned. 'You did it. You beautiful brainbox. It's over,' I said, and I kissed her. Just a quick one though. We had a world to save.

'Gort, open the door,' Pandora said, grinning back at me.

Gort tapped at the panel again and the door slid open, revealing the scene we had seen on camera. The three of us stepped out, wary at first, but the goons didn't move. Only Razor squirmed on the ground like a fish on deck.

'So, uh, what now?' asked Pete. He looked from me, to Gort, to Pandora. It looked like we were in charge.

But before I could answer, Razor gave one last, super-human scream. She shifted the skinny guard holding her just enough to reach one of the guns still on the floor.

It happened so fast. The gun, the shot, the blood. As soon as she had fired it, the other men were on top of her. One of them even grabbed his own gun and fired a counter-shot. Instinct. Old habits, they die hard. Razor's eyes went dull before her head hit the floor, the blood pooling from the exit wound in her back.

'Echo?' Pandora said, but her voice sounded garbled, like it was underwater.

I hadn't been as quick to react as she was. P stood in front of me, just a little, like she was protecting me.

And she had done.

She sank to her knees and I saw the red bloom spreading from her stomach, drenching the front of her shirt fast, too fast. I dropped to her side and leant her back, held her tight, my eyes unable to leave the blood on her shirt, the red bubbles gurgling from her mouth.

'Don't leave me,' I said to her, the only thing I could think to say. 'Dammit, Pandora, don't you dare leave me now. Not just as the world is about to wake up again.'

Her eyes lit up once more, and then closed, her last breath deflating her chest. And then she was gone.

SpindleS.L.E.E.P 3 Release 4.0

Copyright 2075-2080 Aurora Technologies Ltd

All Rights Reserved

System ID = CryogenicSleepingPod6253

Build Time: 31/10/2179 08:34:52

Internal Bio Scan - PASSED

External Bio Scan - PASSED

Subject ready to exit cryogenic sleep

[SELECT] to enter BIOS Setup

[SELECT] to begin waking protocols

I opened my eyes slowly, the sound of the robotic voice still ringing in my ears. It had sounded like . . . instructions? A medibot, perhaps. Light flooded in through the gap in my eyelashes and I squeezed my lids shut again.

'Pandora?' Someone was speaking to me. They knew my name. At least, I think that was my name.

'Pandora, you need to open your eyes if you can hear me.'

I didn't recognize the voice. They sounded persistent and loud and I didn't like that. I just wanted to sleep. Keep sleeping, and never move again. My limbs were as heavy as a corpse's.

'Is she waking up?'

A new voice. Familiar. This voice made me want to move, to run towards it. A warm feeling spread from my chest and rippled out slowly to the rest of my limbs. The new voice was safe. I needed the new voice.

'Yo, don't touch what you can't afford, OK? I need to get through. P needs me.'

Echo. His name was Echo, and he was warmth, and strength, and joy. I knew that voice as well as my own. I opened my eyes.

Pain. Light, and pain. It was so bright I slammed my lids shut again, to protect myself from the brightness and the overall sense that everything was too much.

'She tried to open her eyes. I think she can hear us. Give her a minute.' The first voice was back, the clinical one with the clipped tone.

With my eyes closed, I retreated deep down inside. Dr Kapoor would tell me to breathe. The breathing exercises. *In, one-two-three-four. Out, seven-and-eight.* Relax. Take my time. I tried to move my arms but even the slightest twitch sent pins and needles shooting down into my fingertips. Not that I could move more than that. I felt the straps against my forearms, holding me down.

The pod lurched again and it felt like I was free-falling. My stomach dropped like I was on a roller coaster, but the tracks didn't kick in to catch me. How long could I fall for? It felt like it would never end. The flames and the alarm and the recorded message all blurred into one until it felt like I was floating.

I was going to die. The feeling was like déjà vu, but also I knew it was real. I was in a pod. It was on fire. I was falling to Earth and I was going to die and I was going to do it all alone.

'She's freaking out,' the familiar voice said.

It was closer, so close I could tell Echo, my Echo, was only centimetres away. Was he in the pod? I didn't remember. At least I wasn't going to die alone.

'Can't you do something?' Echo shouted, and I heard some beeps as someone entered something into a control panel. I was still falling, falling but trapped with my arms pinned to my side and no way to save myself. My breathing wasn't even any more because I was hyperventilating.

Panic flooded through me and made me jerk my legs, anything to get up, get out, move away from the danger.

'Pandora. Listen. It's me. Just breathe.' Echo's voice was so close I felt his breath tickle my ear. His breath, because I wasn't falling. There was no drop in my stomach as I hurtled towards Earth.

His fingers slipped into mine and I squeezed them tightly. Echo was here. Everything was OK. I opened my eyes again.

'Welcome back, sleeping beauty,' Echo said.

It was bright, but I was more careful this time, letting my eyes adjust to the light before forcing them open fully. The first thing I saw was Echo, all goofy grin and hideous backwards cap and at least a week's worth of patchy stubble on his chin.

Next, I took in where we were. It was a huge, cavernous room, with a concrete ceiling and bright, hospital-esque lights hanging overhead. Where were we? I twisted my neck to the right and saw the row of pods next to me, seemingly identical to my own, but they were all empty.

They weren't empty last time I was here. General Razor, the gun, the blood. The feeling as life flowed like a river from a hole in my stomach, with Echo holding me in his arms. Now I remembered, I felt it, the slightly itchy feeling of something on my stomach, catching on the fabric of my shirt.

It all came back to me at once. Landing. The city. The car ride. Echo. The camp. The meat farm. The cryolab, the thing I had wanted to find more than anything. Father, his eyes frozen shut, his mouth stilled in a little 'o'.

'Where is he? Where is my father?' I asked. My throat was like sandpaper, every word a struggle.

Echo grinned like a wild thing and stroked my hair. 'You remember. Thank God. And he's safe. They haven't defrosted him yet because they're trying to decide how best to put him on trial. He's safe though.'

'Trial?' I asked. Echo's face fell.

'There's a few things I need to fill you in on. But first, let's get you out of that thing.'

Over the next hour or so, I was interrogated by no less than six scientists in white coats, all armed with clipboards and tablets. I was poked, prodded, bloods were taken and needles were removed. Eventually, they got to my dressing, which explained the itchy feeling I felt when I was still in the pod. On my stomach, just above my belly button, was a small flesh wound stapled shut with six stitches.

'Putting you in the pod was quick thinking on Echo's part,' the nurse said as she cleaned my wound. 'That bullet clipped both your liver and your stomach. Luckily, our surgeons could fix you up with keyhole surgery while you were still partly in stasis, but without that, you would have bled out in minutes.'

'Echo put me in the pod?' I asked. My voice was improving all the time. As Echo would say, this wasn't my first rodeo. 'And then he woke up the surgeons?'

'He woke us all up. And then he uploaded the information about how to wake the humans safely to the bots via his online neural network, so that they could help wake everybody else, too.'

'Everybody else?' I felt like I had so many questions, so much to say, but my brain was too sluggish to keep up.

The nurse smiled. 'We're still setting up the satellites, but it looks like most of the technology survived despite interference. Soon, we'll be able to talk in real time to all the cryo-colonies, all over the world. That boy of yours is something special.'

I smiled. That sounded like Echo.

Another hour of treadmills and oxygen-level tests later, they released me from the small medical bay and back into the cavernous room of cryopods. The side of the room I had woken up on housed row after row of empty pods, but there were whole columns that still had sleepers inside, dressed in the telltale shade of grey that every Aurora product was housed in.

'Hey,' Echo said. He was sitting outside the medical bay on a plastic chair and leapt up the moment I came out. 'How you feeling?'

'Like I want to get out of here,' I said. I couldn't stand the closed-in walls of the bunker for a minute longer. I wanted to see the sun.

'Cool beans. You've been down here a week,' Echo said. He stood and extended his arm like a gentleman asking a lady to dance at a ball. 'Let's bounce.'

A week. A lot less time than the last time I had been frozen, but it had still knocked me for six. I leant heavily on Echo as we made our way over to the lift, the one we had used to break into the bunker in the first place. We passed at least fifty people on our way, all carrying tablets or files and all dressed in Aurora Tech onesies or uniforms, all busy with some task or another.

'This is incredible,' I wheezed.

'Yeah, it's rad,' Echo said. 'Sorry, not far now. I'll call the lift. Hang on a sec.'

We travelled up to the top in silence and then stepped out into the main foyer, the one that led to the outside. Echo held his palm up to that door and it slid open easily.

'The doors actually stick a little sometimes. We're slowly fixing up the electrics. A hundred years can cause a lot of metal erosion. Who knew?' He made sure I was steady on my feet as we stepped outside.

The place looked like it did when we arrived, but even busier. Aurora technicians dashed around, moving crates and unpacking boxes next to building entrances. We walked a little until we hit the raised beds, where some people in plain clothes were raking the earth and shovelling it into wheelbarrows. I recognized Rebecca and smiled; she gave a small wave and ran over to give me a rib-breaking hug.

'Careful, she just survived a shooting,' Echo fussed.

'Oh, right, sorry. I'm just so mighty glad to see you.' Rebecca let go of me and beamed.

'My rescuer definitely doesn't have to say sorry. Rebecca, I can't thank you enough. What you did down there, for a stranger, and for a robotic stranger too—'

'Girl, never you mind. A lot of friendly progress was made while you was sleeping. Even Miles likes the look of these veggies. Says they'll do Rex a whole world of good. Did you know they even had a vet frozen down there in those ice beds? Maybe we can all have pets soon!'

'Rebecca? We need your help labelling these crops for rotation,' a man in a grey Aurora onesie called out behind Rebecca's head, and she waved over her shoulder.

'Duty calls. I'll talk to you later.' She jogged back to her boxes and called over her shoulder. 'I knew you could do it.' She grinned and picked up a crate.

'What did she mean by that?' Echo asked.

I smiled. 'Just friend stuff. Doesn't matter,' I said.

'So they're planting the new crops.' Echo respected my privacy and continued his explanations. 'They're genetically modified to grow in ten days, so say the brain-boxes anyway. We'll be eating fresh veggies by next week.'

'So Aurora Tech and the people at the base are working together?' I said. Maybe they realized they needed each other after all.

'Oh, yeah. When everyone heard what Razor had done – keeping the Chief's death and the bunker and stuff a secret, they were mad angry. Once I showed them the crates of GM crops and explained what they were, they were totally on board with waking up the brainboxes and getting their help in starting over. Some of the top science dudes even think they can fix up the people who have really bad pollution sickness. Miles told me they fixed up old Ron with a prosthetic leg already – 3D-printed it or something. Pretty cool shit.

'Oh! Speaking of Miles, the vet guy thinks there might be dog DNA down there, for cloning and stuff. Miles wants to help. So he said I could look after Rex. Just every now and then, you know. I sort of miss the mutants from the park. When they weren't trying to eat me, they were sort of cute and cool. So yeah. Hope you like lizard–hamster hybrids.'

'That's . . . it all sounds incredible. And I'll get used to Rex,' I said. A tear snaked down my cheek and Echo looked alarmed, but I just laughed. 'Happy tears.' We approached a bench and Echo helped ease me down into it, then he sat next to me and held my hand while I just took in the scene around me.

'I mean, look. It ain't perfect. There are some . . . tensions. Teething issues.'

Echo nodded to two men a little way away by the wall of the compound. They were too far away for us to hear what they were saying, but their voices were raised and they were playing tug of war with a cardboard box. After a few seconds, the box tore in two and what looked like grain spilt all over the floor. Before it could go any further, two women in Aurora jumpsuits ran in to break up the would-be fight.

I looked away. The happiness of hoping that things would settle down quickly was short-lived, then. 'So what's going to happen to Father?' I asked. My chest was tight with the tension of what he was going to say.

Echo squeezed my hand. 'Well, the scientist bros are going to wake everyone else up first, including some old dudes and dudettes that used to be in government. You know, before Aurora Tech. And they're going to decide a fair way to put your dad on trial. There's some support for him, you know. Some people feel like he was just doing what he was told by shareholders. And the fact he saved some people, even if they were the rich ones, and all the seeds and animals and stuff, that counts for something. But some people . . . they're just angry. They need time. I can't honestly tell you which way it might go.'

I nodded. As much as my heart ached for Father, it wasn't for the man frozen inside that pod. It was for the man he was before my mother died and he became too wrapped up in the business and money and Aurora Tech. I knew he was still in there, somewhere, deep down. I just had to find him again. And maybe answering for his crimes would do that, plus help some people find closure. I had to let him go.

'I understand,' was all I managed to say out loud. Echo nodded and put his arm around my shoulders, pulling me in for a hug. He smelt like strawberry laces and aftershave and I breathed deeply. I wasn't alone. We weren't alone. 'And what about the . . . the people that they were . . .' My mouth went dry. The people that they cannibalized? The people that the general murdered?

'We've buried what was left . . . I mean, the remains of the dead. And the science guys in charge haven't woken up their families yet. Still thinking on how to put things to them. But they aren't due to wake up yet, so there's time to find a way to at least try and make peace with it. And no,' he said, reading my mind as he always did, 'we didn't tell the people what they've been eating. Science dudes think it's for the best they don't find out, and I gotta say, I agree. Not sure they won't find out eventually, but while people are still adjusting . . . no one needs to hear that, y'know?'

I cried for what felt like a long time. The sun moved across the sky and more and more crates appeared from underground, all containing contraptions and tools I had never seen before. I watched as scientists put them together and approached small groups of both plain-clothed and Aurora Tech-uniformed people, and started to explain how they worked. No more canned food. No more suffering. There was a long way still to go, and Echo was right – the only thing that would heal us all would be time and forgiveness. Were we capable of that?

'Hey, if you're up to it, I haven't even showed you the best bit yet,' Echo said eventually. I sat up, listening. 'If you can make it. It's not far from here.'

Intrigued, I summoned a last burst of energy and lifted myself from the bench. With Echo at my side, we shuffled in between the buildings until we arrived at General Razor's office building, the place where I started to realize what had been going on. I stopped dead a few metres away and Echo squeezed my shoulder.

'Trust me. We're going to make this someplace where people will never be afraid again,' he said.

I raised an eyebrow at him, hesitated. I didn't want to go back in there, but I trusted Echo with my life. Slowly, we approached the big metal doors, which were propped open, and stepped inside.

They had done a lot in a week. Already, the ubiquitous

concrete walls had been whitewashed with some patchy, possibly home-made paint, and the shutters on the windows had been removed. Inside, several workers moved crates back and forth across the floor, and rugs were being rolled out in the corners of the room.

'What is this?' I asked, confused.

'Well, I sort of had the idea, and then a friend of yours helped me out a bit – maybe she should explain herself.'

I raised an eyebrow. 'A friend? You mean Rebecca?'

'Perhaps he should have said an old friend,' said a familiar voice.

I spun around so fast I stumbled and Echo had to catch me. Standing by the doorway where we had come in was a face I never thought I would see again.

'Yeah. A like, *really* old friend. No offence, Dr Kapoor,' Echo said, running a hand through his hair.

'You're alive.' That was all I managed to say before I burst into tears.

Dr Kapoor had never hugged me before. She had been there for me in more ways than even my own family at times, but she had never hugged me when I was a patient. She did now though, bringing me close enough that I got snot in her pitch-black hair. She didn't smell the same, but that was fair. She had been asleep for one hundred years, after all.

'I can't believe you're here,' I said once I pulled back. I

left a string of snot on her shoulder and almost laughed, but it was a little painful. 'Sorry about that.'

'Nothing to be sorry about. That's what family is for,' she said, and she smiled before giving me another hug.

And in that moment, I understood what she meant. Family are the people that follow you to the ends of the Earth. Literally. My family were all here. Dad was . . . he was something else I had to make peace with. But right now, with most of my loved ones in the same room, I felt happier than ever.

And we talked. Dr Kapoor – or Priya as she insisted on me calling her, which I didn't think I'd ever get used to – told me that she was proud of how well I'd done, out in the big world on my own. And that Echo had filled her in on our 'daring adventure' – to which I said I would explain what really happened another time. She said she was hoping we could resume our sessions soon, but she had a backlog of people, both from the pods and from the New Republic, that needed her help too. I understood. This was a lot to get your head around.

I chatted with her for a little longer before the strain of standing started to take its toll, so she left me with Echo to finish his tour.

'But you're staying nearby, right? I'll see you soon?' I asked.

'Where else would I be?' she said. 'Listen, Pandora, this

world is devastated, but somehow, we will start again. We're human, that's what we do.' She smiled once more, picked up a box of papers and walked out of the room.

'Nice chat?' Echo asked. He had been helping someone with some furniture across the room, and I appreciated that he had given us the space to talk.

'Really nice,' I said. I squeezed his hand as hard as I could manage.

Echo grinned. 'And hey, another surprise. Look up.'

I looked up to a point on the far wall, near to the ceiling, where a worker was painting something at the top of a tall ladder. Even though not all the letters were filled in yet, I could read the message clearly enough.

PANDORA'S BOX
COMMUNITY THERAPY CENTRE
JUST BREATHE

'Do you like it? Oh shit, you don't like it, do you?' Echo's face fell and he bit his lip. 'Listen, I was allowed a favour for, you know, saving the entire human race, and this was it. But if you don't like it, then I'm sure we can change it or I can ask for something else—'

'I love it,' I said, and the tears came again.

I stood on tiptoe and pressed my lips to his before pulling back. I had to laugh, his grin was that wide.

'So what you're saying is, I'm the greatest boyfriend ever?'

'Don't push it,' I said.

From what I could see, there were pods all over the world being woken up, too. A huge world map spread over one wall had green pins at various sites across whole continents. Echo confirmed that these were sites that had not only been revived, but that we had been in contact with through various communication systems.

There were also a handful of red pins. I didn't need to ask Echo what they were, and I could sense he was praying I wouldn't ask. I knew I was lucky I had survived. Plus, surely some of the ships managed to launch into space, and what then? I assumed the HUMANKIND bots knew how to recall them – but space travel wasn't easy at the best of times. Who knew how many would make it back to Earth? I shuddered even thinking about it.

Echo showed me around the rest of the centre. There were already computers set up, and it was only a matter of time before they were connected up so we could talk to people in other centres, all over the world. Echo explained how they were getting the centre ready for training, and that soon every man, woman and child would have access to a weekly wellness check and therapists, to talk through what they had experienced.

'And hey, look who's here.' Echo pointed to a stack of boxes at the far end, where Gort was helping to unload books. He looked up and waved somewhat awkwardly before refocusing on his task. I'm not sure what else I expected, but I was glad to see how well he had healed.

'Hey, Gort. Look who's awake? Dude, get over here.' Echo grinned as Gort carefully replaced the box and made his way over to us.

'I can't believe you thought of all this,' I said, watching a small class of adults jot down notes from a whiteboard, as a scientist explained the therapeutic value of deep breathing.

'Well, it's not just us, is it? It's for everybody,' Echo said, but he was suppressing a cocky grin.

'Greetings, human Pandora. I hope you are feeling better, dawg.' Gort had arrived next to Echo and I tried not to laugh at his new slang.

Echo looked as smug as ever.

'Been teaching old Gort here some new words, haven't I, brother?' Echo punched Gort lightly on the shoulder and for the first time, I saw the corners of his lips twitch upwards.

'Gort, did you just smile?' I asked, laughing.

'Did I achieve it that time? Smiling when with my friends is something that I am working on,' Gort said, and he smiled again, this time a little too wide so his teeth formed more of a grimace.

Echo's brow furrowed. 'Yeah, deffo a work in progress,

but apart from that, things are looking up. One of the brainboxes used to make TeenSynths. He's hoping he might be able to restore Gort's memory, so he'd be more like me, but no promises so far. He also thinks he can upgrade me to a full adult model. Would deffo help with the mood swings. And my moustache.'

Gort nodded. 'Can I go back to my primary objective now, broski?' Gort's face returned to neutral as he addressed Echo.

Echo raised his hands in the air. 'Hey man, you do you. If you wanna do work rather than hang out with your BFFs, be my guest.'

'Thank you,' Gort said, and he turned back to the boxes without another word.

'Uh, like I say. Progress. I'm trying to let him choose rather than telling him what to do, even though he's still just programmed to help the humans. For now, anyway, until we get the uplink set up.'

'That's great news. It would be nice to have a real conversation with Gort, and to know what happened to him in the first place. Oh, and by the way, you are not growing a moustache,' I said, laughing.

He grinned. 'See, that's the beauty. Now you can actually try and stop me.'

We waved goodbye to Gort and walked back outside. The sun was lower in the sky now, and some of the workers were packing up tools for the day.

'So, what now?' I asked.

Echo spun me round to face him, his hands a tight fit on my hips. 'Now? It's dinner time. And because all the animals they froze are still in embryo form, you'll be pleased to hear it's an all-vegetarian menu.'

'Sounds good. And then?' I asked.

'And then, we learn to live again. Together.'

'Together,' I said.

Echo leant in and kissed me hard, and I melted into him. Because despite everything, all the feelings of dread that tomorrow might bring, we had something other people didn't. We had each other, and that's how we would survive. Together.

ACKNOWLEDGEMENTS

I started writing this book in May 2020, during the first lockdown. I had been thinking about it since February, when I did a six-week course with WriteMentor and Alexandra Sheppard (thank you Alex!) and designed two characters: Pandora, from before the fall of civilization, and Echo, for after. Then Covid hit, and my job took a hit too. And that's how I found myself jobless, in full lockdown, with absolutely nothing to do.

I gravitated, as I think most people did, towards old favourite reruns, movies and books to keep my mind occupied on something other than the news. This was what really began to inform the book and Echo's tastes in particular. If it's mentioned in this book, I read/watched/played it when I was writing. There is comfort in old friends from your favourite stories, especially when you're trapped inside twenty-three hours a day.

My wonderfully supportive partner Callum (thanks for everything and more!) was a teacher at the time so he was busy with online schooling and some in-person work. It really was up to me and Zelda, my bassetoodle, to entertain ourselves. And we were lucky. We still had our health, a roof over our heads.

I dug out the fifteen-beat plot plan I'd put in a drawer

several months earlier. Miraculously (who knew that having no other forms of entertainment would be such a boost to productivity?!), I had a first draft in a month. I sent it to my agent, Lucy Irvine, who loved it (the best agent in the world, truly) and after a few edits, it was off out on submission in the autumn of 2020.

And then we waited. It was my third time on submission so I knew the drill: do something else and ignore my inbox. Easier said than done, but I had my amazing writing groups to keep me company (thank you Peak Critique, All Stars, the hubsters and of course the Good Ship authors!). I applied for a job at WriteMentor, which somehow I managed to blag (cheers to my work besties Stuart and Florianne!). Rejections started rolling in. Very nice ones. Lots to love but not quite right – I'm sure if you're a writer, you've heard that before.

That brings us to April 2021. The same month I got my job, but I was part-time to start with and knew I needed something else. I had about £40 in my account when the offer came in (BIG thank you to Kesia Lupo for seeing something in my weird little book).

The email subject line read 'OFFER FROM CHICKEN HOUSE!!!'. Lucy knew how long I had waited for this, so she was as excited as I was. My parents were even more excited, but optimistically, not surprised (they believed in me more than I did – love you, Mum and Dad).

What follows a book offer, as I've come to find out, is two years of hard work. Thanks to everyone at Chicken House – Barry, Kesia, Liv, Jazz and Laura. To Fraser and Sara, my freelance copy- and proof-editors. Thanks to Micaela for the most stunning cover. Thanks again to my family, especially to Callum, Mum and Dad. I love you. Sorry for being so mardy sometimes. Thanks to every one of the writers and authors and friends I've made in the kidlit community. You know who you are.

I hope you enjoyed my book, whether you're an Echo or a Pandora. I hope I managed to mention at least one classic movie you haven't seen. And thank YOU so much for choosing to read my book. Let's do it again sometime.

TRY ANOTHER GREAT BOOK FROM CHICKEN HOUSE

THIS IS NOT THE END by MOLLY MORRIS

Ever since the sudden death of his parents, seventeen-year-old Hugh has developed a serious preoccupation with endings – one that gets a little complicated when he discovers that high-school outcast Olivia Moon can't die.

Hugh agrees to drive Olivia to New York to retrieve a crate of her most treasured possessions – stealing his sister's ice cream van in the process. But the road to NYC is bumpy and full of unexpected turns, including Hugh's growing feelings for Olivia. As the van hurtles towards the finishing line of an unforgettable road trip, Hugh has to face his ultimate fear: unsatisfying, messy endings might just be an inevitable part of life.

This is a road-trip romance with a difference . . . Expect twists and turns along the way.
SUNDAY EXPRESS

Paperback, ISBN 978-1-913696-21-4, £7.99 • ebook, ISBN 978-1-913696-75-7, £7.99